Julie Thomas's debut novel, *The Keeper of Secrets*, was published in 2013, having previously sold in excess of 40,000 copies as a self-published ebook. She is also the author of two other self-published ebooks: *Our Father's War*, her late father's letters home from World War II; and *Stirred Not Shaken*, a collection of short stories.

For over twenty-five years Julie worked in radio, television and film, before turning to full-time writing in 2011. She lives in Cambridge, New Zealand.

Also by Julie Thomas

The Keeper of Secrets
Stirred Not Shaken
Our Father's War

JULIE THOMAS

BLOOD
WINE
&
chocolate

HarperCollins*Publishers*

HarperCollins*Publishers*

First published in 2015
by HarperCollins*Publishers* (New Zealand) Limited
Unit D1, 63 Apollo Drive, Rosedale, Auckland 0632, New Zealand
harpercollins.co.nz

Copyright © Julie Thomas 2015

HarperCollins*Publishers*
Unit D1, 63 Apollo Drive, Rosedale, Auckland 0632, New Zealand
Level 13, 201 Elizabeth Street, Sydney NSW 2000, Australia
A 53, Sector 57, Noida, UP, India
1 London Bridge Street, London, SE1 9GF, United Kingdom
2 Bloor Street East, 20th floor, Toronto, Ontario M4W 1A8, Canada
195 Broadway, New York NY 10007, USA

National Library of New Zealand Cataloguing-in-Publication Data:

Thomas, Julie, 1959–
  Blood, wine and chocolate: a novel / Julie Thomas.
  ISBN 978 1 77554 053 3 (pbk.)
  ISBN 978 1 77549 090 6 (EPUB)
  I. Title.
NZ823.3 – dc 23

Cover design by Keely O'Shannessy
Cover images by bigstockphoto.com
Typeset in Bembo Std by Kirby Jones
Printed and bound in Australia by McPherson's Printing Group
The papers used by HarperCollins in the manufacture of this book are a natural, recyclable product made from wood grown in sustainable plantation forests. The fibre source and manufacturing processes meet recognised international environmental standards, and carry certification.

To Mike, Ann and the team at Destiny Bay on
Waiheke Island for their help and guidance,
to the brilliant Michael Ball for his humour and his
love of New Zealand wine, and to my mum,
who died on Christmas Day 2013, for being
the best everything in the world.

He did not wear his scarlet coat,
For blood and wine are red,
And blood and wine were on his hands
When they found him with the dead ...

Oscar Wilde, *The Ballad of Reading Gaol*

CONTENTS

PROLOGUE

Whakamaria Bay, New Zealand, summer 2015

It was a heart-stopping view.

Michael Wilson looked at his first sentence. It was true, sometimes the view from his deck was glorious, and sometimes it was both glorious and distracting. It would be so easy to close the laptop, decide this project was not for him and go for a swim in the inviting surf that rolled onto the beach a few metres away. Or, better still, he could open a bottle of wine. However, the real reason he had stopped writing was because the term 'heart-stopping' was, perhaps, ill-advised, considering the fact that he had killed three men in the past three years. Not that they didn't deserve it, but still … you could take irony too far.

He had never written a book before and he wasn't sure that he could. The plot was the simple part, so simple he didn't even have to make it up. Truth was certainly stranger than fiction in this case: more murders than you could fire a gun at, two near-drownings, an apparent suicide, gang violence, bent coppers, lots of running away, gallons of wine and pounds of chocolate.

Could he capture the emotion? Could he find the words to explain how much some of it had hurt? The fact that his victims had deserved to die, and that each one of the killings was in self-defence, felt ominously irrelevant. While he loved his wife dearly, he'd nearly broken her heart and lost her, and all because of his damn obsession with doing the 'right thing'. Could you justify all this chaos by having done the right thing? Well, there was no way to find out other than by writing it down.

He squared his considerable shoulders and began to tap at the keyboard again. The place to start was not with the view; it was at the beginning, when he was ten, when he had another name.

PART ONE

THREE LITTLE BOYS

CHAPTER ONE

VINNIE

Vinnie's first real lie was about the death of his father. In 1976, his mother had moved them to Hendon in north-west London and he had transferred to a posh public school. The uniform felt uncomfortable and slightly too small. He couldn't wait to get home and rip it off. On his first day, a spotty kid called Alfie, with braces on his teeth and knuckles grazed from fighting, pushed him against a brick wall and demanded to know how his father had died. Vinnie paused as the options swirled through his ten-year-old brain. How could he impress them and become part of the gang? A group of five boys, all around the same age, were watching him closely.

'Don't you even know?' one of them asked.

'Bet he never had a bloody father,' another said, looking him up and down with contempt.

'Are you a bast—'

'In a car,' said Vinnie. 'He died in a car crash. Some drunk in a Porsche hit him head-on. It wasn't even Dad's fault.' Well, that was easy. Nothing fell from the sky and no loud voice branded him a liar. 'We were awarded compensation and the man went to jail, lost his leg too. It was in the paper and everything. A picture of my mum and me.'

Alfie stared into his face. Vinnie didn't flicker; he gazed back defiantly.

'You? In the paper?' Alfie sounded suspicious.

'Me. In the *Daily Mail.*'

The arm went slack against his throat and his feet took his weight again.

'Wanna join our gang?'

So it became his stock answer. As long as his mother wasn't around, he told people his father had died tragically in a car crash. The truth was somewhat more lurid.

Bert Whitney-Ross, an accountant, had married Mary Crosby, his childhood sweetheart, in a registry office in 1958. After the service they took the two witnesses, Mary's sister and Bert's best friend, for a pint at the local pub. Bert and Mary had grown up as neighbours and had lost their homes and most of their families as children in the Blitz, so they were used to hard times and relying on each other. Marriage was a logical conclusion rather than a passionate explosion. Bert was fond of joking that marriage was an institution and that he had always suspected that, as orphans, they would end up in an institution. They began wedded bliss in a rented two-bedroom terrace flat in East London. Bert worked for Lawrence & Tizdall, a City accounting firm, and Mary was in the typing pool at the air ministry.

After several years of trying for a child, Mary gave birth to Vincent Albert in June 1966. In later years Vinnie liked to say he was named after a Don McLean song, but the *American Pie* album wasn't released until 1971. He was, in fact, named after Vincent Willem van Gogh, the Dutch post-impressionist painter who was the subject of McLean's song. A print of van

Gogh's painting of irises hung in the kitchen and another, of an elderly man with his head in his hands, hung in his father's study.

Vinnie caught whooping cough as a baby and spent many weeks in hospital, with his desperate mother expressing breast milk and feeding it to him through an eyedropper. He survived, but the experience left his mother anxious and overprotective and him with a propensity for chest infections, so she was reluctant to let him play with other children.

Mary was a brilliant seamstress, and after she gave up work she earned extra money by making clothes for the neighbourhood children. She had read to Vinnie from before he was born, and it was an easy step to teach him so he could read to her while she sewed. At weekends his parents took him to museums, art galleries and musical theatre in the West End. They discussed life with him on an adult level, and he learned that adults were amused when you said clever and funny things. If you pleased them, they gave you a treat; if you annoyed them but made them laugh, they forgave you almost immediately. He was the centre of their universe and assumed that this was his proper place.

School, therefore, came as a rude shock. The teachers had to divide their time among many, and seemed somewhat disconcerted by the witty comments of a five-year-old. He took after Bert and was stocky – 'sturdy' his mother called him – and if other children were intimidated by him, he used his humour to defuse the situation.

Not long after the start of his school life he was surprised to be collected at the end of the day by his dad. He knew his mum was due to have a baby soon, and immediately assumed that he was, at last, an elder brother.

He ran towards his father. 'Daddy! Where's Mummy? Do I have a sister or a brother?'

His father bent down to talk to him at his height. He looked very serious and some other feeling that Vinnie couldn't quite understand. 'Mummy's in hospital, Vinnie, and she's sick. I'm going to take you to Aunt Sheila's and she's going to look after you for a couple of days –'

'Has she had the baby yet?' Vinnie demanded.

His father shook his head and stood up. 'Come on, son, we need to get you to your aunt's.'

Two days later he was taken to see his mum. She looked pale and she didn't have that large bump in her tummy anymore.

She hugged him very tight. 'My darling Vinnie. Mummy's brave boy,' she said softly.

He was puzzled. 'Where's my baby, Mummy?'

She stroked his curls. 'In heaven, with Jesus. We're not going to have a baby sister or brother for you, Vinnie. But you'll be Mummy's special boy for her, won't you?'

He blinked against the tears and the intense disappointment. 'Of course!'

His father lifted him off the bed. 'Mummy's very tired and we need to let her sleep. It won't be long before she'll be home again and we'll all be together.'

Once home, Mary became withdrawn and quiet, and, when she was diagnosed with depression, Vinnie began a determined campaign to cheer her up. He adored dinosaurs and created elaborate stories for her around his favourite wooden models. He would set them up on a plastic sheet on the floor and tell her long tales of herds of *Diplodocus*, *Triceratops* and *Stegosaurus*, who were grazing on trees when they were set upon by gangs of *Velociraptor*, *Allosaurus* or his very favourite, *Tyrannosaurus rex*.

'And you think that they're all going to get eaten by the carnivores ... but then –' He carefully poured white vinegar on top of the baking soda and red food colouring in his volcano, and the pink foam flooded out. '– the volcano explodes!'

He picked up little stones and let them fall through his fingers, knocking over the dinosaurs. 'And a meteor shower rains down and kills them all off.'

Mary clapped and smiled broadly at him. He picked up a stone and took aim at the last dinosaur standing.

'I think I need to add palaeontologist to my career list, don't you, Mummy?'

'Absolutely. How many does that make?' she asked.

'Pilot, astronaut, rock star, chef and palaeontologist.'

***

In 1972 Bert's boss, Amos Lawrence, made some unwise investments at the racetrack with his clients' trust funds, the miners' strike hit the economy hard, and the company fell on difficult times. Decisions had to be made and, reluctantly, Amos decided he had to let Bert go. The next day the police arrived at the practice, and Bert realised he had 'dodged a bullet'. While he was looking for another job, he did the books for Monty Joe, his darts partner at his local pub. Monty was a small-time fence with a pawn shop around the corner. He had two sets of accounts, and he paid Bert well to keep the transactions in one ledger hidden and to minimise his tax payments.

The night that changed Bert's life started like any other. He and Monty were drinking in the pub and playing darts.

'How's the job-hunting going, Bert?'

Bert shrugged. 'Had a couple of interviews, but people seem reluctant to take on new staff. Add to their wage packet. Thanks to you, it's not urgent.'

Monty snorted with disgust. 'I blame the bloody Tories. Half a million more unemployed in two years and Heath's too busy with his damn yachts and his orchestras to see what his policies are doing.'

'Times are tough everywhere – my brother-in-law has been looking for six months.'

'Ever heard of Tobias Lane?'

Bert glanced sharply at Monty, but the other man was studiously grooming the flights on his darts.

'No. Should I know the name?' he asked.

'Not necessarily. He's a businessman and, like me, he needs a discreet accountant. You're good at your job. He's looking. I can recommend you, if you like.'

A sudden sense of relief swept over Bert, and he smiled broadly. 'That'd be most appreciated, Mont.'

* * *

Vinnie's memory of his first visit to the Lane home in Richmond was a vivid one. They drove around the corner and there it was, a three-storeyed, red-brick building, partially covered in ivy, surrounded by what seemed like a private park.

'Wow! Look at that, Dad.'

His father seemed very pleased with himself. 'If we lived in a house like that, your mum would spend all day cleaning.'

Vinnie laughed. 'I'd get lost. If we lived in a house that big, I'd get *very* lost.'

They were met at the front door by an elderly butler who saw them into the drawing room. The cavernous space was full of antique furniture, with oil paintings on the walls and a huge Turkish carpet on the polished wooden floor. Bert was examining an impressive bronze of a crouching tiger when Tobias Lane joined them, accompanied by his grandson.

'Mr Whitney-Ross, delighted you could accept my invitation and that you brought your son.'

Tobias Lane was well over six foot, with pale green eyes and black hair, greying at the temples, his prominent cheekbones giving his face a gaunt look.

'Thank you for inviting us, Mr Lane.'

The two men shook hands.

'Vinnie, this is my grandson, Marcus. And Marcus, this is Vinnie Whitney-Ross.'

Vinnie wasn't quite sure what to do. The boy was taller and very skinny, with long arms and legs. Marcus smiled, so he smiled back, and when the hand was extended towards him, Vinnie shook it. What he wanted to say was that the immense oil painting over the fireplace was a very good likeness of Mr Lane, but instinct told him the man wasn't used to children making comments.

'Marcus, why don't you take Vinnie to see Nanny, and then you can go and explore the grounds?'

Vinnie looked at his father, who nodded his agreement.

The stern nanny dressed Marcus in a woollen coat, scarf and leather gloves, as she lectured him about the nippy autumn cold and how he wasn't to take these warm things off. In the corner of the nursery, a little girl with dark curly hair sat on a cushion and played with her teddy bear.

Marcus pointed at her. 'That's Millie. She's my baby sister.'

Vinnie winked at her, and she held out the teddy towards him.

'Bear,' she said.

'He's lovely. What's his name?' Vinnie asked.

She giggled. 'Silly.' She had a slight lisp.

Marcus waited while Nanny finished with his gloves. 'Yes, that's right, Millie, his name is Silly Bear. I named him. Come on Vinnie, let's go.'

As soon as they were outside, Marcus ripped off the gloves and scarf and stuffed them in his pocket. They wandered down the lawn towards a wooden bridge that spanned the stream flowing into the lake. A group of black swans glided around the lake like a ballet on the water. Their intricate movements fascinated Vinnie, and he stopped to watch them. Marcus turned back to face him.

'How old are you?' he asked.

'Six,' Vinnie replied.

'So when's your birthday?'

'June.'

Marcus laughed, and Vinnie could see he was delighted.

'Mine's January. I'll be seven five months before you are.'

Marcus started walking and Vinnie followed him.

'Have you ever played pooh sticks?' Vinnie asked.

Marcus looked at him suspiciously.

'No. What's that?'

'We throw sticks into the water off the bridge, then run to the other side and see whose stick comes out first. It comes from *Winnie the Pooh*, the book by AA Milne. Want to try?'

They had reached the bridge. Vinnie swept up a fat twig at his feet. Marcus hesitated, then ran back up the lawn out of sight. For a moment Vinnie didn't know what to do, and then the other boy reappeared with a big dog turd skewered on the end of a stick.

'Let's see if *this* floats!' Marcus yelled triumphantly as he threw both stick and turd off the edge of the bridge. Vinnie didn't show how surprised and slightly repulsed he felt. They sprinted to the other side as the stick and turd, now separated, drifted past.

Marcus punched the air with a clenched fist. 'Yes! It floats. Let's do it again.'

He ran towards the shrub garden on the far side of the stream. Vinnie paused and then followed him. He was impressed by the boy's confident manner, even if it wasn't what he'd had in mind. When twilight came and it was too hard to see the dog turds in the garden or the twigs floating in the dark water, they chased each other up to the big kitchen.

The cook was exactly what a cook in a house like this should be: plump and rosy-cheeked, wearing an apron and rolling pastry on a kitchen bench.

'Hello, Cookie. This is my new friend, Vinnie,' Marcus said as they burst through the door. She looked up and smiled at him.

'Hello, Master Marcus. What have you been up to then?'

Marcus looked at Vinnie, and they both giggled.

'We've been playing pooh sticks on the bridge.'

The cook was rolling with strong, rhythmical strokes, and Vinnie could see the muscles working in her bare forearms. 'That sounds like fun. Like in the book *Winnie the Pooh*?'

Vinnie nodded. 'Like that.'

'Not quite like that: we used dog poo.' Marcus sounded gleeful.

She frowned and wagged her finger at him. 'For goodness sake, you go straight into that bathroom and scrub your hands with hot water and soap. Get right underneath the nails. Whatever will Nanny say?'

Marcus grinned. 'Nothing, because you're not going to tell her.'

Vinnie followed him into the bathroom and they washed their hands. He scrubbed his as the cook had ordered, but Marcus just rinsed his under the cold tap and dried them on the towel. When they came back, Cookie was pouring two glasses of cola for them.

'Have you made any scones, Cookie?'

She frowned at him. 'It's nearly time for tea.'

Marcus wrapped his arms around her waist. 'Oh please! We've been playing for ages and we're so hungry. Aren't we, Vinnie?'

Vinnie was surprised at how hungry he was. He nodded solemnly. 'Actually, I am, and scones are delicious. My mum –'

Marcus saw an opening and pounced. 'I bet your mum's aren't anything like as good as Cookie's. She makes the best scones and homemade strawberry jam.'

Cookie smiled fondly down at him. 'As it happens, I do have some scones and jam, and even some whipped cream!'

CHAPTER TWO

MARCUS

'What's your name, pretty lady?'

She took a drag on her cigarette and turned to look at him. He was leaning on the bar and playing with a drink coaster; his frame was tall, muscular and powerful.

'What kind of a pick-up line is that, Mr Lane?'

He smiled, and she could see that he was pleased that she knew who he was. 'Just a simple question. You have me at a disadvantage.'

'Melissa Morrison.'

'Now, if I said "pretty name for a pretty lady", *that* would be a lame pick-up line.'

Her laugh was deep and throaty. 'You could just buy me a drink and we'll go from there.'

Melissa Morrison was the daughter of an enforcer who worked for many of East London's gangs, including the Kray twins. A pretty, green-eyed blonde with a sharp tongue and plenty of street smarts, she'd had a tough upbringing, with her father frequently in jail and her mother liking to drink.

Norman Lane was the heir to a well-established dynasty, and that made him a catch. So, he had a temper and a reputation for physical cruelty – Melissa was used to men like that. When Norman took her home, Tobias liked her. She had an old head on young shoulders, and she knew how to calm his son's violent side. Tobias wanted his fiery, impetuous son to marry into the 'family', someone who would understand what her husband did for a living, know her place, and have no qualms about the source of her lifestyle.

Norman was infatuated, and in April 1965 they were married in an elaborate, somewhat ostentatious church wedding with a huge reception. On that day she told her new husband that if he ever laid a finger on her in anger, she would take her revenge with a knife in the middle of the night and he would never see it coming. He laughed, until he realised she wasn't laughing. She fell pregnant on the Italian honeymoon and, on 6 January 1966, Marcus Tobias Lane was born.

* * *

'What's your house like, then?'

Marcus looked at the boy playing across from him in the sandpit in the local park. He obviously didn't have a nanny.

'It's very big, but not as big as my granddad's house,' Marcus said.

'Who lives in your house?'

'The gardener and the cook, they live in a cottage. And Billy, he's the chauffeur, and Mrs Teed, she's the housekeeper and her husband is our butler, Maurice. And Nanny, of course.'

Melissa had hired a woman who came from the 'family' and knew the kind of upbringing the Lanes wanted for their son. His earliest memory was Nanny taking him into the drawing room to see his parents and the large train track that covered the carpet. He ran to the shiny black engine and all the carriages. 'A train!'

His father got down on one knee beside him. 'I'm going to get Maurice to set this up in the playroom. Look at all the things you can put in there. It can pull a passenger train or a freight train.'

The engine felt cold and smooth under Marcus's small fingers. He pushed it along the carpet. 'Make it go, Daddy!'

His father laughed. 'Maurice will, I promise.'

In July 1970 Melissa had a daughter, and they called her Millicent after Tobias's mother. From the moment she came home, Millie was the centre of her big brother's life. He helped Nanny to bath her, dress her and feed her, and he pushed the pram when they went for walks. For a while he insisted that Nanny call him 'Marcus Big Brother', telling his parents it was his Red Indian name. Life was blissful.

Then towards the end of that year he sensed a change in Nanny's behaviour. She told him he was growing up and, at nearly five, he was now too old to sit on his father's lap. And yet she started to give him hugs out of the blue for no reason. It was all very confusing.

'Do you want Christmas to come, Nanny?'

She was feeding Millie and answered without looking at him. 'Of course. All that food and presents and snow.'

Marcus nodded. 'Then it'll be next year. And then you know what happens? My birthday!'

There was a moment of silence.

'Do you know what you're going to give me for my birthday?' he asked.

'What would you like?'

He grinned. He liked this game.

'A real giraffe. Or maybe an elephant or a lion.'

She gave him her usual good-natured laugh.

'Now where would you put a giraffe? We certainly don't have room for an elephant, and what would we feed a lion?'

'Daddy would make Billy build me a giraffe house, like we saw at the zoo. We could feed it branches from a tree.'

'Wouldn't you rather have a seal? It could swim in your granddad's lake.'

He squealed with joy. 'Seal eat fish. I could feed my goldfish to the seal.'

* * *

On 6 January, Marcus was given an enormous stuffed toy giraffe with its own wooden giraffe house. He tried not to show his disappointment at the fact that his goldfish were safe. After a birthday tea with cake and lemonade, he made a snowman in the garden with his parents. Then they explained to him that his life was about to change. The halcyon days with Nanny were over, and it was time for him to start growing into a man; it was time for school.

Later in life he would go to Priory College, an elite public school, but his first school was a primary in the East End. Williams Street was a school with a roll no one talked about, because if the locals talked about where many of the children came from, someone might visit them with a sledgehammer and a not-so-polite request for silence.

Marcus was oblivious to all this on his first day, in his new uniform and shiny shoes, with his writing book and pencil case. He sat very still on the mat with all the other beginners and listened to the rules. At playtime he followed some of them to the bathroom and urinated in public for the first time in his life.

'Who are you?'

He looked up to see two older boys looking down at him. A shiver of unease ran down his back.

'Marcus Lane,' he said quietly.

'First day, Lane?'

The questioner was a thickset boy with longish hair and glasses.

'Yes.'

'Do you know what happens on the first day?'

Marcus frowned. 'No.'

Both boys laughed.

'No one told you about the induction, then?'

'No.'

They grabbed him by a shoulder each and picked him up. His feet, in their new shoes, dangled off the ground. He was about to demand that they put him down, but before the words came out they had carried him into a nearby stall and thrust him head-first into a toilet bowl.

'Welcome to Williams, Lane.'

Marcus decided to obey their threats and tell no one, not the teacher, not Nanny, not his parents, but on the evening of his fourth day something changed.

Nanny was putting him to bed. 'Would you like to get back at those boys who are dunking you in the toilet?'

He looked up at her in astonishment. 'How do you know about that?'

She smiled. 'I just do, and I have a plan.'

The next morning she gave him a plastic bowl and instructed him to pee into it. Then she transferred the contents into a small water pistol and put it in his pocket.

'Just as they go to dunk you, pull free and squirt them both in the face with your gun. Can you do that?'

Marcus grinned at her. He knew exactly what to do. 'I can and I won't miss.'

He was so excited that he could hardly wait until playtime, but he knew part of the 'game' was to appear as scared as ever.

He walked with the other children into the bathroom and waited for his tormentors to approach. They were a little late and he was beginning to worry that they had given up.

'You still using the bathroom, Lane?'

The familiar sensation of being lifted up by the shoulders followed, and he had only a second to slip his hand into his blazer pocket. The gun felt reassuringly hard under his fingers. As they put him down and went to grab his head, he kicked out and spun free. He had a split second to pull the gun out, aim for a face and pull the trigger.

'Ahhhh!' The boy's hands went to his eyes.

Marcus swung around and squirted the rest at the other culprit.

'Shit! That stings!'

Both boys ran out and started washing their faces at the basins. Marcus pushed the gun back into his pocket and straightened his clothes. He paused behind the boys still bent over the taps. 'Don't ever touch me again.'

To his surprise, his classmates came up to him throughout the day and talked to him, asked to be his friend and seemed really impressed with what he had done. Slowly he began to pick up the language of the playground, and when he swore at home he expected Nanny to reprimand him like she used to, but she didn't.

Three boys who lived close to the school asked him if he would like to be in their gang. One often had bruises on his face and arms, but Marcus didn't dare ask why. They were tough kids and they expected him to be tough too. It was time to get some advice.

'Dad?'

His father looked up from the notebook on his desk. 'Marcus. Come in.'

Norman got up and walked over to the sofa, sat down and patted the spot beside him. Marcus missed sitting on his father's lap but understood that he was too old for that now. He ran to the sofa and sat down.

'How's school?' Norman asked.

'Okay, I guess. I want to know something.'

His father nodded. 'Ask away, little man.'

'I have three friends – Mikey, Rory and Tom – and we're in a gang together. They don't like Jimmy Richardson because he's scared all the time. When we talk to him, he cries. Tom wants Rory and me to beat him up. If I don't, they won't let me be in their gang anymore.'

'Do you like them?' his father asked.

'I guess so. Tom's dad hits him, but Rory said Tom deserves it 'cause he answers back. Rory and Mikey do everything Tom tells them. Rory lets me share his lunch, and he shows me his dinosaur books. Tom says books are stupid.'

'Beating up Jimmy – this is Tom's idea?'

Marcus nodded slowly. 'Everything we do is Tom's idea.'

His father studied him for a moment.

'Tom's a leader, but you need to be a leader too. Tom's right – if this Jimmy is weak and cries, then he needs to toughen up. Weak men don't make it in this world.'

Marcus watched his father closely. 'So it's okay, then?'

'What's Tom's other name?'

Marcus frowned and thought hard.

'Tom McGregor.'

Norman smiled. 'Thought so. I know his dad – he works for us sometimes. A good man, a hard man. This is what I want you to do: listen up.'

Marcus nestled closer and focused his full attention on his father.

* * *

The next day he met Tom, Rory and Mikey in their usual place behind the janitor's shed. Marcus could hear his father's words ringing in his ears as he approached them: *Make a tight ball with your hand, lock your wrist and drive from your shoulder, through your elbow.*

He clenched his hand into a fist, walked straight up to Tom and punched him in the chest. The boy doubled over in pain, and Marcus drove his fist upwards in a savage upper cut that knocked Tom to the ground.

'What are you doing?' Rory yelled.

Marcus waited until Tom stood up. Marcus was at least two inches taller, and the height advantage meant he could glare down at his opponent. Tom was rubbing his chin but said nothing.

'I'm the top dog now, and we're going to do what *I* say. Rory and Tom, you're going to beat up Jimmy Richardson – this afternoon, when he takes a shortcut across the back field.'

The other two boys looked at Tom, who shrugged his agreement.

* * *

Eighteen months after he started school, Marcus was a changed boy. His father had taught him how to clench his fist, draw his elbow back and throw a strong, accurate punch. When he had a boy on the ground, he knew where to bite and use his nails to inflict maximum pain. On the odd occasion he came out on the wrong side of a dust-up, he knew how to rub it hard and swallow his tears so no one saw that it hurt.

In class he had raced ahead of his friends. Nanny had taught him well, and from day one he could write him own name and follow simple words in a book. He enjoyed the playground and the sports ground more, the rough and tumble of physical play. His frame was tall and thin, deceptively strong and fit, and undergoing a growth spurt.

Tom had decided that he wanted Marcus as his best friend, so had taken him home to show him where his father hid the guns, chains and baseball bats. Marcus was fascinated by the weapons, the weight of them in his hands, the menace they contained just by their shape and purpose. He had overheard conversations at home, but he had never actually seen a gun before.

'You never point a gun at someone unless you mean to use it,' Marcus said, with the usual authority in his voice.

'What about to scare them?' Tom asked.

'Well, maybe that's okay. But you need to know if it's loaded. I might point this at you for fun and pull the trigger, and someone might have left it loaded and I might blow your brains out.'

One fateful Saturday afternoon they were playing in the garage, pretending to drive one of the classic cars Tom's father collected. The double doors at one end swung open and two men staggered in, dragging a third between them. The middle man was covered in blood. When the two men let him go, he fell to the ground.

'Leave him here until dark. Get the van.'

Marcus tugged on Tom's sleeve and pointed to the footwell below them. Both boys sank down and curled into balls. Tom had more room because Marcus was on the driver's side and some of his space was taken up with pedals. Marcus closed his eyes tight and tried to hold his breath. The men were walking away, he could hear their footsteps on the floor, then something must have grabbed one of them and he tripped.

'Don't leave me! I … won't tell … anyone. I need –'

The voice was muffled as though the speaker had something in his mouth.

'Just shut the fuck up!'

There was a hard whack, the sound of something hitting concrete followed by a loud groan, then more footsteps and the slamming of the doors. Marcus opened his eyes and watched Tom. The boy's face was flushed and his eyes mirrored the excitement Marcus felt. Tom put his finger to his lips and they both waited in silence. Eventually Marcus pulled himself up and peered over the dashboard. He looked back at Tom.

'They've gone,' he whispered. 'Come on.'

Slowly the boys climbed out of the car and shut the doors behind them as quietly as they could.

The man lay face-down on the concrete, a pool of blood spreading from under his head. Marcus reached out with his foot and tentatively kicked the body. It didn't move.

'He's dead,' said Tom in a normal voice.

Marcus stared at the man's scalp: the black hair was matted with blood, and he could see bone sticking out from the wound.

'What did they hit him with?' Tom asked.

'I don't know. A bat, an iron bar.'

He could hear Tom walking to the door, but Marcus's limbs felt heavy and wouldn't move, even if he told them to. It was the most horrible and amazing thing he had ever seen, and he wanted to remember it.

'Marcus, come on! Before they look for us.'

Reluctantly, Marcus pulled himself away and joined Tom in the doorway. He looked over his shoulder, but Tom pulled him around.

'We didn't see anything, we were never here. If Dad finds out, he'll thrash us both.'

CHAPTER THREE

TOM

Tom McGregor's earliest memory was the sound of his father's fists on bone, his mother screaming as she was dragged down the hall by her hair, and his elder sisters shielding him from the fallout. He was the same age as Marcus and Vinnie for part of the year, born in the East End in December 1966 to Dorothy and Stuart McGregor. He was their fourth child and first son, and over the next seven years they had another boy and then twin boys.

Stuart was a brutal, Glaswegian-born enforcer for hire, which meant he worked as a bouncer and as muscle for gangs who needed money collected or if they wanted to persuade clients that protection was worth paying for. He helped pimps establish new territory by persuading existing hookers to leave, and occasionally he boxed bare-knuckle fights for a purse. What he didn't do was kill people, not for any price. If he went to jail, it was for more minor offences and never for very long. If he hadn't had a fondness for drink and a gambling addiction, his family could have lived quite well off the money he earned.

Dorothy took in washing and ironing for people who couldn't, or wouldn't, do their own. Tom spent his early years playing among other people's clothing, which was hanging on lines inside and outside the housing estate flat where they lived. He learned young to share – food, clothes, toys, his bed – and if someone had something he wanted for his family, he learned to take that as well. He was a stocky little boy, strong and fearless, and he could punch and kick almost before he could walk.

* * *

When he was four, Tom volunteered to be the one his father hit if he was angry. His older sisters cried when they got thrashed with Dad's belt, and the younger ones were still babies. He knew what made his dad mad – if he was caught looking at a book, or if he made a sandwich without permission, or if the babies made too much noise. It might start differently, but it always ended the same way.

'Come here, ya little shite!'

His dad dragged him across the room to the small wooden stool. Tom didn't resist – it was better to get it over with quickly. Usually by now he could hear the belt being pulled off his father's trousers, but today that sound was missing.

'I've got a surprise for ya.'

One arm forced him down over the stool and he could see the pattern on the carpet. Once again he started counting the brown roses that intertwined with the green branches.

Thwack!

It was a different sound and it hurt a lot more. He swallowed the shock and the reaction that rose up in his throat. Tears sprang into his eyes, and he couldn't see the flowers.

Thwack!

The second one wasn't so bad, not such a surprise. If he tried very hard, his body wouldn't jump much. Five roses and two branches.

Thwack!

After three blows his dad released his grip and Tom stood up. It was a piece of wood, about half a broom-handle length, round and heavy.

'That should teach ya. Stay out of me way.'

His father stumbled off towards the door. 'I'm going to the pub,' he mumbled as he passed Dorothy, who was watching from just inside the doorway. As soon as the front door had slammed shut, she went to Tom and gave him a hug.

'I don't know why you're always upsetting him. Would you like a cup of cocoa?'

* * *

Just before Tom's fifth birthday his father had a windfall. It was a job that should have gone to someone else, but the usual muscle had been shot in the leg the night before, so Monty Joe rang Stuart one autumn morning and asked whether he could collect a debt.

'Nothing to it. He owes £1000 and the debt's three months overdue, so now its £5000. Rough him up, scare him, take something valuable as collateral, and give him twenty-four hours. Usual story.'

When Stuart got there, the door was open and the man was dead, shot in the back of the head, execution-style. The flat had been turned over, but he found a tin, wrapped in plastic and hidden in the toilet cistern. It contained £150 and a key. Stuart took the money, and was about to leave the key behind when he saw it had a card attached with a series of numbers written on it, so he took it, too. When he was far enough away, he called Monty and told him what had happened.

Monty was furious and took the £150. Stuart didn't tell him about the key, and was about to bin it when instinct told him to check the numbers. They looked like a bank account number, so he started at his local Lloyds branch.

Three hours later he burst through his own front door.

'Dot, ya in there?'

She looked up from the shirt on her ironing board in the kitchen. He didn't sound angry, but you could never tell for sure.

'In here, love.'

He was framed in the doorway, his muscles obvious under his shirt, a stupid grin on his face and a piece of paper in his hand.

'Want some good news for a change?' he asked.

She smiled at him, carefully. 'Course.'

'I found a key with numbers on a wee card. The bank told me it was a key to some box at a Morgenstern bank. All I needed were the numbers I had – one's an account and the other's some sort of ID thing.'

'Sounds very posh. Have you had a look in the box?'

He nodded and walked towards her, still grinning.

'What do ya think is in it?' he asked.

She frowned. 'I haven't got a clue, Stuart. Stop playing games.'

He hugged her. 'Money. Lots of bloody money.'

* * *

Stuart waited a sensible amount of time to see if anyone would talk about the missing money or if it might belong to someone he didn't want to cross. But no one said a word on the street, in the pub, on the phone. He staked out the flat, but no one went near it, and Monty seemed none the wiser. So, eventually,

Stuart withdrew the money and bought a nice house and started a collection of classic cars. Dorothy gave up doing other people's washing. The children still went to Williams Street School, and Stuart insisted they went on the bus. Life was challenging and they had to learn that lesson at a tender age. He considered it his duty to teach them, and their new wealth didn't alter that obligation.

* * *

Tom liked school. It gave him a chance to pass on the anger inside. When he was feeling frightened about going home, he bullied the weaker kids at school, and that made him feel braver. His three friends were Rory, Mikey and Marcus, and together they formed the WSS Gang. Whenever they passed Jimmy Richardson in the corridor, they glared at him, and he whimpered and tried not to cry. That was a fatal error around someone like Tom, and it took just seconds to decide that this kid was their first victim. Tom declared they would wait for Jimmy beside the shortcut he used across the back field and ambush him.

'He deserves a beating,' Tom announced and looked hard at the other boys.

'Why?' asked Marcus.

Marcus was unconvinced, and that annoyed Tom. He didn't like being questioned on his patch.

'He breathes – that's bad enough. Think about it: either you're with us or you're not part of the gang anymore.'

* * *

Marcus had a certain status for Tom: he was Norman Lane's son, and Tom's dad had been very impressed when Tom had told him he was friends with Marcus. The last thing he wanted was to have to deliver on his threat to ban Marcus from the gang. As he saw his friend rounding the corner of the janitor's shed, he knew everything would be all right. Marcus was on board.

Before he had time to react, a fist punched him square in the solar plexus. The pain radiated out in a sharp jolt, like an electric shock, and bent him over at the waist. Another fist appeared from nowhere, hurtling up towards his unprotected chin. The force sent him sprawling on the ground, and he hit his head, hard.

He heard Rory's voice, full of panic, demanding to know why Marcus was doing that. He wanted the question answered, too, and he pulled himself to his feet, rubbing his aching jaw. Marcus stood, hands on hips, glaring at him, daring him to punch back. Then his best friend delivered the knock-out blow: the declaration of the change of leadership.

Marcus taught Tom everything he knew: how to punch more effectively and how to receive a punch, how to lie with a straight face, and how to kick someone when they were on the ground. Tom was a fast learner, and had a deceptive amount of strength in his small body. Rory and Mikey were their acolytes and did what they were told: gave up their superior sandwiches at lunchtime, shoplifted chocolate bars from the corner shop and retrieved balls when Tom and Marcus kicked them out of range.

Tom asked his mother if he could invite Marcus home to play. She said 'yes, but not when your dad's here'. He knew why and didn't argue, because he had no desire for Marcus to see what his dad did. Marcus had undoubtedly seen the bruises but had never commented, and Tom felt sure that if he was thrashed, too, he would have said something. At a subconscious level, Tom had no desire to see his dad fawn over Norman Lane's son, just like everyone else did.

The first few afternoons went well. Then one Saturday they were playing in the garage when they heard a murder being committed by two men on a third. Tom had never seen anything remotely like that, and his main concerns were that his dad never knew he had been there and that Marcus never knew that one of the men was Tom's father. Something deep in his child consciousness told him that his father's response would be more terrible than he could imagine. Marcus had seemed fascinated by the body and was happy to keep their secret, but he never accepted another invitation to visit.

CHAPTER FOUR

RACK AND RUIN

Unbeknown to Vinnie, Tobias Lane had made his father an offer Bert couldn't refuse – five times his former salary. Lane had worked for the Kray twins in the 1950s, but when their rivalry with the Richardson gang escalated into murder, he had struck out on his own. The Krays imprisonment in 1969 left a hole to fill. As well as the usual roll-call of lucrative activities – armed robbery, bookmaking, loan sharking, extortion and protection rackets, drugs, arson, prostitution and fencing stolen goods – he had just begun to branch out into people smuggling. He used secret compartments in his trucks to bring illegal workers into the country and create an underground workforce.

His last chief accountant had suddenly disappeared, and he needed a new one to keep his different sets of books in order, to launder his money offshore, and to make sure the authorities were satisfied with the sanitised accounts. His front as a law-abiding businessman was crucial to his freedom.

Bert told himself, as he listened to Lane's persuasive pitch, that this was a temporary solution, until something else came along. He knew Mary would be horrified, but he didn't need to tell her about the seedy underbelly that resided behind the cover of 'prominent businessman', hidden in the violent shadows. He had no way of knowing how addictive the salary, and the lifestyle it afforded, would become.

Lane's only child, Norman, Marcus's father, was a hugely ambitious man. He hid his desire to take over the reins of the organisation and make changes, especially to the systems used to collect monies owed, but Bert was a sharp reader of people and he could see the signs. Norman was a strict believer in pecking orders, and he made sure Bert understood the consequences of failure. Men in key positions, like Bert's, were paid extra for their discretion and loyalty.

* * *

On Vinnie's third visit, Marcus showed him his hidden den in the hollow trunk of a huge tree. The earth floor was covered by sheets of old newspaper, and dried bird carcasses were hung from the spurs inside the trunk. Marcus displayed his treasures, sealed in a variety of metal tins. They represented the loot from his growing career as a thief, and he offered to teach Vinnie the tricks of the trade.

They began by sneaking into the pantry and stealing handfuls of chocolate chips and tiny marshmallows from the baking jars.

'Never take all of it. That way they won't notice, and they'll just think they've used more than they thought.'

Vinnie nodded his understanding and held out the tin he had taken from his mother's sewing basket. Marcus took a small handful of chocolate and poured it into the tin: 'Carrying it out by hand is no good – it melts.'

33

Then they moved onto taking pound notes from Cookie's petty cash tin in the kitchen. Once Vinnie felt comfortable doing that and had got over his nerves, Marcus showed him where the key to his grandfather's gentlemen's wardrobe was hidden. It was a small key in a tiny lock, and Vinnie's hands were shaking as he tried to insert it.

'Here, let me! You'll take all day.' Marcus pulled the key away and opened the carved walnut door. The space was filled by a series of drawers.

'This one has money, coins and notes.' Marcus took a few coins, put them in his pocket and shut the drawer. 'And this one has old cigarettes. Shall we try one?'

Vinnie nodded silently. Marcus gave him two, and Vinnie stuffed them into his trouser pocket.

'And this one has his dirty magazines. Look at this!'

Marcus took the top magazine off the pile and opened it at the centre spread. He turned it around so Vinnie could see the naked young woman sprawled across the double page. She had a magnificent set of breasts and a come-hither smile.

Vinnie burst out laughing. 'Put it away, idiot.'

Marcus glared at him. 'Don't you want to look at one? Grandpa does. I'll take something from the middle and we'll hide it in the den.'

'I'd rather have cars or motorbikes, or some great paintings.'

Marcus shook his head. 'You're strange – you're not normal.'

The next important lesson was how to lie effectively. Marcus passed on what his father had shared with him. Most people don't lie well, they have a 'tell' that betrays them, but a few can look you straight in the face and look as honest as the day is long. To have a good career as a criminal, it was important to be able to lie convincingly and to be able to tell when you were being lied to. Vinnie liked the idea of being able to tell when people were lying, but he decided to leave the lying part until he found someone in his life he wanted to lie to.

One visit, which he remembered for years, began innocently enough when they took fishing rods and a net down to the lake. Marcus insisted that there were fish in there, but after half an hour of sitting with their feet dangling in the water flicking the lines into the middle of the lake, Marcus got bored.

'Let's take the net and see if we can catch something down that end.'

He pointed to the far side of the lake. As usual Vinnie agreed, so they left the rods on the bank and took the net in search of bounty. It was early summer and there were ducklings swimming among the shallow reeds. Marcus caught one almost immediately. Vinnie wanted to pat it and let it go back to the distressed duck watching them from the lake, but Marcus instructed him to hold it and wait while he caught another one. The second proved a bit harder, and for a moment Vinnie thought the duck was going to attack them. Marcus dropped the net and turned to run back towards the bridge.

'Come on, slow coach!' he yelled.

They carried their fluffy cargo in both hands out in front of them, around the lake to the foot of the bridge.

'I've invented a new sport,' Marcus said breathlessly. 'Duck racing!'

And so the new form of pooh sticks was born. Marcus caught the ducklings in the net and they took them to the bridge and dropped them over the side, then raced to see which duckling emerged first. Vinnie let his go as carefully as he could, whereas Marcus threw his at the water. The drop wasn't very far and the little birds appeared unhurt by the experience, but Vinnie was very glad when the ducklings grew too large for Marcus to catch.

As far as Vinnie was concerned, for the next three and half years he accompanied his father to the Lane house on a regular basis and played with Marcus. He knew his mother wasn't particularly happy, and she never came with them, but, with the innocence of youth, he just accepted it.

* * *

'Do you still want to be a pilot?' Marcus asked.

They were lying on their backs on the freshly mown lawn, staring up at the clouds. It was the summer of 1976 and the massive garden around them was in full bloom. Vinnie could hear bees and insects nearby. His tummy was full of fruit pie and cola and he felt content.

'I think so,' he said, as he traced a pattern in the air with his finger. 'You get to see lots of exciting places. I want to travel to all the places in the atlas you gave me last Christmas.'

He rolled over and glanced at Marcus. The boy's eyes were closed. That meant he was thinking.

'Or I could go into space instead. Do you still want to go into the family business?' Vinnie asked.

Marcus shrugged. 'I guess so. Dad says one day it'll all be mine.'

'All what?'

The boy waved his arm in the direction of the house. 'All this. And whatever it is they do. Granddad says they're businessmen, but I ... Maybe you should become an accountant and you could work for me.'

Vinnie pulled a face. Sometimes Marcus assumed too much. 'Why would I want to work for you? Unless you set up an airline.'

Marcus opened his eyes, turned and grinned at him. 'Maybe I will and you could fly us all over the world.'

Vinnie made swooping motions like a plane with his hand. 'Lane Airways. Or you could put a P in front of it and make it Plane Airways.'

Both boys laughed, and the sharp, happy sound echoed around the empty garden.

'If you become a pilot, then I promise I'll set up Plane Airways and you can be the chief pilot.'

Vinnie was delighted. Marcus always made such sense, and his confident way of treating people – other children, staff and shop assistants – thrilled Vinnie. They did as Marcus demanded, even the adults. No one ever bullied Marcus, and he would have thumped anyone who tried.

'Vin?'

The familiar voice made him roll over, sit up and then get to his feet. His father was standing on the drive with his briefcase in his hand.

'Time to go. Come on.'

His father sounded impatient in his good-natured way. Vinnie looked down at Marcus, who hadn't moved. 'See ya next time,' he said.

Marcus nodded. 'Remember what we say: don't take no shit from nobody.'

Vinnie laughed happily. 'No shit.'

He turned and ran across the lawn to his father. Bert put his arm around Vinnie's shoulders and they walked off together towards the car. Glancing back, Vinnie saw that Marcus had pulled himself up on his elbows and was watching them.

* * *

A week later Vinnie had been out shopping with his mother. He needed new plimsolls, and she had given in to his pleading for some records and books. Life had changed in the past four years – they lived in a much nicer house and held regular dinner parties, and he was used to getting quality toys for his birthday and Christmas. Two years ago Marcus's grandfather had given him remote-controlled cars on a racing-car circuit for Christmas.

Today they had stopped for ice cream, walked beside the Serpentine in Hyde Park, and come home on the tube. He loved these outings: his mother was a fun person to be with, and he hadn't reached the age where it was naff to hang out with your mum. He drew the line at holding her hand, but they had sung their favourite song as they walked down the street from the tube station to the house.

She unlocked the door and went in first. He was just inside when he heard her scream. It was a sound he had never heard before, a shrill, scary noise, a mixture of terror, shock, despair and rage. She was frozen in the doorway to the front room, and behind her he could see his father's lower legs lying at a funny angle on a plastic sheet and bright red blood on the wall.

'What –'

She swung around. 'No, Vinnie! *No!* Come with me.'

She was very white and shaking violently, but she used her arms to push him backwards, her hands against his chest. He was too confused to mount any resistance, and she slammed the door, grasped his shoulder and hauled him outside and down the steps.

'What's wrong? Mum? What's happened to Dad?' he asked, panic gripping him harder than her hand.

'Be quiet. Just come with me.'

She half-dragged him down the path, onto the street and around to the next-door neighbour's house.

'I want you to stay here.'

She banged on the door with her closed fist.

'Why? What's happen –'

The door was opened by Mr Weatherly, half of the pensioner couple who lived there. He was already in his pyjamas and dressing gown, and stepped back in surprise.

'Mrs Ross —'

Mary shoved Vinnie at the old man. 'Please take care of him, Jim. Whatever happens, *don't* let him come back to the house.'

Vinnie spun around and nearly fell off the step. Jim caught him by the shirt and pulled him back.

'Please, Mum! Just tell me —'

Mary shook her head. 'No, Vin. I have to go. Be good and don't look out the window.'

Jim had been joined by his wife. The woman reached across him, took Vinnie's arm and drew him inside the doorway.

'Of course we will, Mary, don't you worry about him … Come on, dear, come and have some lemonade.'

The door shut behind him, and Vinnie followed her reluctantly. His heart was pounding and his throat felt tight.

The ambulance arrived, followed by the police. He heard the sirens and the flurry of activity, doors banging and voices raised, but his guardians wouldn't let him go to the window. They fed him cake, but he didn't feel like eating, and when they tried to distract him with *Blue Peter* on television, he saw nothing and strained to hear what was happening next door.

His head spun with fear and an emotion he had never felt before. Something was very wrong. Every possible reason for what he had seen in the lounge ran riot through his brain. He had brought some artwork home from school — maybe his father had been hanging it up and had slipped, broken a leg and hit his head?

On a more sinister note, Vinnie had a secret. Marcus had given him a cigarette-card collection to hide, something Marcus had nicked from a kid at his school and didn't want in his possession in case someone accused him and demanded his locker be searched. It had some rare cards, and Marcus intended to sell it and split the profits with Vinnie. To make matters worse, Vinnie had shared the secret when he had promised he wouldn't. Had someone broken into the house in order to steal it back? The thought that his father had been hurt because of a card collection made his stomach turn over.

When his mother finally came back, her eyes were red-rimmed and her face was swollen and tear-stained.

She hugged him fiercely, and her body trembled against his. 'We've always been honest with each other, and I'm not going to lie to you now, darling boy. Your father is dead.'

The words hit him like a swift punch in the solar plexus, and it was hard to catch his breath. He had accepted what the old couple had said: that his father had probably broken something and needed to go to hospital. His mother was watching him. She was probably wondering if her words had made sense. Did anyone want the damn card collection badly enough to *kill* for it? His eyes filled with tears, and she took his hands in hers. Her skin felt cold, and that was enough to break his train of thought. His voice was small, and the words were hard to force out.

'How ... how did he ... die?'

'He shot himself. I know it's hard to understand right now, but you will. And we will be okay. We will cope together.'

Suddenly Vinnie could feel something he didn't understand. It seemed to be spreading from his heart, and it made his limbs feel heavy. Her voice sounded unfamiliar and came from a very long way away. For one thing, he couldn't see how she knew that they would be okay. How could anything ever be okay again?

* * *

Over the next few days it became apparent that Bert had been tipped off about an impending surprise audit. His calculations were excellent; his attention to detail, meticulous; he'd hidden money very cleverly, but not cleverly enough to fool the full scrutiny of the forensic accountants of Her Majesty's Revenue and Customs. When his worst fears appeared to be coming true, he transferred money to offshore accounts set up for the purpose, carefully burned all his ledgers and papers in the fireplace of the front room, spread a sheet on the floor to make cleaning up easier and put a bullet through his brain.

His note explained that he knew he would never stand up to intensive questioning and that he had acted alone, his employer was innocent. He had created a double set of accounts but gambled the extra money away. He would never survive jail, so he had taken the easy way out. The essential evidence had been destroyed by fire, and Tobias Lane insisted he knew nothing of what his accountant had done.

Mary was furious and completely mortified. She had suspected that Lane was a crooked businessman, but she'd had no idea he had corrupted her Bert to that extent.

'My husband has never gambled a penny in his life, until now.' She sat very straight in the chair, a handkerchief twisting between her hands, and looked at the stick insect of a man opposite her. Tobias Lane had been just a name, and now she was confronted with the unpleasant reality.

'I understand what a shock this has been and that's why I'm here. I want to help.'

Mary glared at him. 'How exactly do you think you can do that?' Her voice was icy.

He sighed. 'The only way I can. Financially.'

Mary stiffened. How dare he! 'We don't need, nor want, your money.'

He smiled, and she could see a hint of indulgence in his cold eyes. She was a very gentle person, but she had never wanted to punch a man more in her life.

'Come now, Mrs Whitney-Ross. I insist that you let me pay for Bert's funeral.'

'Absolutely not!' She shot to her feet. 'On no condition will I allow that to happen. Bert would be horrified, and I'll thank you to stop patronising me.'

He shrugged. 'Very well. Then please allow me to help with Vinnie. He's a bright lad, he deserves a good education. Will you allow me to pay to send him to public school?'

It was a tempting offer. There was no way she, as a widow, could afford it. Did she have the right to reject such an opportunity for her son because of her hatred for this contemptible man? 'On one condition.'

'Name it.'

'We move away. I want to sell up and buy somewhere else.'

'Still in London?'

'Probably. Possibly. I don't know.' She knew the anguish in her voice was obvious, and it made her feel vulnerable. He stood up.

'Very well, take your time. When you are settled and ready to send him to school, let me know. I am happy to help. Bert was my friend.'

* * *

Vinnie held his mother's hand throughout the funeral, and she didn't cry, not once. He took his cue from her and choked back the tears. Marcus didn't come, but his parents and grandparents were there. Mary shook their hands, but didn't meet their gaze.

Two days later, Vinnie took the cigarette-card collection to his father's old friend, Monty Joe, and sold it for £100.

He suspected it was worth much more, but he didn't know who else to ask. The next day he dipped into his savings box, and took some pound notes, plus the £100, to school. Throughout the day he kept checking his pocket to make sure the money was still there, bundled up and held with a rubber band. After school he walked to the nearest taxi rank and gave the driver the address written down on a piece of paper. His feet didn't reach the floor of the back seat, and he spent the journey looking out the window and practising what he was going to say.

The house was as imposing as ever, and even scarier without his father. He paid the driver and pocketed the few coins left.

The butler answered the door. 'Why hello, Master Whitney-Ross. What can we do for you?'

Vinnie drew himself up. 'I would like to see Mr Tobias, please.'

The butler hesitated, and then opened the door wide. 'Come in, sir. I will put you in the library and tell Mr Tobias that you are here.'

'Thank you.'

Vinnie followed the butler across the massive entrance hall and into the library. He had been here before, and it contained more books than he had ever seen in anyone's house, but none of them looked as though they had been read.

The butler pointed to an armchair. 'Please take a seat. Would you like some lemonade?'

'No, thank you.'

'Very well.' The elderly man left him alone.

The room was silent. Vinnie noticed how the sunlight coming in the window picked up particles of dust in the air. They seemed to be dancing as they fell to the ground.

'Vinnie!'

The booming voice gave him a start and he jumped. Mr Tobias was standing in the doorway.

Vinnie stood up. 'Hello, sir.'

Lane strode across the room and held out his hand. Vinnie shook it and the man's grasp embraced his past his wrist.

'What a nice surprise. How are you? How is your mother? It was a very fitting funeral.'

'We're fine, thank you, sir.'

Vinnie sat down and Lane sat opposite him. There was a moment's silence.

'Have you come to ask me for something?' Lane asked gently.

Vinnie shook his head. 'No, sir. I'm the master of the house now and I wanted to tell you that I'm very sorry. For what my dad did. He wasn't a bad man.'

Mr Tobias was studying him, his head on a slight angle and his eyes kind. He didn't seem mad to find Vinnie here. Something told Vinnie he wouldn't want to make Mr Tobias mad.

'No, of course he wasn't! And he was an excellent father. I could see that because he brought you with him to play with Marcus.'

At the sound of his friend's name, Vinnie smiled and sat forward. 'Is he here? Marcus?'

Mr Tobias shook his head. 'No, I'm afraid he's at his house. Can I give him a message for you?'

Vinnie nodded. 'I just wanted to say goodbye. We're moving away. I wanted him to know that I loved having him as my friend.'

'I'll make sure he knows that, and he will miss you, too.'

Vinnie stood up. 'When I'm older and I have a job and I'm earning money, I will pay you back any money that my dad owed you. I have this, for now.' He took the roll of money from his pocket and held it out.

Mr Tobias said nothing for a moment, and then he sighed. He looked sad. 'Thank you, Vinnie, that's very grown-up of you. I won't forget that, but I won't take your money right now. You give that to your mother instead. Now, how did you get here?'

'In a taxi.'

'Does your mother know?'

Vinnie shook his head. 'I took the fare from my savings.'

Mr Tobias nodded. 'Never mind. I'll get Jones to call you a taxi, and when you get home you can give the driver this and put the change back in your savings and give the other money to your mother.'

Mr Tobias gave him a £20 note.

Vinnie's eyes widened. That was a lot of money! 'Thank you, sir.'

That night, as he lay in bed and thought about his day, it occurred to Vinnie that Mr Tobias hadn't asked him where the money had come from. Maybe Marcus had told his grandfather about the cigarette-card collection, so Mr Tobias already knew. It was a very grand house and Mr Tobias obviously didn't need extra money, so maybe he had told Marcus to forget about it. Either way, Vinnie felt uncomfortable about the money and unsure what to do with it. If he admitted to his mother that it was the proceeds of a crime she would be heartbroken, and he couldn't cause her any more pain. Best to hang on to it for now – you never know when you might need some capital to set up a little sideline business.

* * *

Mary sold the house and most of their possessions and bought a flat over a shop in Hendon, far away from the scene of her husband's betrayal. Vinnie missed his dad and Marcus very much, but being close to the RAF Museum was a bonus, and he visited there every weekend. The irony was not lost on Mary that they were also very close to the police college.

Vinnie found his own way of coping, part of which was lying about the way his father died. He had no way of knowing that if he had told his mother this, she would have been immensely relieved.

CHAPTER FIVE

MARCUS GROWS UP

Marcus did tell his mother about the body in the garage at Tom's, and she decided he wouldn't play there anymore. He was just getting tired of thinking up excuses when his grandfather introduced him to a new boy, a boy who didn't go to his school, a boy who came to visit with his grandfather's accountant, a boy who was easily led, a boy called Vinnie Whitney-Ross.

To start with, Marcus thought Vinnie was a bit of a softie. It seemed that the boy could *read* proper books, all by himself. That impressed Marcus, but he decided not to show it. When they played games, like running races, he won and that was what mattered. Vinnie was funny and clever and liked listening to his stories. He knew an awful lot about dinosaurs, and that meant they could play at being *Diplodocus* and *T-rex* on the lawn.

Once or twice he considered telling his friend about the time in the garage and the man on the floor, but he wasn't sure how Vinnie would react. Something told him that Vinnie wasn't fascinated by dead bodies, and he might decide not to come back.

The years flew by and Marcus grew more and more confident. No one questioned him when he ordered the servants around or reprimanded them, and even the teachers at school seemed a bit scared of him. He became aware that being 'Norman Lane's son' had advantages, and he used them to the hilt. Vinnie was a willing subject, and Marcus enjoying teaching him how to steal and how to tell when people were lying.

When he was ten he changed schools to Priory College Junior School, the feeder for the public school where he would spend his senior years. It was full of gullible, spoiled boys from wealthy backgrounds who were eager to show how grown-up they were, and it made for rich pickings for an articulate, manipulative boy like Marcus. Within days he had a group of acolytes who hung off his every word and delighted in bullying anyone who appeared weak.

During that summer his grandfather called him into the great big library. 'I have some news that might make you sad. Bert Whitney-Ross has shot himself. So Vinnie won't be coming to play anymore.'

Marcus hardly blinked, so used to hiding his emotions had he become. 'Vinnie has something of mine, something I want back. I can sell it.'

His grandfather looked surprised. 'What is it?'

'A collection of cigarette cards.'

'Is it yours to sell?'

Marcus shrugged. 'It is now.'

'Why does Vinnie have it?'

'In case someone wanted to search for it and found it in my locker. He's looking after it for me.'

Tobias smiled. 'Don't worry. I'll pay you for it. How much do you want?'

'Some of the cards are hard to find. I think £200 sounds fair.'

Tobias was obviously surprised again. 'Do you? I think £150 sounds generous. Now, run along and scam someone else.'

Later, Marcus went down to the garden and ripped the heads off all the carnations. Then he sat down on the lawn and cried with frustration. He knew crying was weak, but that strange emotion of missing Vinnie, the feeling he was so used to between visits, now seemed overwhelming. After a few moments he wiped his eyes and ran to the end of the lake where the net lay waiting. He played duckling racing by himself, as he considered how he would have liked to tell Vinnie that a gunshot was a noble way to die.

* * *

While Marcus's natural leadership skills made him popular at Priory College, his thinly veiled temper got him into trouble. He played rugby in the winter and cricket in the summer, and took great pride in wearing the purple house colours of Mortimer on his school tie. As he matured, the lesson about actions and consequences was reinforced: if you didn't commit the action, you weren't held responsible for the consequence. This seemed like a tremendous stroke of luck, so he found less intelligent boys who would take care of the physical side of discipline and punishment for him.

He styled his gang on the Italian mafia, and gave each boy a codename. He was 'Mario' and his compatriots were 'Luigi', 'Carlo', 'Vincenzo', 'Roberto' and 'Paulo'. He gleaned information from many sources and put it into action: homemade gunpowder led to homemade fireworks that flew higher than any shop-bought ones, and he even made a brief, if unsuccessful, foray into homemade napalm. But his most creative and popular invention was the matchbox bomb.

'How many should we use as flints?' The boys were staring at the contents of a matchbox, laid out on the table.

'Half and half,' Marcus replied.

They watched with quiet fascination as he prepared the matches and packed them back into the box, then wrapped it tightly in foil.

'Now what?'

Marcus smiled at the boy who had dared to ask the question.

'Now you get to try it out.'

The first one failed to ignite, so he packed it more snuggly and bound it into a hard silver ball. This time the elected perpetrator threw it into a wastepaper bin in the school playground and the explosion was immediate and dramatic.

Eventually, Marcus came to the attention of the Order of Bacchus, an association of senior boys who took their drinking seriously. They met fortnightly in a locked common room, and he knew the invitation to attend was a rare honour for a fourteen-year-old. The boy leading him there knocked on the door with a complicated sequence of rhythms.

'Enter.' The voice from inside was clear and strong. Marcus recognised it instantly but said nothing. The boy took a key from his blazer pocket and unlocked the door.

The room was bare, apart from five large chairs at one end. Each chair was occupied by a senior pupil dressed only in a toga made out of a white bed sheet, and each had a garland of plastic grapes and leaves on his head. Marcus's first reaction was to laugh out loud, but he knew that would be suicide.

'Name?' It was the same voice – the sports star of the senior year.

'Marcus Lane.'

'Age?'

'Fourteen.'

'Form Four. You're advanced for your age.'

Marcus always listened to his instinct, and this time his instinct was to keep quiet unless he was asked a direct question.

The boy to the left of the one speaking pointed at him. 'I hear you have a gang of thugs who follow your orders. Is this true?' he asked.

'I ... can persuade my fellow pupils to do what I ask them to do.'

All the boys smirked at him.

'So, if we wanted some enforcers to help with the initiation ceremony, you could help us?' asked the leader.

Marcus thought for a moment: be brave or be sensible? 'What's in it for me?' he asked.

The leader smiled and looked at the floor. 'What's your father's name, Lane?'

'Norman Lane.'

'And your grandfather is Tobias Lane.'

It wasn't a question, so he didn't answer it.

'We help our initiates to experience the pleasures of the drunken state. Sometimes they want to stop before we want them to stop, and it would be useful to have boys to ... help them to continue. Do you understand?'

Oh yes, Marcus thought to himself. *I understand perfectly. You want some of my gang of thugs to hold down new members and pour alcohol down their throats until they can't hold any more.*

'Yes,' he said. Better to keep things simple at this stage.

'Do you drink, Lane?'

He frowned. 'Not often. I find being drunk diminishes my power over others.'

They all smirked again.

'Bright lad. We'll pay you £10 every time we use one of your boys.'

Marcus frowned again. Be brave.

'I need to pay them, and there is some danger involved. If they get caught they risk expulsion, not you. Make it £15 and you have a deal.'

There was a moment's silence, and he began to contemplate how difficult these seniors could make his life. Everyone seemed to be waiting for the boy in the middle to make up his mind. He studied Marcus.

'Takes balls to drive a bargain with me. I like that. Fifteen quid it is. But I want your best muscle – strong and dumb. Understood?'

Marcus smiled at him. 'Perfectly.'

'You can go now.'

He nodded, turned on his heel and left the room. As he walked up the corridor, Marcus thought about how long it would be before he sat in a position like that, a senior, an intimidator, an enforcer. He knew he was already feared and respected, and he took great pleasure in living up to his brutal reputation, but age would enhance that. Three more years and he would be the king of this place. The thought gave him deep satisfaction.

* * *

The winter Marcus turned sixteen, his life changed in a few moments.

He wasn't even at home – he was at boarding school – but the reach of family was long. His father and grandfather were sitting together in the drawing room of the Richmond house. It had been a very profitable year and the two men were indulging in a glass of port and a Cuban cigar.

'I think it's time Marcus left that school and joined the family,' Norman said.

Tobias frowned and took a gulp of port before he answered. 'You know Melissa's very keen for him to get good qualifications, maybe even go to university –'

Norman snorted with barely concealed disgust. 'What on earth for? By sixteen I was earning money from my own patch.'

'He's bright, he enjoys learning.'

'She's always pampered him and Millie. No, I think that's completely unnecessary.'

Norman wanted to tell Tobias to keep his thoughts to himself, but his father was one of only two people who could make him hold his temper in check, and Melissa had counselled him against upsetting Tobias.

His father didn't answer; instead, he put his glass down on the table at his elbow.

Norman glanced at him. 'Are you feeling okay, Dad?' he asked.

Tobias seemed to stare at the rug for a moment, then pulled himself to his feet. His face was turning grey and a light sheen of sweat had appeared out of nowhere.

He held out a hand towards his son. 'No ... I ... have –' Suddenly he clasped at his chest and his knees buckled. He slumped slowly to the floor and onto his side. Norman gripped a shoulder and rolled Tobias onto his back. Then he sat down again. His father was opening and closing his mouth, but no sound emerged and his eyes were bulging. He continued to clutch at his shirt, but his grasp was weakening.

Norman took a slug from his glass and inhaled his cigar. 'I want to watch you die,' he said softly. His eyes never left his father's face as the life ebbed out of the older man. The process had always delighted him, but never to this extent. No death had ever changed his life the way this one would.

Tobias's eyes were nearly closed and his breath was nothing more than a gurgling sound.

Norman leaned forward and whispered: 'I'm going to change everything.'

When it was obvious that his father was dead, Norman got to his feet, bent over and picked up the other man's wrist. There was no pulse. He walked briskly from the room, calling his mother's name as he left.

**

After the funeral, Norman, Melissa, Millie and Marcus moved into the imposing Richmond house, and Tobias's widow moved into their old home. Melissa fired most of the servants and hired new ones. Norman gave her an open chequebook to redecorate, while he set about modernising the family business. Against Melissa's wishes, he also decided that it was time Marcus left that 'damn expensive school' and learned his trade.

'But I like school!'

His father glared at him. Norman Lane was a colossal man at over six foot five, lean and muscular, with hands that balled easily into fists. 'What use is it going to be to you? Damn history and Latin and geomet–'

'It helps me understand the world, how it works –'

'Bullshit! You need to learn to shoot well – not for game but at people, with a damn pistol. Learn how to make people obey you, be a leader. Learn not to be impulsive.'

That was rich, coming from his father. There was no sense in resisting, though, Marcus knew that, but somehow he had to have one last go.

'Can I finish this year?'

'No! Young Tom McGregor, the boy you went to primary school with? He left school in December and joined us. Dan says he's making excellent progress, and I don't want you to lag behind. I'm going to put you with Dan and Tom, and you can start shadowing Dan's clients.'

'But –'

'Don't you dare contradict me!' his father roared.

Marcus saw the fists clench, bit his lower lip and said nothing more. Dan had been his grandfather's second-in-command, and he knew the criminal underworld, from every disused warehouse to every crooked landlord. He would be a hard taskmaster but, if you planned a life of crime, there could be no better teacher. Accept the inevitable, that had been his mother's advice, and he had to admit that the idea of firing a gun at real people was just a little bit more exciting than watching thugs kick the crap out of younger boys.

CHAPTER SIX

TOM GROWS UP

As Tom grew older he learned to control his fear, and his father lost interest in him as a victim. He started to single out Tom's younger brother, one half of the set of twins and weaker and sicker than his siblings. Tom was furious but, try as he might, he couldn't get Stuart to redirect his anger back towards his eldest son. It was the terror that Stuart needed to see.

Dorothy had taken refuge in prescribed tranquillisers and vodka, and sometimes didn't get out of bed all day. Then one night it all changed.

Stuart was working for the Clerkenwell gang, clearing a street of hookers who worked for rivals, and he got knifed by a pimp. The hunting knife missed vital organs in its journey from the back of his body to the front, but he was in a bad way when the gang dropped him at the doors of the local hospital. The police rang, but Dorothy was in no fit state to go, so Tom went. He was fifteen and wary of anyone in authority – policemen, doctors, teachers, he hated them all.

'I'm afraid the knife blade severed your father's spinal cord and the damage appears to be permanent. He'll come home eventually, but will be confined to a wheelchair.'

Tom looked at the doctor who was sitting opposite him and trying to break bad news gently.

Don't show your joy, they won't understand. Tom swallowed. 'Paralysed?' he asked in a small voice.

'Yes, son, from the lower chest down. You'll get some help on the NHS, but your family will have to do a lot for him.'

Tom nodded slowly.

'What would happen if we couldn't manage? My mum's very sick – she's in bed all day sometimes – and my older sisters have left home, and he wouldn't like it if his kids had to do private stuff for him.'

The doctor paused and consulted his notes.

'He would qualify for residence in a rest home, but we would need to talk to your mum about that.'

Tom considered the hell he could create for his father, but it would take work and it would slow down his life plan. So he made sure that Dorothy was unable to hold a lucid conversation with the medical establishment, much less look after her invalid husband.

After much consultation it was decided that the best place for Stuart was a care unit at a local rest home. Stuart protested violently to anyone who would listen, but the staff ignored him and his children didn't visit. Tom took away his mother's drugs and booze and booked her into a rehab clinic. She had nothing to hide from now. As a parting gift, Tom told the rest home staff that Stuart had been violent and was not a nice man.

* * *

The day he turned sixteen, Tom left school and went to see Tobias Lane. He was prepared to start at the bottom and work his way up.

'I want to learn, sir.'

Lane studied him.

'It's hard work and it's not pleasant.'

'I'm not squeamish, and I know how to fight and shoot.'

'Very well, I'll put you with Dan. He'll teach you everything you need to know. When do you want to start?'

'Tomorrow. There's something I have to do this afternoon.'

* * *

Tom went straight from the Lane house to the rest home where his father lived. It was four in the afternoon and Stuart was dozing in his wheelchair, facing the window overlooking the garden. He looked smaller, hunched and pitiful. Tom stood and watched him for a moment, then took the chair by one handle and swung it around. The movement woke Stuart up.

'Tommy! About bloody time. Ya've come to take me hame.'

Tom shook his head. 'No. You'll die in this place. I've come to pay a debt. I want to thank you for teaching me to be a hard bastard.'

He balanced himself beside the chair and punched his father in the side of the head. Stuart's body was sent backwards by the force, and the chair nearly overbalanced. Tom grabbed it and pulled it back down. He continued to punch with a closed fist for over a minute. Stuart's face whipped from one direction to the other and blood spilled from the cuts. Finally Tom's fury was spent and he stepped back.

CHAPTER SEVEN

VINNIE GROWS UP

School and Vinnie went together like oil and water. He had grown into far too much of a show-off to fit into the rigid public school system. But while he had no interest in sport and was too lazy to be overly academic, he could act and sing. It was clear that he was quick-witted and clever, and his teachers were frustrated by their inability to capture his interest. He could play the class clown to perfection, and his philosophy was 'make others laugh with you before they laugh at you' – a talent that saved him from being bullied.

Vinnie was just sixteen but he looked older at around five foot ten, thickset and barrel-chested, muscular and sturdy, with curly hair, pale blue eyes and a strong face. When his father had once told him that he, too, had a 'Roman nose', he had pored over books about famous Romans to find his nose on pictures of busts of Augustus, Agrippa and Julius Caesar, and finally decided it was a good thing. He was growing more like his father as his body matured; sometimes it made his mother draw a sharp breath when he walked into the room.

Those formative years around Marcus had rubbed off. He knew how to lie convincingly, cheat at cards and shoplift successfully, but he also knew that the danger lay in getting caught, so he took on the role of Fagin rather than that of the Artful Dodger. His charm, wit and flair for drama enabled him to explain the techniques required for successful thievery in humorous detail. He found a coat on a market stall that had pockets inside and out, and used it to teach his patsies to lift wallets, hide things up their sleeves, slip things into their pockets and evade detection. Soon he had the younger boys completely under his spell, and persuading them to carry out the crimes was easy.

Sometimes circumstances gave him the chance to make a profit and be a hero. One of his protégés, Joseph, had an older sister, Clara, who was particularly attractive and was devoted to books. However, she wasn't very practical and was renowned for losing things. When her brother told Vinnie that she had borrowed an edition of *The Annals of Imperial Rome* by Tacitus, Vinnie persuaded him to 'steal' it and bring it to him. As luck would have it, there was no name inside it, nothing to distinguish it from any other copy.

In no time, word came back that Clara was distraught at the thought that she had lost someone else's book.

Vinnie waited a day or two, then knocked on her door. 'Good morning, Mrs Hill. Is Clara there?'

The middle-aged woman regarded him with suspicion. 'What do you want with my daughter?'

Vinnie smiled. 'My name is Vinnie Whitney-Ross, and I might be able to help her with a problem.'

Clara appeared in the background. 'Who is it, Mum?'

Her mother turned around. 'Vinnie someone. He says he might be able to help you with a problem.'

Clara beckoned her mother away and came to the door. 'Hello, Vinnie. What problem?'

By way of an answer Vinnie pulled the book out of the bag he was carrying. She leapt forward and grabbed it from his hands.

'My book! Where did you find it?'

'Actually, it's not your copy. I help on a second-hand book stall, and we had it in stock. Joseph said you had lost your copy, so I've come to the rescue.'

She was flicking through it and looking at the inside cover. 'That's wonderful, thank you! How much do you want for it?'

Vinnie hesitated. 'Ordinarily we'd want a tenner but, as you've had a traumatic loss, let's call it eight quid.'

She rushed down the steps and threw her arms around him. 'Vinnie, you're my hero.'

She planted a big kiss on his cheek, and he hugged her back.

'So pleased to be of service.'

When Vinnie's classmates brought him their ill-gotten gains, he smuggled the loot out in hollow books and took it across the city to Monty Joe, his dad's old client, who could sell it in his chain of shops, on the market or down the pub. The smaller items, stationery, sweets and grubby magazines, Vinnie sold to other schoolboys through an intricate network of ever-changing empty lockers and coded messages. He gave the thieves thirty-five per cent of his proceeds, and it proved to be a good little earner. He had over £2000 in a well hidden shoebox by 1982, when it all came to a grinding halt.

His own preferred hunting ground was his friend's book stall on the Portobello Road Market. All the punters thought Vinnie was a rookie trader with a very good line in patter. What set him apart were some cracking first editions, nicked for him from bookshops, parental bookcases and the lockers of his rich fellow pupils.

One cold Saturday morning he was visited by a heavy-set, balding man wearing a Burberry raincoat.

'Morning, sir. Looking for some classics?'

The man was perusing the books on the table and didn't look up. 'Poetry. I like poetry,' he said quietly.

'A very noble gift, being able to write poetry. Anyone in particular? We have some TS Eliot, a nice volume of John Donne, Robert Graves if you prefer something mod–'

'Robert Frost. Got any Robert Frost?'

The man looked up, and Vinnie could see that he was sweating. His eyes flickered sideways and telegraphed his wish to be anywhere but here.

Something deep in Vinnie's brain warned him that this interaction was not right. He turned and dug into a box of books on the chair behind him. 'Actually, I might … ah yes, here it is. This came in only last week. *In the Clearing*, published in 1962.'

He handed the book over, and the man's face lit up. 'Excellent! How much do you want for it?'

'It belongs to my friend. This is his stall and I mind it sometimes. I believe he said not to accept less than fifteen quid.'

The man extended his hand. 'Done.'

Two days later Vinnie arrived at school and was sent straight to the headmaster's office. It was a room he was familiar with, and he stood silently in front of the huge desk, hands behind his back, studying the carpet and waiting for the elderly man to finish writing.

Without looking at him, the headmaster opened a drawer, took out the book of Frost poetry and tossed it onto the desk in front of Vinnie. 'Where did you get this?' he barked.

Vinnie felt a net starting to close around him. 'I'm not sure I know what you mean, sir.'

The old man raised his head and fixed his watery brown eyes on Vinnie. 'Then let me explain, young man. I gave this book to my godson, Bartholomew, and told him to brag about it and then leave it in his locker. Sure enough, it was stolen. Last Saturday I sent my neighbour to a stall at the Portobello market and he purchased it for £15. From you. How do you explain that?'

Vinnie's expression was one of complete surprise. 'I can't, sir, it's not my stall. I simply look after it sometimes for a friend. And I believe he gets his stock from a pawnbroker, sir. Perhaps Bartholomew actually pawned it … sir.'

The headmaster stared at him for a long moment, and Vinnie's face remained serene. What he wanted to do was burst out laughing: it was a sting and he was less stupid than he appeared, this old man. Finally, the headmaster gave a resigned sigh and went back to his writing.

'I've called the police. They'll want to take you down to the station for a chat. Consider yourself expelled. Don't come back, Whitney-Ross.'

* * *

Once again, Mary was mortified; it appeared the acorn had not fallen far from the tree. All those years of public school, a gift that had kept her secretly tied to a family she loathed, and he had learned to be a thief? Vinnie used his patter to persuade her that this was just the turn of events he needed, and that school was doing nothing but cramping his entrepreneurial style. He was sixteen, he was allowed to leave, and he desperately wanted to be out on his own, living his life and making a crust. So he took a tiny room in a boarding house in Islington, with a shared bathroom and a communal TV lounge. He remained completely unaware that his gruff old landlady telephoned Mary every week to reassure her that he was fine. While his mother still worried that he had inherited traits that would lead to his downfall, she accepted that it was time to stand aside and let him fly.

He got his own stall on a weekend market and a local lockup for storage. At night he drove a delivery van for a friend who asked no questions when the odd box went missing. A neighbour at the market put him in touch with a contact in the importing business, and he used his savings to buy pallets of fashion and accessories knock-offs and sell them on without ever touching the goods, but always taking his cut. He haggled hard. If the seller thought he was going to put one over 'the kid', then he was mistaken. More importantly, Vinnie loved every minute of it, and when he dropped, fully clothed, onto his single bed to sleep, he couldn't wait until the next day, the next challenge.

Mary sold up and moved to a small cottage down a village lane in Sussex, complete with flower garden. She sometimes felt she should wear a straw hat and ride a bicycle with a wicker basket on the front. Her eccentric neighbours all reminded her of characters in Agatha Christie or Dorothy L Sayers novels, but to the best of her knowledge none of them were murderers. She drank at a local pub, the Maypole Inn, and worshiped in a tiny stone church with a Saxon font. It was a peaceful, quintessentially English, village life, and the only thing she missed about London was Vinnie.

PART TWO

THE MIDDLE YEARS

CHAPTER EIGHT

MARCUS AND VINNIE

'Get the knife.'

Marcus glanced desperately around the room. The floor was covered in debris swept from the table during the struggle. His companion was holding a thrashing man in a choke-hold on the floor.

'There!' The exasperation was evident in Dan's voice. He was nodding towards an object sticking out from under a dirty plate. It was the handle of a knife.

Marcus lunged forward, grabbed it and tried to stuff it into Tom's closed fist.

'Not him, you fucking idiot. *You.*'

Marcus looked up at Dan; he was moving his finger from the man to Marcus and back again.

'Go!'

Marcus went to Tom's side. The man he was choking was slowly turning a deep shade of red and his eyes were open very wide.

'Cut off his ear,' ordered Dan.

Marcus recoiled in shock. 'What?'

Dan snorted with contempt. 'Oh, for fuck's sake, grow a set of balls! Cut off this bastard's ear.'

The man squirmed even more, but the hold was secure. Marcus looked at the long, thin-bladed knife in his hand. He moved in beside Tom and put the knife flat against the man's head just above his ear. The voice in Marcus's brain was battling with the desire to gag and the bile in his throat: *You can do this! You were born to do this!*

He looked up at Dan, who nodded.

'That's the place. One swift cut. Bring it down with force. If it's blunt, you might have to saw a bit.'

Marcus closed his eyes and drove the knife downwards. There was resistance at first but he pressed harder and the cartilage gave way. Blood spurted everywhere and the man tried to scream, but he didn't have enough oxygen. The outer ear came away in Marcus's hand and he dropped it and the knife onto the floor.

Tom let the man go and both hands went to the wound and the blood streaming down his neck. He let out a noise halfway between a wail and a cough.

'That's your one warning. Pay what you owe or we'll be back for the other ear – or worse,' Tom said as he climbed to his feet.

Dan nodded at Marcus. 'Bring the knife and the ear so he can't have it reattached.'

Tom strode towards the door, and as he drew level with Dan he stopped. 'I wouldn't have bloody hesitated,' he muttered.

Marcus's eyes met those of the terrified and bloodied man. For a second they held each other's gaze, then Marcus grabbed the knife and the mound of flesh and ran after Tom.

* * *

The first time Marcus was told to put the frighteners on a pimp who had kept too much money, he didn't go far enough and the man was back on the street that night, proudly showing off his bruises.

'Where did you hit him?'

Marcus frowned. 'Arms, legs, with the bat.'

'Didn't break any ribs?'

'No. I guess I was scared I might kill him.'

Dan nodded. 'You need another lesson with the dummy: how to avoid permanent injury but still inflict pain. The word is that the pimps think their lives are much easier now that you're in charge of prostitution.'

The contempt in his voice infuriated Marcus.

'How dare they! What do I do?'

'You need to establish your authority. If you can't inspire fear, I'll give the job to Tom.'

A week later the same pimp stole some girls from their best illegal club, and Dan instructed Marcus to teach the man obedience by breaking his legs. The weapon he was given was a baseball bat, but he swapped it on the way out of the store cupboard for a lead pipe.

The pimp was drinking in a pub and Marcus waited in the car park until closing time. As the man put a key in his vehicle door, Marcus struck him from behind in the small of his back.

'Ahhh!' He fell against the car and slumped to the ground.

'Too fucking soft, am I?' Marcus growled.

He raised the pipe and brought it down on the unprotected head. It made a delicious cracking sound. When he stopped, the pimp was a bloodied pulp, long dead.

Dan was furious and made Marcus dispose of the body himself on a construction site, but Norman took him aside and told him he had made his dad a proud man.

Marcus was surprised by his own reaction: he had felt no fear, no desire to vomit, no remorse – just satisfaction that he had done the job and cleaned up after himself.

* * *

The next five years passed like a bolt of lightning. By his twenty-first birthday, he was running the enforcement and protection side, had done his first drug deals and had created a city-wide reputation for his chilling ability to menace. When Marcus told you he had you in his sights, the best thing to do was leave the country.

He and Tom worked well together. They knew each other's strengths and weaknesses. Marcus was aware that if he wasn't brutal enough, Tom would step in and claim the honour of dispensing justice. Tom recognised that Marcus was the boss's son and was destined to lead, whereas Tom was destined to be his second-in-command. The leader was hot-headed and very bright, whereas the follower was manipulative and lived by his wits.

Melissa made it her business to cultivate her son's sense of style. He liked Italian suits and shoes, luxury watches, and wore a pinkie ring with a massive diamond. There was intense speculation about his sexuality, fuelled by the fact that he was never seen with a girl on his arm. He was aware of the gossip and didn't care, life was too full and too brutal, and he was a focused control-freak. Women were not part of the plan at this point. His one indulgence, though, was his love for his sister.

Millicent, or Millie, was now a seventeen-year-old bottle blonde who loved parties and music and enjoying herself. Marcus knew that at some point she would be married off to someone 'appropriate' from the crime underworld, and he was determined that she would be treated right or she would be a young widow. He was also obsessed with keeping her safe from the scourge his family peddled onto other young girls. He lectured her constantly about drugs and alcohol, and vetted any young man who came near her, to the point where she complained that they were all terrified of him. His evident satisfaction at that state of affairs only annoyed her more.

When he heard that Millie had been seen in the company of the son of one of the Clerkenwell Gang, he went straight to his father. 'Things have changed, Dad. We need to address the new threats.'

'What threats?' His father had the ability to make any word dismissive.

Marcus bit his tongue. *Stay on subject.* 'What threats? The Irish, the Turkish Cypriots, the Yardies. I see evidence of them every day.'

'What do you suggest we do? Murder them all?'

'Assert ourselves. Send some enforcers out to give them a clear message. They need to stay out of our business and off our patch.'

Norman nodded slowly. 'It's a big risk, could escalate into some kind of bloody revenge war, and a lot of bystanders would get hurt,' he said.

'Not if we show enough force. They won't dare retaliate if we hit them once, hard and clean, and re-establish our dominance.' Marcus knew he was sounding too impatient, and he was aware that was a dangerous thing to do to his father.

Norman seemed to make up his mind. 'Talk to Tom, make up a gang, and hit their muscle. The Clerkenwells use Afro-Caribbeans and they're dangerous. Use experienced men. No killing unless it can't be avoided.'

On three consecutive nights, Marcus, Tom and a gang of their best enforcers hit rival gangs as they left the pubs where they drank. It was a well co-ordinated attack: broken limbs, ribs, noses, jaws, smashed teeth and some minor internal bruising, things that sent a message without doing any permanent damage. Marcus made sure that the young man who had dared to escort his sister was one of the Clerkenwells targeted. He inflicted that damage himself and delivered a very clear 'stay away from Millie Lane or I will kill you' message into the distressed fellow's ear as he landed the blows.

The next day he was visited in his office by the police. This was a rare occurrence; Norman was acquainted with many politicians and senior police officers, and was well known for helping them look the other way. But his visitor was a young detective constable called Ron Matthews, who was clearly keen to make an impression.

Marcus looked him up and down with a thinly veiled sneer. Matthews was chubby, clean-cut, not much older than Marcus, and trying to appear authoritative.

'Where were you last night around eleven, Mr Lane?'

Marcus smiled, but the warmth didn't reach his eyes. 'Drinking in my local until around ten – any one of about a hundred people could vouch for me. Then my driver took me to a club in Soho – again, plenty of witnesses.'

Matthews nodded and made a note. 'And the night before?'

'Come now, Constable, you can't expect me to remember that long ago. I believe I ate a very good rib-eye steak at Le Caprice, or was it Le Gavroche? I eat at both so frequently I forget which it was.'

Matthews drew himself up and snapped his notebook shut. 'Thank you, sir. I'm sure you're aware of a rash of serious physical assaults over the past few nights. Between members of the criminal underworld. If you should come into contact with anyone involved, I trust you'll tell them that reprisals would not be a good idea. The police are watching.'

Marcus let out a short bark of laughter; it was humourless and without warmth. 'Oh, I shall! I'm sure whoever they are will be quivering in their shoes, Constable.'

* * *

It was the summer of 1992, and Vinnie was drinking in his favourite pub and playing darts with Monty Joe, just as his dad had done years before. As he was about to take his turn, his cell phone rang.

'Sorry, Mont, I need to take this.'

Monty Joe scooped up their glasses. 'No problem, I'll get another round in.'

Vinnie answered his phone. It was one of his best suppliers.

'Vin, thank goodness! I need a favour. In about an hour I'm going to drop off an oversized crate at your lockup. Can you hold it for me? It's top-quality stuff, shoes and handbags. I'll give you twenty per cent of the stock.'

'How long do you need?' Vinnie asked.

'A week, maximum. Got a shipment going out Friday and that'll make room.'

You scratch my back and I'll scratch yours.

'Twenty-five per cent, and it's there for as long as you need.'

'Done. Don't open it until I'm ready to pick it up, though. Apparently, it's packed pretty tight.'

* * *

'Some of the latest Colombian shipment has been stolen.'

Dan looked up at Tom. 'What do you mean, *stolen*?'

Tom shrugged. 'What I said. When the truck was unloaded, a crate with three bricks was missing.'

'What does the driver have to say?'

73

'Not much. He picked up from three trucks at Dover. It wasn't until he unloaded at the warehouse that he realised a crate was missing.'

'A crate of what?'

'Knock-offs, handbags, shoes.'

Dan nodded slowly. 'Leave it with me. I know who might be able to track that.'

* * *

Across the city, Vinnie was doing an inventory of his double lockup. It was almost full of stacked boxes and packing crates, and he needed to shift them. Stock sitting in a lockup was not earning any money. Over the years it had become harder to buy and sell without seeing the goods. In the old days he had been like a futures broker, doing deals on his phone and taking a cut as it went through, but nowadays 'cowboys' were ruining it for everyone by selling non-existent stock. People needed to eyeball what they were buying, touch it, feel the quality and count the items. This had led to him holding a lot more stock, and stock made him nervous. If it was slightly the wrong side of the law, you ran the risk of being raided.

He tore open a box and rifled through the contents – T-shirts embroidered with the logos of popular bands. They sold well on the market stall, and he made a thousand per cent profit on each one.

'You own these two lockups?'

The question broke through his reverie, and he spun around. Two large men in suits, with badly hidden shoulder holsters, stood in the alley just outside his doorway. Muscle. Gang muscle.

'Yes, gentlemen. Can I help you?'

'We're looking for crates.'

He frowned, genuinely perplexed. He had kept well away from the gangs.

'Of?'

'Something you shouldn't have.'

The speaker pulled a very large crowbar from behind his back and stepped into the lockup.

Vinnie sighed. 'Be my guest.'

He stood and watched them as they tossed boxes aside like kindling and pulled crates off piles. About ten minutes into the search, one of them jemmied open a large wooden crate to reveal handbags and shoes. They stopped abruptly and looked at each other. Vinnie felt a prickle of unease, as if a cold shadow had passed over him.

'Knock-offs, for the pub and market trade. Made in China, via Eastern Europe,' he said in his most reassuring voice. The men started digging, throwing the contents over their shoulders. Vinnie was about to try a weak protest when one of them straightened up and turned towards him. In his hand, he held a brick-shaped packet, wrapped in black plastic.

'What's this?' he asked.

Vinnie raised his hands, palms towards them. 'Whoa! I have no idea. Never seen it before, I swear.'

The other man pulled a second brick from among a twisted pile of handbags. 'Never seen this before either?'

'No! I'm a two-bit hustler with a market stall. I *don't* do drugs! I'm holding that crate for someone else. I haven't even opened it.'

The two men went back to the crate and within a minute had found the third brick. They kicked handbags and shoes out of their way and walked back to Vinnie.

'Save it for the boss.'

Vinnie felt his knees literally start to tremble. 'Which boss?' he asked quietly.

'You're coming with us.'

They put a felt hood over his head and shoved him into a car.

He couldn't believe it. That scene in the movies where the baddies put a hood over the good guy's head? It was real. Honest to God, they did that. He was aware of the seriousness of his position, but still couldn't help wondering how many of his friends would believe that detail. After about twenty minutes of what felt like inner-city driving, with lots of tight turns and periods of being stationary, they stopped. The door was opened and someone grabbed him and pulled him out.

The men took hold of an arm each and marched him across uneven ground and through a doorway. The temperature changed, and the floor was smoother; he was inside. His nostrils were assaulted by an acrid combination of smoke, old urine and gasoline. He stumbled forward until they pushed him down onto a chair and whipped the hood off. He was in an open expanse, a warehouse or an abandoned parking building. The lighting was dim, but he could see that the concrete walls were covered in graffiti.

The two men stood, arms folded across their chests, one on either side of the chair. He was about to comment on how well they had decorated the place when a car stopped outside, multiple doors opened and closed, and footsteps crossed the gravel to the exterior doorway in the gloom at the end of the room.

A third man walked towards Vinnie and stopped in front of him. He was about Vinnie's age, immaculately dressed and yet he looked uncomfortable in his clothes. The trace of expensive cologne made Vinnie's nose twitch. This one was definitely higher up the chain of command.

'Vinnie Whitney-Ross,' the man said.

A hundred smart responses rushed through Vinnie's brain, but his throat felt very tight, so he just nodded.

'Do you know why you're here?'

Vinnie nodded again. 'The packing crate,' he whispered.

'The packing crate.'

The man walked around him and said nothing more. Vinnie's patience gave out.

'If you think I –'

The man flicked the back of his hand across Vinnie's cheek. It stung briefly.

'When it's your turn, I'll ask a question.'

Vinnie nodded slightly.

'Handbags and shoes and three bricks of cocaine. That crate belongs to us. How did it get in your lockup?'

At last, a chance to explain.

'Because … someone called and asked me to hold it for him. He offered me twenty-five per cent of the contents. He said shoes and handbags, and he said a week, maximum.'

'When?'

'Three nights ago. I was in the pub when he called me. I was with Monty Joe.'

The man frowned and stared hard at Vinnie. 'Monty Joe on the fence?'

Vinnie nodded. 'Everyone knows Mont – he'll vouch for me. What I do. A market trader, nothing more.'

'This "someone", does he have a name?' the man asked, and Vinnie could hear the disbelief in his voice.

Now the tricky bit. 'In a manner of speaking.'

The frown turned into a glare. 'Don't play fucking games with me!'

'I'm not! He's called The Finn. Everyone calls him The Finn. Always have. He was introduced to me as The Finn. I asked him his real name once and … it's The Finn.'

The man pulled a gun from his under-shoulder holster and put the muzzle against Vinnie's knee. For a split second Vinnie thought his days on two legs were over, before he could protest his innocence.

Suddenly he caught movement in the shadows.

'Stop! Don't shoot.' It was a cultured accent, a public school accent.

The other man stepped away. Marcus Lane walked into the light and straight up to the chair. Vinnie reeled back in shock. Marcus! My God, he was so tall.

'Vinnie.' Marcus offered his hand. Vinnie took it and stood up. Marcus was wearing a heavy coat, and Vinnie felt the other man's body warmth as he was embraced in a bear hug. He knew Marcus would sense he was trembling. He didn't know what to say.

'Marcus.'

'Long time, old friend. What are you doing in a hell-hole like this?'

Vinnie didn't know whether to feel relieved or terrified. Emotions surged through him, and he ran his hand through his curls. 'They think I stole some drugs, cocaine bricks in a packing case. I *don't* do drugs, Marcus. I hustle low-end stuff on a market stall.'

Marcus smiled down at him. 'Of course you don't. It's a misunderstanding.'

Marcus turned to the interrogator, who was watching with obvious fascination. 'Tom, have our men return Mr Whitney-Ross to his lockup and tidy up whatever mess they made.'

Vinnie shook his head emphatically. 'That's not necess–'

'Oh, yes, it is. If anything's broken, you show them and they will pay for it.' Marcus extended his hand again. 'It's good to see you. I'm so sorry our paths crossed under such circumstances. How is your mother?'

Something made Vinnie want to shiver. 'She's fine. Thank you for turning up when you did.'

Marcus gave him a small nod as he turned away.

The sight of his long body lit a light bulb in Vinnie's brain and he grabbed the opportunity. 'Marcus?' he said, his voice steadier.

Marcus swung around. 'Yes?'

Vinnie drew his wallet from his back pocket and pulled out two £50 notes. 'I owe you this.'

Marcus came back to him, and it was obvious by the frown that he didn't remember. 'For what?'

Vinnie held out the notes. 'A packet of stolen cigarette cards.'

A large grin split the other man's face, and he took the money. 'Thank you!'

'Don't take no shit from nobody.'

A look passed between them and the years melted away.

'No shit.' Marcus said softly and turned away again. As he passed Tom, he stopped.

'The man you want – The Finn – is Simon Fish. Find him and ask him why he stole from us, and you don't have to be polite.'

'Yes, boss.'

Marcus tapped Tom's shoulder with his finger. 'And be very glad that you didn't harm my friend, because that would have made me angry.'

CHAPTER NINE

MILLIE

'I want you to turn over every club, every brothel and every jazz joint – *anywhere* she might be. Search them all. Do you understand?'

The room full of men nodded.

'Don't come back until you find her and find out who took her.'

One by one they filed out. Marcus punched his fist into his palm to stop the rising tide of fury that threatened to engulf him. It had all been going so well. While the newer gangs had continued to expand and spread their tentacles into Lane territory, Marcus had been very careful with his responses. Reprisal was a dangerous business, and more than one hot-headed boss had ended up in jail for murdering his rivals. Marcus preferred sabotage, fire-bombing and guerrilla warfare.

But now everything had changed. Someone had taken his Millie. She was twenty and the apple of her parents' eye. For a while it had looked as though she might be happy to marry Tom;

however, Norman had found the handsome son of a prominent businessman who would inherit his father's gambling empire, and Millie had accepted his proposal.

Two nights ago she had gone to a nightclub with friends and hadn't come home. Within twenty-four hours, every street thug in London knew that Marcus Lane was on the rampage.

Norman let all his contacts in the Met and at Westminster know that he required their help, and the word quickly filtered down to the police snouts who lived on the streets. Countless doors were broken down and guns pointed in faces, but there was no sign of Millie anywhere.

Eventually Marcus, Tom and Norman sat around the dining table in the Richmond house and studied the reports that had come back.

'She's not in London. If she was, someone would've coughed something by now,' Tom said.

Marcus winced. The strain was taking its toll, and both he and his father were exhausted. 'So where do you think she is?' he asked.

Tom shrugged. 'Maybe a London gang took her and sold her on – Manchester, Birmingham, Dublin, Liverpool. Or maybe someone bought in a contractor and told him to hold her out of Lon–'

'So, why haven't we heard from them yet?' Norman asked.

'Don't know, boss.'

Marcus looked at Norman. 'What do we do now?' he asked.

His father frowned and considered the report in his hand. He sighed. 'We offer money, through every channel we know. Tom, put the word out. The kind of money that opens mouths. One million pounds to the person who brings me proof that they know where she is and who took her.'

* * *

81

Four weeks later, the Manchester police staged a raid on the house of a known member of the Cheetham Hill Gang as part of a drugs bust. The Noonan brothers formed the core of the gang, and for several years they had ruled the narcotics market in central Manchester.

Five young men were playing cards at a table in the lounge. As two policemen burst through the door and another two came smashing through the windows, all five gangsters drew their weapons and were shot as they rose to their feet.

There was a moment of eerie silence, and then the kitchen door flew open and a man and a woman ran out, each brandishing a pistol and coming straight at a policeman.

'Drop your weapons now!' the policemen ordered in unison.

They kept coming, the woman screaming, 'Die, pig!'

The policemen opened fire, and the man and woman were killed instantly.

* * *

Marcus stared down at the young blonde lying on a mortuary table, a sheet drawn up to her chin. She looked like a china doll, white, perfect, still and dead. The sour taste of rage and grief rose in his throat.

He swallowed hard. 'Yes', he said quietly, 'that's my sister, Millicent Lane.'

'Do you have any idea what she was doing in that house, sir? In Manchester?'

Marcus turned towards the questioner. The chubby face was vaguely familiar and Marcus wracked his memory banks. Of course, it was the smarmy cop who'd interviewed him after the raids on the other gangs. He'd been promoted to detective sergeant Ron Matthews. Not so young and eager anymore, and definitely not a rooky.

'Obviously not, Detective. But I can tell you one thing: someone is going to pay. Dearly.'

* * *

'Do you think he has something to say?' Tom pointed to the naked man tied to a chair. He had a gag around his mouth and a large knife imbedded in each muscular thigh. He was shaking his head from side to side and trying to say something.

'Not sure,' Marcus replied as he caressed the man's cheek with a third knife. 'I hate Manchester. The sooner we get out of this dump, the better.'

Tom smiled and pressed down on one of the knives. The man's scream was impeded by the gag, but his body writhed. 'Hates the rain, my friend, and it's rained since we got here. He's angry enough without adding bad weather.'

The man's eyes flicked from one tormentor to the other.

'Do you have something to say, scum? Where should the next one go?' Marcus asked.

The man's speech was indecipherable, but the straining of every fibre of his body was not. Marcus raised the knife above the exposed genitals, and then at the last moment whipped the gag off.

'Don't! No more! I'll tell you. *Please!* No fucking more.'

Marcus stepped back.

'One chance. Go.'

The blood was running down between the man's legs and pooling on the ground.

'We took her. From outside some dive in London. But she weren't by herself, like. The man … the one who died … he came with her.'

Marcus bent down and studied the face. It was contorted with agony. 'Hakan Turan?' he asked.

The man nodded vigorously. 'The Elmas brothers ... he's, like, their cousin. They hired us 'cause they couldn't hide her in London.'

Marcus sighed and stood up. 'But why would they?'

Tom shook his head. 'What use was she without a ransom demand?' he asked.

Marcus swung round to face him. 'It makes no sense ...'

The man in the chair gave a short humourless laugh, as though he couldn't help but be amused. 'Oh, that's, like, priceless. You don't fucking know.'

In one gesture Marcus turned back and had the knife at the man's exposed throat. 'Know what?' he demanded.

'Kill me and you'll never fucking find out.'

The blade pressed harder.

'I won't kill you, but I will cut out your tongue. There are some things worse than death. You have thirty seconds.'

'All right!'

Marcus pulled the knife away.

'We didn't take her against her will. She was, like, dead happy to come. She was in love ... with that Turkish idiot, Turan.'

Marcus and Tom glanced at each other.

'That's a lie!'

Even as the response escaped, Marcus knew Tom believed it. He started to pace, his mind was whirling.

'She wouldn't. I'd have known. She'd have told me.'

'Would she, though? What would the boss have said? Not like she just dropped money at the casino. He'd have done his nut at her.'

Marcus shook his head. 'There *has* to be another reason.'

'At least we know who to blame.'

Marcus strode back across the room. The man's head had dropped onto his chest and the colour was draining from his face. He was losing a lot of blood.

'Two things are going to happen. You're going to die unless we call an ambulance, and I'm going to fire-bomb every property your gang owns, unless ...' His voice trailed off.

The head raised enough for the man to look at him. A last attempt at hatred burned in the eyes. 'Unless what?'

'Give me a name. Someone who knows something I can use against the Elmas.'

The man nodded.

* * *

Detective Matthews was called back to his desk to take a phone call. It had been a long day and he was on his way home, but experience told him it was better not to miss phone calls.

'Detective Matthews, it's time for someone to pay for the death of Millie Lane.'

Matthews checked his watch, grabbed a pen and scribbled on his desk pad. The male voice wasn't polished enough to be Marcus Lane.

'Who is this?' he asked. Experience also told him he wasn't going to know.

'The Elmas Gang will rob a Securicor van in Reigate tomorrow. They'll have shotguns and they'll be wearing masks, Winston Churchill masks. If you want to arrest Boran and Murat for armed robbery, I suggest you be there.'

'When –'

The phone clicked and Matthews heard the dial tone. He wrote down the details. It wasn't Marcus or Norman Lane, but the information had clearly come from their organisation.

* * *

Boran Elmas, who was driving the getaway van, was shot by police but lived. His companion in the van was killed.

Murat gave up without a fight. Jailed for armed robbery, the gang's ability to function was temporarily disabled. However, there were other brothers in the family, and they stepped up. Marcus was satisfied with the outcome and felt ready to initiate stage two of his plan.

Norman's contacts had identified each member of the police anti-drug squad who had entered the Cheetham Hill house the night Millie died. Throughout the 1990s a series of drug raids in Manchester and London went bad, and those four officers died. On two occasions Marcus was there to pull the trigger himself; the other two he hired out to hit men. Each time he made sure that there was enough collateral damage to hide the true target. Only one man joined the dots nearly a decade later, and became convinced that the Lanes were behind it. But no matter how hard he tried, Detective Chief Inspector Ron Matthews couldn't prove that Marcus Lane was a killer.

CHAPTER TEN

ROMANCE

Two days before Vinnie's twenty-sixth birthday he decided to do something spontaneous and take a holiday. It was time to get away, far, far away, and cool his heels somewhere exotic. The brush with Marcus and his operation had left him badly shaken. The Finn never came back to claim his packing case, and the fake Prada, Gucci and Chanel handbags and shoes were too good an opportunity to miss. They were brilliantly made, and he sold them for £90 each.

At the same time he was offered two dozen bottles of fine wine in exchange for a bathroom lot of Italian marble tiles literally off the back of a truck. The wine proved to be a superb drinking experience, so, on the spur of the moment, with a full glass in hand, he decided on a crash course in wine appreciation.

That same day he flew to Paris and hired a car. He drove slowly through France to Italy, stopping at vineyards and châteaux, sampling at wine shops and cellar doors, and questioning anyone who spoke enough English. When he posed as a rep for an importing business, he found the owners were more than happy to talk and ply him with samples.

After three weeks on the road, he arrived in Tuscany and found a local pensione. The delightful hosts recommended an isolated family restaurant in the hills behind the villa, so he drove up there and ordered an evening meal. The view over vineyards and olive groves was rustic and peaceful, a long way from the sterile concrete of the city. He settled back and surveyed the scene as he sipped his Prosecco and nibbled on a plate of antipasto. There was something about wine, food, the setting sun …

'Swap you half this tart for what's left of your pasta.'

The accent was American. He turned to his left to observe them, two women in their early to mid-twenties. One was blonde; the other, taller, a brunette.

After he finished his antipasto, he got up and walked over to them. 'Excuse me for interrupting, but, as the only other English-speaking person here, I thought I would introduce myself. I'm Vinnie Whitney-Ross.'

The brunette looked up and smiled. 'You're excused. I'm Anna, Anna Adams, and this is Belinda Miles.' Her accent was English.

The blonde gave him a small smile.

'Are you here on holiday?' he asked.

Anna nodded. 'We've rented a villa down the road for a few days. We've just finished a cookery course in Rome. Would you like to join us?'

He saw the slight irritation cross Belinda's face, but his interest was elsewhere so he chose to ignore it. 'I'd love to. Will you criticise the food I've chosen?'

She laughed. 'Only the dessert. I'm a chocolatier and Belinda's a pastry chef'.'

He waved to the waiter then fetched his chair. The man brought him new cutlery and his half-bottle of Prosecco.

'Dessert is probably the hardest course to match. I'm on a wine trip, and food matching has been a fascinating part of the journey,' he said.

Belinda waved a forkful of pasta in his direction. 'Depends on the dessert,' she said.

'White chocolate crème brûlée with raspberries – love brûlée, chocoholic. You do know that chocolate absorbs alcohol in the bloodstream?'

Belinda looked at him as if he were an idiot. 'Who told you *that*?'

'Every chocoholic in the world knows it for a fact. And chocolate biscuits leak calories if you break them. Two of the world's most necessary food groups – wine and chocolate.'

Anna shot him a stunning smile, and he felt his stomach give a slight heave, as though a trough full of butterflies had suddenly been released.

'I was very tempted by that dessert myself,' she said, 'but I've ordered the mousse.'

'An aged Tokaji or a Muscat,' Belinda said, 'with white chocolate.'

There was a pause.

'So, what prompted a wine trip?' Anna asked.

He settled back in his chair and sipped the wine. 'As W C Fields said: "What contemptible scoundrel stole the cork from my lunch?"'

Anna gave a bark of laughter, while Belinda looked as though she had heard the quotation a hundred times before. 'So you're a wine buff?' There was an edge of sarcasm in her question.

'No. I think I'd have to say I'm a wine *bluff*. But I intend to learn as much as I can, as quickly as I can.'

Suddenly Anna looked up and pointed at him. 'Actually, we're going to Castello Banfi tomorrow. There's a museum in the castle and a taverna for lunch, with some truly exceptional wines. Why don't you come with us?'

Belinda was about to open her mouth, when Vinnie leaned across the table and shook the hand that was still pointing in his direction. He smiled into her eyes. Result.

'Miss Adams, I'd be delighted to accept your invitation. You are too, too, kind.'

CHAPTER ELEVEN

ANNA

People disappointed Anna Adams. Almost without exception, they failed to behave the way she expected them to. How hard was it to do the right thing, a good thing, or a thing that demonstrated thoughtfulness? Not that hard, and yet they almost never did.

She had been born as the 1960s came to a close, her parent's fourth and last child and only daughter. Her mother, Sybil, was in her thirties when Anna was born, and her father, Colin, was in his forties. He was a doctor at a rural clinic in the Hampshire village of Torbay, and everyone loved him and confided in him. He was bearded and he bellowed when he laughed, and he swung her up in the air as he called her his 'Little Princess'. Her brothers spoiled her and pulled funny faces to make her laugh. She used to sit on the handlebars of their bicycles as they peddled through the village. Her mother was a homemaker, and baked and sewed and gardened and read to her. When they walked to the shops, people patted Anna on the head and told her she was a 'pretty wee thing'.

Life was idyllic and quiet for four years, and then one day it wasn't anymore. She had been building a castle in her sandpit. When she went inside, her mother was crying and her eldest brother was trying to comfort her.

'Go and play in your room, Anna,' he said, his voice stern.

'What's wrong with Mummy?'

At the sound of her voice, her mother wailed into her handkerchief. Her second brother came through from the kitchen and put a cup of tea on the table beside her mother's chair.

'Come with me,' her eldest brother said, more kindly, and he ushered her up the stairs to her bedroom. Once again she asked what was wrong with Mummy, and this time she was told that Daddy had left. Colin had run off to London with his much younger nurse because he 'needed more excitement'.

During the years that followed, Colin divorced Sybil, remarried and had another three daughters. He paid for his three sons to go to a public boarding school, while Anna kept her mother company and went to the local village school. She was happy with that solution – she loved being at home, and the idea of coping at a boarding school was too terrifying to contemplate. Besides, Sybil was passing on her excellent cooking skills. In her heart, Anna knew she was not an exciting person – if she had been, Daddy wouldn't have left because he needed more excitement.

It was always a time of great joy when the boys were due home for holidays. Biscuit tins were full to overflowing, and Mummy had jerseys knitted in winter and new cricket whites made for summer. Invariably the boys saw their friends, ate her home cooking, and then wanted to go to the city and stay with Daddy and their half-sisters, who were so much more exciting. Anna would have liked to go, too, but it seemed disloyal to her mother, so she stayed at home and baked for the local Women's Institute competitions and painted pictures.

As Anna progressed through her unexciting teenage years, one by one her brothers grew up, got jobs and got married. It was like going to the weddings of strangers, where her father gave her an awkward hug and introduced her to her giggling half-sisters, as though she hadn't met them at the previous wedding.

Sybil was very proud of her three boys. The eldest, twelve years older than Anna, was a junior banker in the City of London; the next was ten years older and an accountant living in Leeds; and the youngest boy, eight years older, was a trainee journalist with a newspaper in Liverpool.

* * *

The day Anna turned sixteen, she and Sybil celebrated with dinner at a local pizza parlour.

'I'm leaving school at the end of the week.'

Sybil put down the slice of pizza she was eating and stared at her daughter. 'Says who?'

'Says me. I'm sixteen, I can make up my own mind.'

'Can you now? And what are you going to do if you're not going to school?'

Anna gave her a satisfied grin. She had been waiting for this night, this moment, for weeks.

'I've got a job.'

Sybil was obviously even more shocked at this news. This was all going very well. 'Doing what?'

'In that new café delicatessen place on the High Street. I went to see the owner, and asked if I could cook something for him. He said, "Yeah, if you like." So I made the hummingbird cake and he loved it!'

'Did you tell him you were going to leave school?'

'Of course. He doesn't care. He says I can cook and bake and serve behind the counter.'

Sybil shook her head. 'You've got it all worked out then, I see.'

Anna nodded. 'It'll be wonderful, Mummy. I'm going to work so hard and show them what I'm made of – it's my big chance!'

* * *

Food was Anna's passion, and she kept her word and worked all hours. As well as cooking and baking and serving, she gave out advice about the trendy new products she chose out of catalogues. At night she read cookery books and biographies of great chefs. The café became a showcase for her cakes and desserts, and regular customers began to ask her to create something for their special occasions. She enjoyed the surprise when people came into the shop and enquired about something they had tasted, and the owner introduced them to the tall, gawky, awkward teenager with brown plaits and green eyes, who blushed at any praise.

When she was eighteen, her maternal grandparents died in quick succession and everything changed again. Sybil was left their cottage and suddenly had some real money of her own. Anna expected most of it to be divided between the four children, and she was sure that was what her brothers expected when they rang to see if their mother needed anything. To Anna's astonishment, Sybil had other plans.

'We're moving. We're going to sell this old house and move to the city. To London.'

Anna couldn't speak for a full minute. 'Why?' she eventually whispered.

'Why do you think? So you can follow your dream. A proper career in food.'

Anna's joy knew no bounds. Her eldest brother found them a funny little cottage in Chelsea: two bedrooms, peeling wallpaper, worn carpet, a sloping kitchen floor and an overgrown backyard. It needed a lot of work, but was a very good buy in an area that would only appreciate in value.

For the next four years Anna worked all the hours she could. Five days a week she made desserts for a catering company, and at night she went to cookery courses. On Saturdays and Sundays she cooked for a local French pâtisserie, and when she couldn't sleep, she experimented in her own kitchen. For the first two years she had an on-again, off-again relationship with one of her brothers' old school friends, a divorced man who tried, and continually failed, to stay sober. Eventually she got sick of her mother asking her whether she had 'doormat' engraved on her forehead, and she gave him his marching orders.

Her day-to-day existence was far too busy for loneliness, or for any feelings that she was missing out on the social life that her workmates had. But, as she fell into an exhausted sleep at night, she was often overcome by a sense of being in limbo, of being in training for some other kind of life, something else and something bigger.

* * *

That something else was 1991. One freezing February day she came home to the news that her father and his second wife had been killed in a car accident. She knew she should feel grief, but in reality she had grieved for her father many years earlier. Now it felt as though a friend she had kept in vague contact with had died tragically; sad but distant.

The family gathered at the beautiful Victorian church St Paul's in Knightsbridge. Anna sat at the back of the congregation and held Sybil's hand. One by one her brothers spoke, beginning with her eldest brother.

'I know you'll all agree with me when I say that Dad was a fine man. He cared deeply for his patients, and his family meant the world to him.'

Her next brother carried on the theme. 'We have all got where we are today because of the schooling we had, a gift from our father. He was a wonderful husband and a devoted father. I know we shall miss them both deeply.'

The youngest boy was concerned for his half-sisters. 'I want you all to know that we will take care of you. We are just as much your family as your maternal relations, and we are all here for you.'

At the wake Anna passed her only comment to her family: the cake was from a third-rate commercial bakery and tasted like plastic, and the egg filling in the sandwiches was far too salty.

Two months later she joined her siblings at the offices of a lawyer for the reading of Colin's will, and was surprised and delighted to be left a £40,000 legacy and his golf clubs. Their conversation about her wanting to make the time to take up golf had slipped her mind but, obviously, not his. While she still didn't have time for golf, she was touched by the gesture.

'Anna?'

She was about to take her leave, and turned back to see one of her brothers standing by the table. He was frowning and he looked uncomfortable.

'Yes?'

'I'm sorry to be a pain, but I took Dad's clubs from the house before the funeral and I'm already using them.'

Anna smiled. Nothing about this surprised her. She toyed with making it harder for him, making him suffer. 'That's fine. Maybe we could swap them for something else? What about that boat painting I gave him for Christmas? It was in his study.'

Her brother shifted and his embarrassment was palpable. 'Actually, it's already in the house in Cornwall – it looks great there. Why don't you take some of the money he left you and buy something to remember him by?'

She smiled again. Really she should make him squirm, but what was the point? 'Why don't I do that?'

Anna wanted to make some improvements to the cottage, but her mother insisted she leave the money in the bank for the moment and consider her future. She did look for a keepsake of her father, and the fact that she couldn't find one only served to reinforce how little she had known him.

CHAPTER TWELVE

LIMBO

It was a hot Saturday in June, and Anna was whisking crème pâtissière over heat at the local pastry shop. Her concentration was broken by the sound of the telephone. The kitchen was empty.

'Damn!'

She put the saucepan aside and picked up the receiver. 'Hello?' She knew her tone was brusque.

'Is … is that you, Anna?'

It was her neighbour, and she sounded upset.

'Yes, sorry Jill, it's me. I was up to my elbows in custard. What's wrong?'

'It's your mum. Apparently, she's had a fall. Philip rang here looking for you. She's been taken to hospital. I think you had better get there.'

As Anna drove through the streets, she imagined a broken hip or wrist or ankle, hospital care and lots of TLC and rehabilitation. Her mother was a strong woman and very determined.

When she got to the hospital and gave the staff at the emergency desk her name, a nurse ushered her into a room, where she was joined almost immediately by a doctor.

'What were you told on the phone, Ms Adams?'

She gave him a puzzled frown. 'My neighbour said that Mum had had a fall and my brother was looking for me.'

'You brother is on his way, but is not here yet. I'm sorry to be the bearer of bad news ... Ms Adams, your mother suffered a cerebral haemorrhage in the lower part of her brainstem, which damaged her vagus nerve. I can, and will, give you a more detailed explanation, but for now all you need to know is that death was almost instantaneous. She was dead before she hit the pavement.'

As shock set in, Anna really didn't hear anything more he said. She spent the night sitting beside Sybil's body and found the fact that the woman couldn't answer back strangely liberating. Although they had been as close as a mother and daughter could be, neither of them had been very good at expressing emotion. Now all that seemed to fall away.

'I know you sacrificed a lot. You could have found someone else and led another life. Been loved again. But you chose to devote yourself to my happiness. I don't know why I've never thanked you for that. Maybe you should have reminded me once in a while.'

She leaned forward and kissed her mother on the forehead. It was a strange sensation, kissing human skin that was not blood warm. Sybil's eyes were shut, but her mouth was slightly open. They had brushed her white hair, and it formed a halo around her head on the pillow.

'But you knew, and I know, that you were my world and I was yours, and we loved each other to bits. I will make you proud of me, Mum, I promise you. Someday I'll do something important and I'll know that I've made you proud.'

Once again the family gathered, but this time Anna was in charge, and the church was smaller and the vicar knew Sybil. Two of her brothers tried to insist that the situation would be too much for her – she wouldn't be able to speak, or she would go on for too long, and that would be embarrassing. Anna didn't get angry, but she told them that if the funeral was too embarrassing for them, they were welcome to pay their respects long distance, as they had for so much of their mother's life. They stared at her open-mouthed. She didn't feel overcome by grief at any stage – this was what her mother would have wanted, but it had nothing to do with her own mourning. In the end she was the only one who spoke.

'I was my mother's best friend. When I was four, her other best friend left and found a new life. So it was just Mummy and me. Family came and went when it suited them, ate our cooking and made polite conversation, but we stuck it out together.'

She watched as her brothers squirmed in the front pew and rubbed their faces, and she couldn't help a small smile.

The food at the wake was spectacular and drew many compliments.

When a patient of her father's asked her if Sybil had had bad circulation, she couldn't resist. 'Well, she does now,' she replied, without a shadow of a smile. The woman was horrified at such sacrilege, and Anna wondered if the whole world had lost its sense of humour.

Everything her mother owned was left to her, and the limbo was over. Anna waited a week, then handed in her notice at work and took the entire contents of her wardrobe, and her mother's wardrobe, to a local charity shop. The next day she went shopping for dresses, shirts, trousers and skirts in bold prints and large blocks of bright colour – everything her mother had objected to. She bought new makeup, chunky jewellery, fashionable shoes with heels and silk scarves. On the way home she bought a bottle of Krug, and that night she spread all her new possessions out and looked at them while she drank the whole bottle.

Over the following weeks she had the kitchen remodelled to give herself more bench space and bought new appliances. Then she redecorated the rest of the cottage with new wallpaper, curtains and artwork, ripped up the carpet and polished the wooden floors, added rugs, cushions and a home entertainment system. She gave away her mother's bed, took down the curtains to let in the natural light, and turned the room into a studio, with an easel, canvases and paints. Colour, creativity and music exploded throughout the house.

There were a few pieces from the family life – the old kitchen table, a carved glory box, a fine china dinner set, some portraits – which she send to an auction house. She informed her brothers that if they wanted them, they could bid.

If she concentrated on what she had to do and didn't think about her mother, she could keep the grief at bay and assure everyone she was fine. When she made herself think about conversations, car trips, holidays and birthdays, she felt as though she was standing on the edge of a black pool of grief, waiting to dip even the tip of her big toe in.

The discovery that stopped her in her tracks for a whole day was made when she opened the bottom cupboard of her mother's bedside cabinet. It was full of letters, nearly seven hundred letters, each one written by her mother to her father. Every fortnight, from the day he left until the day he died, she had written to him and then put the letter in her bedside cabinet. Anna sat on her bed and read about how her mother had felt through the years, about her pride in Anna's achievements, how much she had missed seeing her sons regularly, and how her pain had slowly diminished. To start with, she had blamed herself for their separation and wanted to know what she could do to entice him back, then she had blamed him and cried out to know how he could have left his family so easily, and then, at last, she had accepted his actions and forgiven him, and told him about the life going on in the world he had walked away from.

Anna's tears flowed as she read, and she ached to take her mother in her arms and comfort her. There were no living objects for her anger and sorrow, apart from her siblings, so she had some of the letters copied and sent them on, then swore to herself that she would have nothing more to do with any of them.

In August she went to an auction sale with half a mind to buy some chocolate-making equipment. Chocolate was her passion, and as soon as she saw the stock being auctioned, it became clear that the magic of chocolate was calling to her. In quick succession she bought a table-top chocolate tempering machine, a tempering table, a vibrator to get rid of air bubbles, moulds, tins, thermometers, and other useful bits. She had leaflets printed, offering free samples of the unusual and amazing chocolate creations she could supply for upmarket dinner parties. If you wanted an Anna Adams creation, you had to be in quick and pay for the privilege.

* * *

Anna worked seven-day weeks and was exhausted, mentally and physically. Then her best friend, Belinda Miles, suggested a busman's holiday. Belinda, originally from San Francisco, was a pastry chef working for Harrods, and she loved everything Italian. From chocolate cannoli, sfogliatelle, zeppole and farfellette with powdered sugar to a croquembouche cupcake, Belinda's delicate and sweet pastry creations were mouth-wateringly delicious.

She had found an advertisement for a week-long dessert cookery course in Rome, and suggested that afterwards they could go to Tuscany for a few days, rent a villa and relax, drink wine, eat food and read anything but cookery books. The Anna of old would have found a hundred reasons to decline – clients who required her expertise for their summer parties, equipment she needed to spend money on – but the 'new' Anna saw the possibilities and grabbed the opportunity.

Anna and Belinda couldn't have been more different. Belinda was petite and blonde, tanned, witty, sarcastic and full of nervous energy. Anna was taller, curvier, a fair-skinned, green-eyed brunette with a gentle, lazy bohemian chic. Her confidence seemed boundless, and only she knew that it was less than a year old.

The course was amazing and inspiring; she perfected a towering dark chocolate cake made of layers of lace-thin crêpes. She also discovered that she adored Rome, from the square pizza to the crumbed mushrooms to the bowls of pasta to the gelato.

The villa in the Tuscan hills was delightfully crumbly and dusty, but the pool was refreshing and the kitchen garden held many new delights.

One night Belinda suggested they go to a family restaurant in the hills to have dinner. The food was bursting with garlic, herbs and ripe tomato flavours. Then halfway through the main course, a broad-shouldered man got up from a table across the room and walked over to them.

CHAPTER THIRTEEN

MARRIAGE

It all happened in what seemed like the blink of an eye. Vinnie and Anna exchanged phone numbers after a day of tasting wine at Castello Banfi, and promised to contact each other in England. He didn't wait: he started calling her at home while he was still in Europe. He told her what he had ordered for dessert and asked her what wine he should choose, but he didn't tell her that dessert was often all he ordered. The conversations got longer and longer, and he described what he saw and tasted, in Rome, in Naples, at Pompeii and on the island of Sicily.

When he couldn't reach her for a whole day, he drove to the nearest airport, handed in the car and flew home. Their first night together was his first night back, and he didn't leave her house for a week.

It was her bohemian chic that first attracted him: she seemed comfortable in her own skin and loved to indulge her passions – chocolate, colour, art, music and, very quickly, her passion for him. She had a rich, deep laugh that reminded him of a chocolate waterfall, and they laughed a lot and at the same things. They were intellectual equals, and the verbal sparring was confirmation for them both that the relationship was strong and stimulating.

When he was, finally, on his own, Vinnie took a long, hard look in the mirror. For the first time in his life he wanted someone more than he wanted financial security. He'd had relationships before, but as soon as the woman had got serious, he had found a reason to run for the door. He had been called a commitment phobic so many times that he had begun to believe that he was. But this time he was willing to accept, even after one week, that she wouldn't leave him if he could be worthy of her.

What would that take? Perhaps an honest pay packet for an honest job and to keep out of trouble? It was clear that she had her own standards of behaviour, and that she wouldn't be there to post bail if he got nicked. She'd had a long-term relationship with a dependant alcoholic and had given up hope of him staying sober; she knew what she didn't want.

When he needed to think, he walked, so he spent a whole night wandering aimlessly around his city, through the park, up to the theatre district, down to the river and across a bridge, planning and working out what he would have to give up and where he could turn to get a job. It wasn't an easy decision – the life he led was the only life he had known. So what was he good at? Talking, selling stuff to people, convincing them that they needed what he could provide. What did he enjoy talking about most? Apart from himself, wine. Where did people like him go for wine? The Wine Warehouse! He had the passion, he had tasted some spectacular wines, and he had the kind of brain that retained facts and dates. All he had to do was bluff until his knowledge caught up with his bravado, and persuade the manager of his local branch of the Wine Warehouse to give him a job. Simple!

The next day he paid his neighbour to be a customer and take notes on all the bottles prominently displayed in the shop, and then Vinnie hurried to the library and researched those wineries in books. When he was ready, he marched into the shop and asked to speak to the manager.

'Good morning, sir. My name is Vinnie Whitney-Ross, and I'd like to take ten minutes of your time to show you how I would sell some of your best wines. You won't regret it.'

He was hired on the spot, and told to return at 8.30 the next morning. An hour into his first day, he was arranging bottles of Chianti when he felt a light tap on his shoulder. He spun around to find Anna standing in front of him, a list in her hand.

'I was wondering if you could help me, sir. I need some wine to go with a chocolate dessert. For a very exclusive dinner party.'

Her green eyes danced mischievously at him. He glanced over to where his new boss was flicking through a magazine and watching him furtively.

'Certainly, madam. What kind of chocolate?' he asked.

'Valrhona. I'm a chocolatier.'

He paused for a moment and looked at the shelves. 'Which Valrhona are you using?'

She raised her eyebrows in genuine surprise. 'The recipe has three different components, all Grands Cru. The truffle is Le Noir – slightly acidic and intensely chocolate, lovely soft, spicy notes, but a definite after-taste, some would call it bitterness.'

Vinnie nodded thoughtfully. 'And the other two?'

'Er, Jivara – very creamy, tastes of vanilla with a malt finish. And Araguani – raisins, chestnuts and liquorice, intense, long palate.'

'Which is the dominant flavour? Which one do you want to match?'

She shook her head in amazement and smiled at him. 'The log is the centrepiece, and that's the Araguani.'

He studied the shelves. 'I was going to suggest a Californian Zinfandel, relatively new here and quite scarce, but very drinkable ... but there would be too much competition between the different chocolates and the wine.'

As he spoke, he gestured for her to follow him across the shop. 'So instead, I would go for a Cabernet Sauvignon or a Pinot Noir or perhaps even a vintage port. A Cab Sav should have some Syrah in it, which will give you raisin, cinnamon and liquorice notes.'

They stopped beside the French red wine section. He pulled out a bottle and handed it to her. His expression was very serious.

'Château Saint Estève d'Uchaux, Vieille Vignes. All you need to know is that it's sixty per cent Syrah and forty per cent Grenache, and comes from vines that are forty-five years old. And it is magnificent.'

She turned the bottle over in her hand.

'How much, per bottle?'

He smiled at her. 'How many do you need? Five glasses per bottle.'

'Ah ... three. No, better make it four.'

'Can be up to eight hundred quid a bottle in some places, but we'll sell you four bottles for two thousand.'

'And it's worth that?'

'It's worth double that – it'll make your dessert sing like Callas.'

She nodded and gave him back the bottle.

'Done. Can I pay by credit card? Callender's, they're one of London's best-known catering companies.'

He took another three from the rack and gestured towards the counter. 'Certainly, madam. Right this way. Let me give you one of our special customer cards, then we'll know you have a discerning palate.'

As they returned to the counter, the boss beamed at him and walked away.

* * *

'Is there anything I could tell you that would put you off me?'

Anna rolled onto her side and looked at him. Vinnie was lying on one elbow, the sheets crumpled around his body, smiling at her. She frowned.

'Do you want me to be put off?' she asked.

'No! Not one little bit. But I want to know what sort of thing would put you off.'

She sat up. 'Ever killed anyone?'

'Nope.'

'Ever slept with anyone under sixteen?'

'Nope.'

She smiled down at him. 'Ever stolen anything?'

'Ahhh. Now, that's where we get into a grey area.'

He sat up, and she could tell by his expression that he did want to tell her something.

'If you have stuff you want to tell me, Vinnie, just do. I'm not that fragile.'

'Okay.'

She watched him and waited. Instinct told her not to rush him and not to interrupt. They'd had a lovely two months, and she didn't want anything to be a deal-breaker. Not this time.

'You know my mum's a widow and she lives in Sussex. What you don't know is that my dad died from a gunshot wound – a self-inflicted gunshot wound. He was an accountant and he got involved with a dodgy client and some gambling, and he killed himself. I was ten.'

He paused and she nodded slowly.

'You poor thing!'

'Then I got into some … trouble at school. Kids stole stuff and I fenced it, not drugs, just things. Nothing major, but I made money, a bit like Fagin! I got caught and I got expelled. I was sixteen.'

Again he paused, but she said nothing.

'So far, nothing to get too worked up about, I guess. I wanted to make my own way, so I worked as a trader, meaning I traded stuff. People sold me things, and I sold them on to other people. Some of it wasn't very legal.'

His eyes betrayed his anxiety, and she nodded again.

'I worked the markets. I took deliveries and sold them on to people I knew had outlets, pubs, clubs –'

'What sort of things?' she asked.

'Mainly clothes, handbags, knock-offs, household goods –'

'Not drugs?'

'No! Never anything like that. The odd case of wine, but never drugs.'

She smiled. 'Nothing else matters to me, sweetheart.'

He looked relieved and she wanted to hug him, but it was too early in the conversation – there was more.

'I went to Europe because I needed to stay out of sight. I nearly got caught up in a war between two rival gangs, all to do with some cocaine in a crate of very good knock-off designer stuff. I had been asked to store it and had no idea what it contained.'

She raised her eyebrows. 'Close call.'

He nodded. 'Yep. I decided to have a holiday and learn more about wine. I met you.'

'Why are you telling me all this, Vinnie?' she asked.

He sighed. 'I guess I don't want us to have secrets.'

'In that case, I have a confession. I used to steal mint chocolates from the corner shop and put them in my sandwiches.

I was the only kid in my class with chocolate sandwiches and all the others wanted to trade.'

He laughed. 'You brazen hussy. Were you ever caught?'

She shook her head. 'Nope, and Mum never suspected a thing. Wow, this is not what I expected at all. And you gave up all that because you met me?'

He nodded and took her hand in his. 'And I got a real job,' he said.

'I know! But you do enjoy it, don't you?' she asked.

'Absolutely! So far it's been great.'

She had to smile at that. He was like a puppy sometimes. 'But what if you get bored? It's the same thing, day in and day out, and that's not what you're used to.'

'It's a stepping stone, babe. I already have plans for my own business, but I need to do my basic training. I need to learn what customers want.'

She put a hand up and stroked his face. 'I'm amazed that you've changed all that for me. I don't know what to say, except thank you for being honest about the past. I think we're off to a great start.'

* * *

The next weekend he took her to Sussex to meet his mother. Mary was as tall as Anna and had a kind face, gentle eyes and her son's wit. They got on well from the first moment, and she could tell that Mary was delighted with the relationship.

Bit by bit and day by day, Anna fell more in love with Vinnie. Part of her kept waiting to be disappointed, for him to show his feet of clay, but it didn't happen and eventually she stopped believing it would. For their six-month anniversary he took her for a long weekend to a hotel in the Lakes District, and they shared a magnificent meal and a bottle of Château Lafite-Rothschild.

'Dear Lord, this wine is good!' she said, as he raised his glass towards her.

'A toast?' he asked.

'Oh, absolutely! Sorry, just ignore the fact that I've had a sip or two.'

He laughed gently. 'You're forgiven. To us.'

She raised her glass and touched it against his. 'To us. The best us I know,' she said.

'Good.'

He put his glass down and hesitated for a second, then got up and moved around to stand beside her. For a moment she thought he was going to take her hand and draw her to her feet, but instead he knelt down on one knee. She couldn't hide her surprise.

'Vinnie –'

'Anna. You know I love you, you're my soulmate. I can't imagine my life without you now ... Will you marry me?'

She nodded, speechless.

He grinned. 'Can I get up now?' Vinnie asked.

She wrapped her arms around his neck and they kissed. '*Now* you can get up.'

They stood, hugged and kissed again. He dug into his pocket and pulled out a small black box. 'I should've had this ready. You can see I've never done this before.'

He opened the box and offered it to her. In it was a lovely cushion diamond, surrounded by smaller diamonds, in platinum, an art deco style, the style she loved. She gasped with delight.

'Oh darling, it's gorgeous!'

He looked relieved as he took it from the box and slipped it onto the third finger of her left hand.

She kissed him again. 'I love you, too, and thank you for being romantic.'

* * *

They were married in the little stone church with the Saxon font in Mary's village. He was twenty-seven and she was twenty-four. It was 1993 and the world was in a hedonistic whirl. She and Vinnie wrote their own vows, and promised to be there for each other and never lie to each other and to follow one another to the end of the earth.

If the ceremony was simple, the wedding breakfast was far from it, and was a stupendous success. Vinnie matched each of the six courses to a different wine. He introduced the vintage and proclaimed it more wonderful than the preceding one, and Anna took the opportunity to tease him. She designed and made her own wedding cake: five tiers, and each one a different flavoured chocolate filling, with white chocolate and sugar-paste flowers wrapped around each tier, and a solid chocolate wine glass and dipping spoon on top instead of a bride and groom. Its unveiling drew a round of applause from the delighted guests.

They honeymooned in Paris and hunted for rare wine and chocolates, went to the Louvre and took a boat ride down the Seine. Anna had never been happier in her life; at last she had found a man who didn't disappoint her and would never lie to her.

After the reception, Mary sat in her lounge and cried with joy. At last the spell of the past, the curse of the Lanes, the devastation wrought by her husband's stupidity, had been broken. For twenty years she was right.

PART THREE

BLOOD

CHAPTER FOURTEEN

DOWN THE MARKET

February 2012

Vinnie looked up from his graphic novel and smiled as he questioned his wife. 'And what is it today, dear? Bovril and tomato? Parsley and mascarpone? Really, I should get danger money.'

He sat in a deck chair beside his stall in Covent Garden Market. She stood over him and frowned back in mock disapproval, a plastic tray of round chocolate balls in her hand. Her green eyes glittered at him.

'Oh, very funny. My concoctions go down a treat with *discerning* punters.'

He dropped the book into his lap and investigated the balls by poking at them and making them roll around. He did this because he knew it annoyed her.

'Maybe *they* should get danger money,' he said as he closed his eyes and she slipped a ball into his open mouth. The first hit was intense chocolate, and the next made his eyes open in surprise.

'Ah, let me see: tonight, Matthew, I can taste … *basil*?'

She punched the air with her free hand. 'Yes! Sweet basil. Try another one.'

He shook his head vigorously. 'Not until you tell me what they are. I need my taste buds.'

She pointed to each ball as she identified them. 'Ginger and wasabi for the Japanese, pink peppercorn, lime and chilli, smoked Earl Grey tea, salted caramel and Pinot Noir.'

He took the last one she pointed to and held it up. 'You could've started with the best one first, silly woman.'

'It's got some of that New Zealand wine –'

He pretended to choke. 'You put Crystal Creek Pinot into a *chocolate*? You philistine!'

She gave a gasp of mock astonishment and put the tray in his hand. 'All this time I thought you were just a wine snob, but you're actually a full-blown wine nerd.'

He looked up at her out of the corner of his eye and grinned. It was definitely a game day. 'I keep a pipette in my pocket.'

She emitted a short laugh and covered her mouth with her hand to smother it. 'I'm not sure that's the most flattering term for it, my darling.'

He popped another ball into his mouth. Round one to him.

'And here's me about to compliment your salted caramel. I'd pay real money for this one.'

Vinnie's cart was built like a miniature gypsy caravan, with a side that opened up, shelves that folded out, and big hooks on the poles that supported the roof. A sign read 'Vin Extraordinaire' in a flowing script, and the contents on display included decorated wine glasses, books, wine stoppers, corkscrews, wine racks and more. It was an extension of his real job – sourcing and supplying fine wine to wealthy clients – but he enjoyed it and he made contacts.

Anna's cart stood next door, identical in structure. Her sign read 'Anna's Chocolate Pot' in the same script, and her wares were edible and delicious: handmade truffles and chocolates, racks of chocolate bars, moulded shapes in chocolate, dipped fruit …

A couple strolled slowly across the piazza towards the two stalls. The man was older and the woman was a trophy.

Vinnie stood up and smiled broadly at them. 'Morning, my lovelies. Would you like to try a really unusual chocolate?'

They gave him a confused shake of the head. He put down the tray and picked up a pack of cocktail mats, painted with wine bottles and grapes. 'Genuine china, Italian-made. Very classy, good value, too. Only a tenner.'

The busty blonde took them from him. 'Gosh, feel 'em, Ronnie! 'eavier than they look.'

'Aren't we all, my lovely? Special treat, for today only: they come with a song. Where else would you get service like that?'

The painted fingernails clinked against the china as she turned them over. Her companion picked up a book on French wine and looked at Vinnie.

'Does this come wiv a song?' he asked.

New money, desperate to impress, reads wine magazines, wants a top-class cellar and doesn't know a cork from a screw cap – Vinnie's bread and butter. He shrugged dramatically.

'Go on, you've twisted my arm.'

The blonde held out the mats towards her husband.

'I really like 'em, Ronnie. They'd go beautiful on that new coffee table – it's Italian, too.'

She turned to Vinnie and smiled sheepishly. 'Cost a lot more than a tenner.'

Vinnie winked at her. 'Worth it, though. Is it marble?'

'Yeah, it is! How'd you know that?'

He shrugged. Hooked.

'You look like someone who knows the best when she sees it. Italian marble, it's the best.'

Her husband hesitated and nodded. 'Go on then, the book and whatever it is Barbara wants for her damn table. But I want that song.'

Vinnie beamed, took a card from his top pocket and handed it over. 'If you ever want any help sourcing fine wine, sir, I'm your man. Vinnie Whitney-Ross, best labels, best prices.'

The man took the card gratefully and read it. Landed.

'Thanks very much, Vinnie. I'll be in touch.'

Vinnie spread his arms wide and sang the first verse of 'Little Ole Wine Drinker Me' a capella in a rich baritone voice. At the conclusion, he took the blonde's manicured hand and raised it to his lips. She gave an excited giggle, and the few people who had gathered applauded.

'Gosh, you should be inside, busking with one of 'em CD players.'

Anna wagged her finger at the woman. 'Oh, stop encouraging him!'

The blonde turned and glared at her. 'Don't be mean, he deserves encouragement. Thank you, Vinnie, for being so lovely and singing to me.'

* * *

On a late winter evening Vinnie and Anna strolled hand in hand through Richmond Park. Gently rolling green hills flowed in every direction as they walked along a dirt track towards a stand of bare trees, the branches stark against a leaden sky. Anna carried a dog lead in her free hand, and Vinnie a plastic bag in his.

He was now forty-six, still a muscular, heavy-set build. He smiled and laughed easily, people warmed to him quickly and he liked to be the centre of attention. Part of this was that old defence mechanism: if they laugh with you, they won't laugh at you. He had a soul that loved music, art and wine, with a performance flair that Anna had brought to life.

The fact that she didn't have a maternal bone in her body had surprised him, as she was empathetic with most people, and kids were naturally drawn to a chocolatier. She had remained firm on the issue, though: she didn't mind his past, she was available, but having children was not on the agenda. Motherhood meant sacrifices she was not prepared to make. She had three siblings and three half-siblings, but never saw any of them, so nieces and nephews were not on the agenda either. He found it amazingly easy to agree, and they came to a compromise that suited them both.

The newest compromise bounded up to them, his tail wagging furiously, a chocolate Labrador puppy called Merlot. It was the one name Vinnie had suggested that didn't immediately sound like a wine label. They stopped and both patted the dog with obvious affection, then watched as he raced off. Deer were grazing in an open field, and their heads shot up in alarm as Merlot ran between a stand of trees.

'Are you at the club tonight?' she asked.

He nodded. 'For a while. Why don't you join me and I'll treat you to a curry?'

She hooked her arm through his. 'You spendthrift, you. I could be persuaded to do just about anything for a prawn korma.'

* * *

The Golden Circle was an underground supper club and cocktail lounge, with a loud atmosphere, lots of coloured lighting and, occasionally, clouds of dry ice. At one end of the elongated space, tables and chairs were scattered around the periphery of a packed, under-lit dance floor. An enormous mock-candle chandelier swung above the dancers. The five-piece band played on the slightly raised stage, and music boomed from the speakers, which were partially hidden by heavy velvet drapery. At the other end of the room, people were drinking and flirting, clustered around a circular gold-coloured Perspex bar. One long wall was lined with deep booths filled with men in ill-fitting suits conducting business hidden from view.

Vinnie sat at a table and sipped a glass of cranberry juice as his gaze swept from the dance floor to the bar and back again. He supplied the wine for the club and had an informal arrangement with the owner, David Kelt, which meant he spent three nights a week chatting about wine and encouraging people to try the more expensive bottles. He found new clients among the patrons on a regular basis, and it allowed Kelt to advertise a discerning wine list. Vinnie could also spot trouble before it erupted and give a wink to the bouncers, who sorted it out. Kelt knew he was an observer, a wise and experienced head who had made it to the peaceful harbour of an honest living.

Anna was squeezing her way through the crowd of people. As she reached the table, he stood and kissed her.

'So sorry, my love,' she said. 'Traffic was crazy.'

She sounded stressed and tired. He rubbed her arm, pulled out a chair and she slumped gratefully into it.

'You're in perfect time, she's the real star.'

He indicated towards a redheaded woman, dressed in a fringed jacket, jeans and cowboy boots, busy lowering the microphone and preparing to sing.

'Oh, please! How many dying dogs and abandoned lovers can she fit into a three-song set?'

Vinnie laughed. 'Darling, you'd be surprised. Do you want a drink?'

'Is it one of yours?'

An affectionate glance of understanding passed between them.

'Absolutely, only the best for our VIPs. With an obscene mark-up.'

An elegant brunette put her bony hand on Vinnie's shoulder and leaned down to whisper in his ear. 'Mr Kelt wants to see you in his office, as soon as you're free, sir.'

Vinnie nodded and stood up. 'I'll just get Anna a drink.'

'I'm quite capable of looking after myself!'

Vinnie winked at her. 'It won't hurt him to wait, and I'm supposed to be encouraging the clients to drink.'

'But they're supposed to pay for it,' she said to his disappearing back.

* * *

Vinnie stood in the open doorway. David Kelt sat behind an antique mahogany desk and wrote figures into a black leather notebook with a Montegrappa fountain pen. He was taking obvious care to write slowly and create perfectly rounded numbers. Vinnie liked the man, who was in his late sixties, rotund, with a thick head of grey hair, an impressive moustache and a face flushed by the regular intake of fine wine.

The thin brunette was stacking several bundles of banknotes into a very full wall safe, and when Vinnie coughed the woman rapidly closed it up, punched numbers into an electronic keypad and swung an oil painting back against the wall, covering the safe.

'You wanted to see me, David?' Vinnie asked.

Kelt closed the notebook, looked up and smiled broadly. 'Hello, Vin. Got time for a drop of the good stuff?'

'Always!'

Kelt motioned for the woman to leave as he went to the sideboard and poured two glasses of red from a delicate crystal decanter.

'It's that '85 Grand Vin Château Latour, from the auction. A great year.'

Vinnie sat down and accepted the wine. His eyes glistened as he held the glass up to the light. *God, I love my job*, he thought to himself.

'Thank you. Indeed it was! A very hot, dry summer. Harvest was between 30 September and 11 October, with light rain between 4 October and 9 ...'

His voice trailed off and Kelt smiled and cocked his head to one side.

Vinnie shrugged with embarrassment. 'I have that kind of brain, David. When I read about harvests, tasting notes, reviews, it just sticks.'

'Good God, don't apologise. It must be something of an advantage. I've been meaning to ask you: Israeli reds, any you'd recommend?'

Vinnie raised an eyebrow. 'One or two. Why?'

'I tried a Syrah at a dinner party. Seahorse, or something like that. Rich, very intense, peppery even. I thought it was a real surprise.'

Vinnie nodded and sipped the wine. 'Dear Lord, that's good!' he exclaimed. He took another sip, let it roll around in his mouth, and then swallowed slowly. 'One you should definitely try is the Flam brothers, from the Judean Hills of Upper Galilee. Golan is a Master of Wine, and Gilad is the businessman. Their father, Israel Flam, was the chief winemaker for Carmel, Israel's largest winery. He was a pioneer in Israeli winemaking, and the boys are a credit to him. Superb reds. Merlot reserve, Cab Sav reserve, but the star is the Syrah – just exquisite.'

Kelt took a long sip of the wine and also savoured it. 'Maybe a mixed case? To start.'

Vinnie nodded. This departure from a lifetime devotion to French reds was something he had been trying to foster. There was so much more to sample if he could just get his clients to take a chance. 'Excellent! I'll drop it around tomorrow night. Nice to see you experimenting.'

Kelt beamed at him and raised his glass. 'Live dangerously, Vinnie. Your palate will thank you.'

* * *

It took Ronnie and Barbara two days to get back in touch after their purchases at the market. Vinnie's website, also called Vin Extraordinaire, listed his services, and among them was a page called 'Wine Match'. If you were having an important party, anniversary, birthday, wedding, product launch – any event where quality and flair were important – you gave him your menu and he suggested exciting and impressive wines matched to each course, and, naturally, supplied everything he recommended. He offered bubbles, red and white wine, boutique beer and non-alcoholic choices, and could match any cuisine.

Ronnie and Barbara were having an anniversary dinner party for clients and friends, and they wanted wine that would surprise.

Vinnie sat on an over-stuffed sofa and scrutinised the menu Barbara had just handed him. She was wearing a one-piece lounge suit in a very loud bird print, a vivid green turban, a stack of thin gold bracelets on each arm and two rings on each of her fingers. Vinnie couldn't help but wonder what knock-offs he would have been able to sell her in his former life.

'So, Vinnie, what you think of the food?' she asked anxiously.

He looked up at her and shook his head with genuine surprise. 'Beautiful, my lovely.'

She smiled, the relief rippling across the part of her face that wasn't botoxed. 'I chose it from all the lists 'em caterers sent round. But their wines were all French. Ronnie wants some of that new stuff everybody's talkin' about.'

Vinnie nodded. 'New World. Australia, New Zealand, Chile, Argentina, South Africa, America.'

'Really? All 'em countries make wine? Well, I never.'

'I think you should go with some of my favourites, from New Zealand. That trio of salmon to start? The roulade and the vodka-cured salmon in particular need a crisp, strong, gutsy wine … a lovely Marlborough Sauvignon Blanc.'

She watched him with a mixture of fascination and thinly veiled desire. 'Got any samples?'

He winked at her. 'Of course. In the car. Got any smoked salmon?'

She smiled and touched his knee with her long green talons. 'Of course. In the fridge.'

CHAPTER FIFTEEN

DAVID KELT

David Kelt was a very good client of the Lanes. Tobias had loaned him the money to buy his first club, and David had paid back the debt on time and with interest. When he had decided to expand, he had raised the issue with Norman and discovered that the interest rate had trebled. After a couple of days of thought, he went back to Norman with a proposition.

'I need a capital injection and you need an efficient laundromat. I have a very good system in place, sending money offshore and bringing product back which is sold for clean, legitimate profit. I can give you several references from satisfied customers.'

Norman puffed on his cigar while he considered how to make the deal work for him. 'What do you want for this service?' he asked.

'A lower interest rate on my loan.'

Norman nodded. 'I think we can make this work, David. How about you open one of your famous bottles of wine and we start talking percentages?'

The end result was the Golden Circle and a very successful money-laundering system. Kelt brought Norman potential contacts and received a 'finder's fee' along the way. This symbiotic relationship worked well for several years, until the manager of the Golden Circle decided to retire in mid-2011.

Kelt had one major flaw: he had a roving eye, and his current squeeze was a young brunette with ambition. She decided she wanted to run the club and, if Kelt didn't agree, she'd take her favours elsewhere. She was intelligent, attractive, witty and an extremely good lover with no desire to get married, someone he really didn't want to lose. So he agreed to her demands and set about teaching her how to run the club. To his surprise she proved to be an excellent learner. By February 2012 she had mastered all aspects – staff, ordering, cashing up, booking acts and running the illegal high-stakes gambling in the back room. There was only one thing about her he didn't know: she was also sleeping with Marcus Lane's 2IC, Tom McGregor.

'He runs a really good legit business,' she said as she lay next to Tom in his bed.

'So, there's no creaming off the top before he pays us?'

'No, not at all.'

'What about the money-cleaning side of it?'

She frowned. 'He does all that himself.'

'In his head?'

'No, in his notebook.'

Tom rolled onto his elbow and looked at her.

'What notebook, sweetheart?'

'He has a black leather notebook. I searched his desk to see if I could photocopy it for you, but it's always in his pocket. He writes numbers in it – dates, amounts, bank accounts.'

Tom smiled and pulled her towards him. He kissed her passionately. 'Good girl, that's very interesting.'

***

Vinnie sat in his car and watched people walking down the wide pavements. Some were exercising dogs and others were hurrying home, laden with carrier bags or briefcases. He could see yellow beams of light from cracks between curtains in several of the bay windows. The cars were expensive, shiny, almost daring someone to try and break into them. Mayfair at twilight was a beautiful sight. This was the London he loved, peopled by those who knew how to enjoy the finer things in life.

He sighed deeply and turned to Merlot, who sat on the passenger seat beside him. 'How many wine cellars do you think there are in this street alone, boy? How many bottles of Pétrus just waiting for a corkscrew?'

He rubbed the dog's head, then opened the car door and pulled himself out. The black Mercedes was a hatchback. He lifted the boot and picked up a cardboard case of wine, held it under one arm and slammed the boot shut. David Kelt's house was a semi-detached Georgian three-storey mansion, elegant and perfectly maintained. The door was painted black, and the handle was brass that shone like gold. Kelt answered almost as soon as Vinnie rang the bell.

'Vinnie! Come on in. Eliza's away for the night, so I have the house to myself.'

Vinnie followed him into a black and white tiled entranceway. A wide oak staircase rose to the upper floors.

'Delighted to see you branching out,' Vinnie said as he put the box down on the floor. 'I've got some stunning New Zealand reds, too – Central Otago Pinots and Waiheke Island Bordeaux blend. I know I harp on, but I'd love you to try a couple. Some of them are up with second-growth Bordeaux.'

Kelt laughed. 'Baby steps, Vinnie. Let me get my head around the Middle East before I go any further south.'

'Fair enough. Shall I take them down?'

Kelt leaned over and pulled a bottle from the box. 'Leave one up here – I'll try it later. The rest can go on the south wall. And do a little checking for me, if you wouldn't mind.'

The size of the basement wine cellar spoke of a serious collector. Three brick walls were covered by double-depth, floor-to-ceiling wine racking. Two walls were full, and the third was about half full from the bottom up. A central light threw out a dim glow. Columns of dust danced in the light and then settled on a new bottle. A carved wooden podium, supporting an open ledger, stood in one corner.

As Vinnie's eyes adjusted to the gloom, he could see the bottles, lying in rows, waiting, always waiting. The temperature was constant, just under 13 degrees Celsius, and the air felt dry on his skin. He could smell that heady aroma, the mixture of ageing cork and the residue of hundreds of bottles opened in this room. It was a combination of what he called 'wine memories' – chocolate, tobacco, cut grass, citrus, leather, plum, spice, tropical fruit, ginger – a hundred scents melded into one. It also smelt of money, the smell a cellar has when the owner will spend £30,000 on one bottle. He got to handle them, and sometimes, when Lady Luck smiled, he got to taste them.

One by one he lifted the bottles out of the case and slid them into gaps in the rack. After each addition he went to the ledger and wrote in it with a fountain pen. When he had racked all eleven bottles he rested for a long moment, his hand on the nearest corner.

He glanced at his watch, then started to move around the room, turning bottles in their racks, kneeling down and pulling a bottle from a rack near the floor and putting it into a gap higher up the wall. He handled the bottles with reverence, and with some he wiped dust off them and read the labels. It was a magnificent collection.

A muffled noise broke the contented silence. Vinnie hesitated, bottle in hand, listened, and then resumed checking. It was time he wasn't there, time to turn from wine-merchant Vinnie to husband Vinnie and meet Anna at their local pub. It was quiz night and his general knowledge –

Indistinct voices from upstairs crashed into his reverie again. He straightened up, walked over to the heavy door and pulled it open. The sounds were much clearer now, and he could hear that the tone was distinctly aggressive. Kelt shouted something that sounded like 'Get out of my house!'

Stay down here and wait until it was over, or go and investigate? Maybe David needed his help, and he wasn't one to walk away from a friend in need.

Vinnie started to climb the twisting, brick-lined stairwell. The steps were slate and he made sure his shoes didn't click on them. His hand brushed against the cold wall as he moved upwards, closer to the noise. As he reached the top step he could see bright yellow light shining from under the door. He paused, his hand resting on the knob. There was a sudden crashing sound, glass breaking, but it wasn't in the kitchen, it was at least one room away. He twisted the knob slowly, very gently pushed the door open and stepped into the kitchen. It was minimalist, well lit and empty.

'Where the fuck is it, scumbag?'

The accent was American, and the angry voice came from the next room. Vinnie bent down, untied his laces and slipped out of his shoes. He moved noiselessly across the slate floor to a serving hatch built into the far wall.

'Where the fuck is *what*?'

It was Kelt's voice, a mix of frustration, fear and fury. Vinnie squeezed himself into the right-angled corner of the two kitchen benches and moved a metal knife block slightly to hide his shadow and create a clear view into the dining room.

The drawers of the ornately carved sideboard were pulled out, and folded linen, cutlery and small boxes lay scattered over the polished wooden floor. A shattered mirror covered the scene in shards that twinkled like snow in the light from the overhead chandelier.

Kelt sat in an upright chair with his back to the long table. He had a raised red welt across one cheek and a rapidly swelling eye socket. The two intruders were side-on to Vinnie, and he could see only one man's profile. The taller of the two men, mid-thirties with a shaven head, leaned forward and poked Kelt in the chest, hard.

'You got sixty seconds and then I'm texting. Boss won't be best pleased.'

Kelt threw his hands up in a gesture of despair. 'For the last time, I don't bloody know what you're talking abo—'

The leader slapped Kelt hard across the face with the back of his gloved hand, and Kelt's head jerked back. Blood spurted from his mouth.

'Tell the boss.' He took a cell phone from his pocket and sent a text message. The smaller man licked his lips, and his hand flickered towards Kelt in anticipation.

'We taking him in, then?' he asked. He was the American.

The fear on Kelt's face was obvious, and Vinnie instinctively pulled back into the shadows, which obscured some of his view. What the hell should he do? Go back downstairs and call the police? Would he get cell coverage in the basement? Probably not. If he tried for the hall and made any noise, he would be rumbled and they wouldn't want a witness. He felt genuinely afraid for Kelt, but his desire to stay alive was stronger.

'Look, I told you —' Kelt's desperate plea was cut off by the loud beep of the leader's phone.

'He's here. Go and let him in. Now!'

Kelt moaned. 'Oh, sweet Jesus Christ!'

As the second man left the room, his associate bent over and punched Kelt in the stomach.

'Say your prayers, you lying bastard,' he sneered.

Kelt grunted in pain. 'Ahhh … I swear. I have no idea what –'

The door swung open and the second man returned. All heads in the room swivelled to watch the man who followed him. Vinnie could see a black cashmere coat open over a dark suit, black leather gloves and highly polished black shoes. Mob boss. As the man picked his way through the debris on the floor to stand directly in front of Kelt, Vinnie could tell that it was a very tall, very erect body, with slicked-back black hair. Somehow, even from the back, he looked more like a stick insect than any man Vinnie had ever seen.

'He's not fucking singing, boss.'

The boss stood very still and scrutinised Kelt closely. 'Good evening, Mr Kelt. I'm truly sorry we have had to intrude on your peace and quiet. I believe you have something important. Something I need to see.'

The voice was as smooth as melted honey and the accent was clipped, but polished by the public school system. About four words in, the realisation hit Vinnie in the stomach with the force of a kick and pushed him back against the bench. Bile rose in his throat until he could taste it, and for a second he thought his bowels were going to open. It was Marcus! This monster was Marcus Lane.

Kelt swallowed and ran his hand over his ashen, bruised and swollen face. Then he raised his other hand towards his interrogator. 'You seem to think I keep some kind of record –'

'I know you do. So *where* do you keep it?'

'If I did … do … have a record, do you really think I would bring it home? Risk my wife?'

Marcus didn't move or speak.

Kelt bowed his head. Vinnie could see that he was trembling.

'It's … in a … in a secret drawer in my office desk.'

Marcus nodded slowly. 'The bad news for you is that I believe you. Our arrangement is over.'

He turned to the leader and snapped his gloved fingers. 'Kill him.'

He started to walk towards the door. Kelt half rose, his arms following Marcus's retreating body.

'No! I haven't –'

The leader pushed him down onto the chair, pulled a Walther PPK from his holster and fired at the centre of Kelt's forehead. The gun made a hollow clicking sound.

'Shit!'

Marcus turned around at the door.

Kelt pleaded, half-rising again. 'Listen to me! It's not incriminating –'

The leader tried again, but the trigger was stuck and he fumbled with it. 'Sorry, boss! It's fucking jammed.'

Marcus strode back across the room, taking a Glock from his coat pocket. 'Do I have to do everything?' he asked. He shot Kelt in the head and the man slumped to the floor, taking the chair with him.

Then Marcus swung around to face his muscle. 'It's so hard to get decent assassins. I've told you before: I don't tolerate swearing and I prefer a Glock.'

He fired two bullets into the heart of the leader at point-blank range. The man fell to his knees, an expression of stunned surprise frozen on his face, and then keeled over.

Marcus shook his head, turned to the remaining man and clicked his fingers again. 'Clean the house, no trace. And I was never here.'

He pocketed the gun and stalked out.

* * *

Vinnie stared at the body of David Kelt and the legs of the other man, framed by the hatch in front of him, his hand clamped tightly over his mouth and his brain reeling. What the fuck was that? *Marcus*? Was that actually Marcus, after all these years? It had to be a nightmare – any moment now he would wake up in a cold sweat and get up for a glass of water. By the time he got back to his warm, comfy bed, he wouldn't even remember the scene.

As the front door slammed, he jerked into motion. Nightmare or not, if he was found here, he was dead. He crossed the room on the balls of his feet, moving swiftly for a big man, carefully picked up his shoes and went through the door to the stairwell, closing it silently behind him.

CHAPTER SIXTEEN

PÉTRUS

The wine cellar was in total darkness. Vinnie sat against the brickwork in the far corner, his knees drawn up to his chest, a bottle of wine, gripped by the neck, resting on them. He concentrated on breathing deeply in through his nose and out through his mouth, to try to still his racing heart.

Marcus was a cold-blooded murderer. His childhood friend was able to end the lives of two men without, apparently, a second thought, and he was the boss of a gang of very frightening men. The idea made Vinnie feel nauseous.

More importantly, he was now trapped in the cellar. What was the chance that the remaining thug would come down here? Almost nil. He didn't look like a wine connoisseur, but one could never tell these days – some of his best clients were the most unlikely-looking wine drinkers. He forced his terrified mind to focus in the present and concentrate on staying alive. He was in no doubt that the man wouldn't leave witnesses. How long had it been since the attack? Twenty minutes, an hour, two, three? He couldn't see his watch, and his mind had lost all track of time.

Suddenly the thud of heavy footsteps on the stairwell echoed around the room; they seemed twice as loud as normal in the darkness.

'Oh Christ,' Vinnie muttered.

The door opened and the dim glow from the stairway silhouetted the second man's bulk in the doorframe. Vinnie shrank back against the wall and held his breath. He could hear a strange roaring in his ears, and the neck of the bottle moved in his slippery grasp.

The man switched on the soft central light, walked into the room and surveyed each wall in turn. 'Well, I'll be damned. What've we got here?'

He pulled a couple of bottles halfway out, read the labels and slid them back in. The third bottle he pulled all the way out. 'Oh, come to Papa!'

He put the bottle on the ground and pulled out another. 'Oh yeah!'

He grabbed the discarded cardboard box and started filling it with bottles. Vinnie watched from the shadows as the man roamed the racks and chose his loot. On two occasions he came within inches of the corner and Vinnie sucked in his breath. Surely he would hear the pounding heart?

Finally the man gave the room another sweeping glance and stood at the door, his hand on the light switch. Vinnie breathed as slowly as he could. His tight shoulders slumped with relief, touching the rack and causing a couple of the bottles to rattle deep inside their slots. The man stared hard in his direction and put the box down.

'Hey, who's there?'

He started to walk towards the sound. Vinnie moved to a squat, tensed his muscles and prepared for the next step. Timing was crucial. When the thug was three steps away, Vinnie smashed the bottle hard against the rack and it broke in half.

Cold liquid gushed over his hand and streamed onto the floor, his nostrils were filled with the pungent smell of red wine.

Vinnie propelled himself forward and upward, the jagged bottle held by the neck out in front of his body. His momentum carried him with extra force, and the weapon caught the unsuspecting man in the upper stomach. Vinnie drove it in as hard as he could, up under the ribcage, and gave it a vicious twist. It stuck fast, almost entirely embedded in the man's torso.

'Ahhh ... What the –?' The man grabbed frantically at the neck with two hands, but couldn't move it. 'Get it out!'

A sudden rush of fluid spurted in a stream through the neck of the bottle. Even in the dim light Vinnie could see that it was blood. The sight sickened him and he swallowed against the nausea.

The man stumbled sideways, his fingers still clawing at the bottle, and blood ran out of his mouth. Then he fell backwards, his head hit the floor with a dull thud and his eyes stared blankly up at Vinnie.

'Oh, fucking hell! Why did you come down here? You greedy bloody little moron.' A wave of adrenaline and revulsion flowed through him, and he seized the rack to steady himself. The rows of bottles swirled as he shook his head to try to clear it. It didn't work. He took three steps and vomited violently into the corner of the room.

When the reaction passed, he knelt down and put two fingers on the man's neck, feeling for a pulse. None. The thug was dead, as surely as Vinnie would have been if his self-defence hadn't worked.

He felt a strange mixture of horror, numbness, adrenaline, anger at the man for making him do such a thing, but the immediate fear had passed and his mind was clear. As he stood, he noticed the bottom half of the bottle lying on the ground and picked it up. The label was cream and there was grey engraving, a red word, the jagged crack right across the red seal –

'Pétrus? Oh, Christ! I would have to pick the most expensive wine in the whole fucking world.'

He stared down at the corpse and shook his head. 'Killed by a bottle of Pétrus. You dumb lucky bastard. I could have bought half a house with the price of that bottle!'

With one hand he pulled the other half from the body, and then he turned back to the ledger.

'Now think, Vinnie. Come on man, *think*! Just the very best. Rack Two.'

He went to the rack and starting pulling bottles out to make a collection in the centre of the room.

* * *

David Kelt's dining room was in darkness, but moonlight flooded in through the bay window. The chandelier over the table flicked on. Vinnie stood in the doorway, a tea towel wrapped around one hand. The blood spray was gone, the chairs were pulled up under the table, the drawers had been pushed back into the sideboard and the boxes and glass had gone from the spotless wooden floor.

He gave a low whistle. 'That's some cleaning job.'

He moved rapidly to the sideboard, put his wrapped hand down the back, found a spot and pushed. A carved gargoyle on the front corner popped out and swung open. Vinnie used his covered hand to pull out a black leather notebook. He flicked through the pages then pocketed it, shut the compartment, turned out the light and left.

* * *

The water streaming from the showerhead was hot, and steam enveloped Vinnie as he scrubbed his body with a long-handled brush. Was it a nightmare? It still felt like a nightmare. If he got out of the shower and called David, would the man answer? He knew what happened when you tangled with the Lanes; his mother had lectured him about corrupt businessmen, about gambling away their money – you ended up putting a bullet in your head. And he still remembered that warehouse, that moment when he would have had his kneecap shattered by a bullet if it hadn't been for Marcus.

He was scrubbing too hard and his skin tingled with the pressure. Tonight felt dangerously like times past, times forgotten. He felt a need to wash it all away, to cleanse himself again.

* * *

Half an hour later Vinnie sat in his lounge and stared out the window at the moon, a glass of scotch in one hand and the notebook in the other. Merlot sprawled across the carpet in front of the empty fireplace and chewed on a battered slipper.

The notebook was full of lists of names, including the Lanes, with amounts of money, Swiss and Cayman Island bank account details and dates beside them, some in red ink and some in black. He recognised some of the other names, too – politicians, entertainers, lawyers and sportsmen. It was what Marcus had come looking for, and it was why David had died. What was David doing? Laundering, blackmailing?

So what was his next course of action? Logic said talk to Anna, go to the police, explain what happened before the body was discovered and his fingerprints … of course his fingerprints were everywhere in the cellar, from when he had racked all the bottles. He wasn't the slightest bit concerned about them arresting him for murder: if he hadn't done what he did, the man would have killed him.

More importantly, did he identify Marcus? Did he owe his childhood friend anything? What was that intervention in the warehouse worth? He would be a cripple now if it hadn't been for Marcus. If he described the killer as bald, short and fat, there was no one to contradict him, but then David's real killer would never be caught. And if he did describe him accurately, did he tell them about their childhood? Would Norman Lane come after him? Was Norman still alive? His car boot was full of the best of David Kelt's wine – literally thousands, if not hundreds of thousands, of pounds worth. What did that make him? A thief or a man desperate to fund his escape?

So many questions battled to be heard inside a brain that flipped from icy calm to desperate panic and back again. He drained the scotch and let the notebook slip from his grasp. A long-suppressed Vinnie, almost like another man entirely, was rising from his past to take over and formulate a plan.

* * *

Vinnie and Anna's bedroom was as cluttered as the rest of the house. Books and magazines filled a bookcase; more were piled on top of the wardrobe and stacked on bedside tables. A TV flickered in one corner, the drama muted.

Anna sat on the bed and held her husband's hand. He was sitting up in bed and gazing steadily at her while she was staring blankly at the wall.

'You killed him.'

It wasn't a question.

'I did.'

'Dead. With a bottle of wine?'

'Very. With a bottle of Pétrus.'

'Oh my God! Well, at least I understand why you didn't make it to the pub quiz.' She turned to him and rubbed his hand gently. 'I'm so sorry I was angry.'

He smiled at her. 'Don't be a goose, you didn't know.'

She nodded slowly. 'And you didn't know David had anything to do with these people?'

'Not a clue.'

'What was he hiding, do you think?'

'Not a clue.'

'You didn't recognise them … from the club?'

He frowned. 'Nope, I've never seen them in the club.'

Another long moment of silence.

'Have you told me everything?' she asked suddenly.

He nodded. 'Everything.'

'Promise?'

He could see her anxiety.

'For God's sake, yes! I promise.'

'You're going to call the police.'

Again, it wasn't a question.

He shrugged, but he was watching her closely. 'Do I have a choice?'

She grasped his other hand, and held them both tightly in hers. 'Yes, of course you do, darling. You brought the bottle home, there's nothing to link you, and, anyway, you deliver wine all the damn time.'

He shook his head emphatically and pulled his hands away.

'My DNA is all over that bloody cellar. As soon as someone checks they'll –'

'Of course it is. Maybe David surprised someone in the cellar and then killed him.'

'I vomited. If they don't believe my version I'm really in trouble.'

'It was self-defence! You don't work with murdering thugs! You don't hide illegal things from some crim–'

She was becoming agitated, and he wrapped his arms around her, stroking her hair rhythmically.

'And they'll accept that. But only if I talk to them before Eliza discovers that they're down one bottle of remarkable wine … not to mention the body that's lying in a pool of what's left of it.'

She pulled back. The protection of shock was receding, and her expression was finally one of panic and terror. 'Stop it! Don't make a joke! It's not a laughing matter, Vinnie. David is dead and you're a witness to murder. You'll be in terrible danger. *What have you done?*'

It took a great deal to make her cry, but she was on the verge of tears now.

He took her face in his hands and kissed her gently. 'No one can make me do anything I don't want to do. I'll go to the police station. Everything will be fine, I promise.'

* * *

Vinnie's Mercedes sat at one end of a narrow alleyway that ran between two abandoned warehouses in East London. He stood beside the open boot of the car and watched as a short, bald man bent over the three boxes.

Brian Davis was what Vinnie would have become but for Anna. He moved across the line of the law as if it didn't exist. If it didn't make a quid, it had no meaning; everyone had a price. He was strong and wiry, with quick, aggressive movements.

He lifted wine bottles out of the boxes, examined them, and then returned them. When he stood up he exhaled in a low whistle and gave Vinnie a very hard stare. 'A '94 Pétrus, '78 Romanée-Conti, '48 Mouton-Rothschild, '96 Lafite-

Rothschild, '88 Latour, '56 Margaux. You sure you're not having a laugh?'

His voice was high-pitched for a man and at odds with his appearance. It sounded as though someone had his balls in a vice. Vinnie smiled slowly at him.

'Told you it was worth getting up early for.'

'Where'd you get a collection like this, Vin?'

Vinnie shrugged and ran a hand through his curls. 'Times are tough. This isn't the whole collection. If a client needs to liquidate some assets fast, he's going to call me.'

'But they'd make a bloody fortune at auction.'

'No time. He needs cash. No questions.'

Davis nodded and touched the nearest box. 'Understood. Hell, I'll take 'em all. Name your price.'

CHAPTER SEVENTEEN

DCI RON MATTHEWS

Detective Sergeant Peter Harper was an ambitious man. He had known that he wanted to be a policeman at an early age, not only because his stepdad was one or because he wanted to rid the world of bad guys, but because he liked firing guns, solving mysteries and telling other people what to do.

Life as a beat copper was not for him, though. He wanted to be a detective. So he got a university degree in social sciences and joined the police force. His rise was rapid: commended as a young constable, CID after three years, and now he was a DS for one of the best detective chief inspectors on the force, Ron Matthews. Next step was a DI, and he had a plan.

Harper was in his early thirties, single, with short back and sides, clean-shaven. His easy-going manner made him popular with his colleagues and disguised his dedication to his job. He had disposable income and wore a Rolex, very good suits and handmade shoes. On this particular day he was the duty DS, and he sat at his desk and surfed the internet. The weather was still crap and he was heartily sick of winter. Why couldn't he get a decent case, somewhere warm and exotic, with great wine, sandy beaches and women who smiled invitingly? His desktop was stacked with folders: minor fraud, armed robbery, rape … Serious enough, but not as challenging as a murder. DS Scott had a murder, a pub brawl that had escalated, and Harper kept his jealousy to himself. The case was nothing to get really excited about. He wanted a murder with a twist, like the ones in the books he read, or the cases he had solved in his imagination when he was a kid – missing dead bodies, multiple suspects, gangsters, red herrings, foreign diplomats …

* * *

The police station reception was busy. Three uniformed officers manned the long counter, and people milled around, both civilians and officers. Vinnie imagined that this was the norm. He hadn't been inside a police station for a very long time, and he didn't feel comfortable about returning.

A policewoman looked up and smiled at him. 'Morning, sir. How can I help?'

'I'm Vinnie Whitney-Ross. Who's the DS on duty?'

She hesitated. 'DS Harper, sir.'

Vinnie handed her a sealed envelope.

'Can you give him this, please? It's a signed statement. I'll take a seat and wait.'

'Can I let him know what it's about, sir?'

'I killed someone.'

Her expression didn't alter. She gestured towards a cluster of chairs, some occupied, some empty. 'Thank you, sir. I'll let him know you're here.'

He nodded his thanks and took a seat.

* * *

Two hours later a car drew up outside David Kelt's house. DS Harper got out and bounded up the steps to the door.

The bell sounded somewhere deep inside. A petite, elegant woman in her late fifties opened the door and looked him up and down. 'Yes?' she asked.

'Mrs Kelt?'

She frowned. 'Yes, can I help you?'

He took his badge from his pocket, opened it and held it up for her to see.

'DS Harper, the Met. May I come in?'

She took a step back in surprise, and then opened the door and stood aside for him.

'Certainly.'

'Thank you.'

He followed her into a sitting room off to the right of the tiled entrance hall. The room was exquisitely furnished and spotlessly clean.

'What's this about, detective?'

'Is your husband home, Mrs Kelt?'

She shook her head. 'No. But that's not unusual. I've been away and I've only just got home myself. Do you want to speak to him? I can give you his mobile number.'

'Thank you. I've tried it. It goes to voicemail. Would you mind very much if I had a quick look around? Nothing formal. Have you noticed anything out of place?'

She glanced around the room, baffled and concerned. 'No, nothing. What on earth are you looking for?'

He followed her gaze. 'There could have been a disturbance last night. May not be your house, but I'd like to check.'

She shrugged. 'Be my guest.'

He walked into the dining room, stopped, sniffed and bent down to touch the wooden floor. He looked at all the chairs in turn and ran his hands over the sideboard. Then he went to the service hatch and looked through it into the kitchen, finally examining the bench and the knife block. When he turned around she was standing in the doorway watching him.

'I'll just have a look at the cellar. Would you wait up here, please?'

* * *

Detective Chief Inspector Ron Matthews sat behind a tidy desk; he liked order. He was bearded and overweight, in a rumpled suit and no tie.

The knock on the door made his fingers hesitate over the computer keyboard. 'Come.'

Harper put his head around the door.

Matthews looked up sharply. 'How is he?' he asked.

Harper shrugged. 'Remarkably calm.'

Matthews reached for his phone and nodded at his DS. 'Good. Give him a coffee and put him in Room Two. I'll be five minutes.'

'Yes, sir.'

'And remember, kid gloves, Peter. He's about to have his world turned upside down and I don't want him spooked. I've waited a hell of a long time for this. We need him.'

* * *

Vinnie's foot tapped nervously on the floor, his tongue flicked over his dry lips and he ran his hand through his hair. The police officer was watching him from the other side of the table. Two disposable coffee cups sat between them.

He had been told nothing. The DS had ushered him into a room and asked him to go over the events of the night before in his own words and in his own time. He hadn't been asked any

146

questions, so he had just relayed what had happened as he had written it down.

There were one or two omissions, of course – nothing about the notebook – so he had indicated he had no idea what they were looking for, and he hadn't told them about his own raid on the dead man's cellar. Harper had brought him a stack of magazines and excused himself. After a couple of hours Vinnie was getting impatient, but, just as he had set off to complain, the detective had returned and escorted him to this room. Then, again, they waited.

The door opened and Matthews came in, a folder in his hand.

Harper got to his feet. 'Vinnie, this is DCI Ron Matthews.'

Matthews extended his hand, and Vinnie half-rose to shake it. It felt firm and dry.

'Sir, this is Vincent Whitney-Ross,' Harper continued.

'Mr Whitney-Ross. Wrong time, wrong place, eh?'

They all sat down, and Matthews put his folder on the table.

'Call me Vinnie. I don't use my surname much.'

'So, Vinnie, you say you killed a man last night, with a bottle of wine?'

Vinnie could hear the suspicion in his tone. 'There's a body, I told you. In David Kelt's cellar.'

Matthews shook his head. 'No, there isn't. Without your statement we wouldn't know a crime had been committed. So, why have you come to us?'

Vinnie sipped his coffee and eyed the two men up before he answered. This was insane!

'Eliza deserves to know. And David deserves justice … And to be honest, I thought you'd find my DNA all over the cellar: I vomited, and I have two halves of a rather blood-soaked bottle of '03 Pétrus.'

Matthews lifted an eyebrow and smiled. 'What a waste!'

'Tell me about it. It was dark – I grabbed the first bottle I could find.'

'Your wife knows you're here, presumably.' It wasn't phrased as a question.

Vinnie hesitated, and then nodded. Instinct told him to tell the truth.

'Good,' Matthews continued 'You work for Kelt?'

'*Worked*. The man in question is dead. I supply wine for the Golden Circle, one of his supper clubs. I work the crowd, encourage people to drink –'

'What's the clientele like?'

Where was this going? The older man was absolutely impossible to read, while the younger one was trying not to show how excited he was.

Vinnie shrugged. 'Ordinary people after a good time, drinking, dancing. Lots of stag and hen nights.'

Matthews watched him for a moment, and then gave a brief nod, apparently satisfied.

Vinnie rubbed his face with both hands. He suddenly felt very tired.

'And how long have you been on Covent Garden Market?' the DCI asked.

'Three years, part-time. My wife, Anna, has a chocolate stall, but it's a hobby for me. Mainly, I run a subscription fine-wine club. I plan wine lists for events, buy wholesale and sell on.'

'And that's what you were doing at Kelt's home. Delivering wine?'

Vinnie nodded again, with growing confidence. 'A mixed case – Flam brothers, Israeli reds. A chance to broaden his collection, he's a major client – *was* a major client.'

Harper shifted in his seat, and Matthews threw him a sharp glance. The younger man wasn't happy about the obscure questions, and the older one wanted him to shut the fuck up.

Vinnie sipped his coffee, more for something to do than because it quenched his thirst. *And they don't even know that I know who —*

'And you don't take drugs, smoke dope?' Matthews asked suddenly.

Vinnie stopped mid-sip and put the cup on the table, harder than he meant to, slurping some of the liquid. 'No, I don't! Look, if you don't believe me, I'm very happy to call it quits.'

'Except they came back and cleaned up the body, didn't they? So they know someone else was there. But you took the bottle, so they can't track you down. That was very clever.' Matthew's tone was noticeably sharper.

'So you *do* believe me?' Vinnie asked. He leaned in towards the table.

The two men exchanged looks, and the senior officer gave a slight nod. 'I tested both the cellar and the dining room for a chemiluminescence reaction with luminol,' Harper said.

'And?'

'Huge areas glowed bright blue. That means there's been significant blood splatter.'

His statement hung in the air for a moment. A peculiar sense of dread started to trickle like iced water down Vinnie's spine, and his stomach felt as though he was free-falling in a lift.

Matthews opened the folder, took out a black-and-white photograph and slid it across the table. It was a candid shot of Marcus, walking down a crowded pavement towards the camera. Vinnie couldn't hide his reaction, his eyes widened and he started back slightly. Just the sight of the angular figure made him feel sick.

'Do you recognise that man?' Matthews asked quietly.

Vinnie regarded the photo as his brain decided what to say. Instinct told him that the next few minutes would determine how the police viewed him and treated him.

Finally, he sighed and looked up at the two men across the table. 'Yes, I do.'

'Is this the man you saw kill David Kelt?' Harper asked.

'Yes, it's Marcus. Marcus Lane.'

The DCI looked angrily at his junior officer. 'Who told you his name, Vinnie?'

'No one. I recognised him as soon as he spoke. My dad worked for his granddad.'

'As what?' Matthew's tone was suddenly heavy with suspicion.

'An accountant. I was a kid. Marcus and I played together for around four years. The house was owned by Tobias Lane then. My dad shot himself when I was ten.'

The subject his mother never talked about, the betrayal he'd never understood. Their expressions had changed, hardened. For some reason Matthews was annoyed.

'You realise the significance of this, don't you? This could be our chance to at last put the Lanes away.'

'I remember Marcus's dad – he was a cruel bastard. And you want me to testify against his son?'

Matthews leaned forward and prodded at the photo with his finger. 'Not want, need. We *need* you to look at some mug shots and then pick him out in a line-up to make doubly sure, and then we *need* you to testify at his trial. Without you, we can't place him there. Without you, David Kelt is simply a missing person. *With* you, Marcus Lane is guilty of double murder. He'll get mandatory life. Throw away the key, as they say.'

Vinnie looked away. 'And Norman will hunt me down and have me killed,' he said softly, almost under his breath.

Harper shifted uncomfortably again and opened his mouth.

Matthews raised a hand to silence him and then spoke urgently, aggressively. 'I'm not going to insult your intelligence. You're obviously a bright man and you know these people.

You're a witness. If we can find your DNA, so can they. Lane will have you killed anyway.'

Vinnie threw up his hands. Did they have to be quite *that* honest? 'Oh, so I have bugger-all choice!'

Matthews acknowledged the point with a small nod. 'Admittedly. But listen to the proposition first. If you testify, we give you immunity over the murder you say you committed – and we believe you did. You live in a safe house and we rush the case to trial. Afterwards, we put you and Anna into witness protection, which means you get new identities, new passports, a lump sum and we relocate you. A new life, somewhere safe.'

Vinnie hauled himself to his feet and walked to the window that looked out over the street. He stared down at the pedestrians and the cars. People were coming and going from the front of the station, getting on with their lives, being normal. Suddenly he ached for Anna, to talk to her, hug her, see her reaction, get her opinion. All those years he had longed to start again, clean the slate.

He turned back. 'I don't suppose these windows open. That seems like a better choice.'

Harper looked alarmed, but Matthews smiled slightly.

'We both know you don't mean that, but just in case: no, they don't.'

An expression of silent understanding passed between the two men, respect and resignation.

'You wear a balaclava and a boiler suit and testify from behind a screen. You are referred to by an initial. No one sees you, only Harper.'

'What if Marcus recognises my voice? I knew his.'

'It'll be a closed court, the judge, the jury and the lawyers. He'll never hear you. We can make sure everyone else has to leave, to ensure your safety.'

151

'Remember, Lane already knows someone was in the house. Someone killed his thug,' Harper reminded Vinnie.

Matthews frowned at his DS. 'But *how* does he know? Marcus can't be innocent and have his lawyer accuse you of anything. And he doesn't know you ever left the cellar, not for sure; he doesn't *know* you witnessed the murders. He may think his thug just surprised someone.'

Vinnie ran his hand through his hair and started to pace. 'It's a bloody big ask. I happen to like my life. And what about Anna? She wasn't keen on me even coming to see you. And I didn't tell her it was Marcus. She'll freak! She might refuse to come, and I couldn't lose her, not now.'

Matthews made another slight gesture of acknowledgement. 'I understand all of that. Vinnie, the Lanes don't make mistakes. We may never get a chance like this again. God knows how many lives you'll save.'

Vinnie threw him a wry grin. 'No pressure, then.'

'Some years ago Marcus's sister was killed in a drug raid in Manchester, shot by police –'

'Millie? I remember her – she was very sweet.'

'All the men who took part in that raid are dead, all killed in the line of duty. I know that Marcus Lane is responsible; I just can't prove it. You'll be avenging a great deal more than David Kelt.'

Peter Harper pointed up at him. 'Think about what you both gain. A new life, wherever you want. What would you do? Open a wine store?' he asked, as he smiled hopefully.

'And think what you both lose if you take your chances with Lane. He might decide to punish you by hurting Anna,' Matthews added.

Vinnie came back to the table and sat down heavily. It was starting to make sense. A germ of an idea was forming in the back of his brain, but he wasn't about to let them see that. This was a game of poker, with terrifyingly high stakes and only one chance.

'Can we take our dog? He's just a puppy and he means the world to us. If we had children, you'd let us take them, presumably.'

Once again the two policemen glanced at each other.

It's a routine, a well-practised routine, Vinnie realised. They're the dogs and I'm the sheep, and they're getting me ever closer to the damn holding pen. Like a lamb to the slaughter. Well, two can play at that.

'Possibly,' answered Harper.

'But we sever contact? With friends, famil—'

'When witness protection goes wrong it's because people go back. They call family, revisit their old haunts, despite being told not to,' Matthews said.

Vinnie held out his hands in a gesture that he hoped adequately expressed his exasperation. '*Goes wrong?* What exactly does that mean, Detective Chief Inspector?'

Matthews remained aloof. 'You stay away, you stay out of contact, and you will stay safe. Simple.'

'And how do we explain this sudden and permanent departure to our nearest and dearest?'

For the first time the DCI hesitated.

Aha, a chink.

'Only those very close know the truth. In a case like this, everyone else, they think you're dead. It's the easiest way.'

Vinnie gave a low whistle. Dead? For real?

'Thirty-six hours from the time of arrest, then we have to charge him and we need to hide you.'

'I have one other problem.'

Matthews looked concerned. 'Which is?'

'Not a which, a who. My mother. She's a widow and she lives in Sussex. Because it's the Lanes, she's also at risk. They know her. If anything went wrong and they identified me, their first call would be her cottage.'

'What do you want to do about that?'

Vinnie hesitated. 'I'm all she has. Could I take her, too?'

The two men looked at each other, and then Matthews gave him another small nod. 'Yes. Under the circumstances.'

Time to set up the final demand.

'What do I get compensation for?' he asked.

Matthews used his fingers to count them off.

'Your house – professional valuation, minus mortgage which will be paid off – your wholesale wine business, both market stalls, the website and your client list. Then you get a payment for your inconvenience and sacrifice, plus a payment to resettle. I think I can confidently say that, in this case, it will be a very generous payment.'

Vinnie nodded thoughtfully. 'Do I really have a choice?' he asked.

'Your signed statement will be in Kelt's missing person file. Norman Lane has a bloody long reach, and you have a named bullet.' Matthews said bluntly.

'Can I withdraw my statement?'

'No.'

'Christ, that's a definite, then! And if I testify?'

'The name in the file goes away. Every reference becomes Witness A, and all traces linking the statement and the testimony to you vanish.'

Realistically, this was his safest option.

'That's what I thought. Thank you for being honest.'

Vinnie picked up the empty cup and started to shred it. Time ticked away and no one in the room moved. Let them sweat; let them think he was still making up his mind.

Finally he swept the pieces of polystyrene onto the floor. 'Okay, here's the deal, gentlemen,' he said quietly. 'Anna and

Mum have to agree, too. If either one says no, then we'll take our chances with the Lanes. I'll identify him and I'll testify. But I want new identities and I want real money to relocate outside the UK.'

He paused, but Matthews still didn't react.

'I have some resources of my own and I want to buy a winery. In New Zealand. I don't want to sell wine anymore, I want to make it.'

Harper looked at his senior officer, and Vinnie could see alarm and fascination in equal measure on the young man's face. Matthews still scrutinised Vinnie.

Come on, you old bugger, you know you really want this guy and I'm your only chance. Give in a little. Vinnie tried not to look as though he was holding his breath.

Slowly Matthews leaned forward and extended his hand across the table.

'Deal.'

CHAPTER EIGHTEEN

NICKED

When his henchman didn't answer his cell phone, and hadn't returned home to his wife by 4 am, Marcus ordered a search of the scene. He should have had confirmation that the clean-up was complete, and the fact that he hadn't bothered him. It was time to reinforce the rules, because people were getting sloppy. If the truth be known, he regretted killing Lenny – the man had been a loyal assassin for years – but the lesson had to be driven into Harry's head: obey the rules or pay the price. If he had gone on a bender, Marcus would have to make an example of him, too.

Kelt's house was empty and spotless, and the team was reporting in before leaving when Marcus asked whether they had checked the wine cellar.

'Call yourself a clean-up crew? Check the damn cellar and call me back. When I get my hands on him, I'll wring his bloody Yankee neck.'

'Yes, boss.'

Five minutes later his phone rang again.

'He's dead, in the cellar.'

'How?'

'Stabbed in the stomach with something – no weapon here.'

Marcus scowled, but kept his temper on the phone. 'Let me know when it's clean. I want to see his body before you dump him.'

* * *

Marcus examined the wound closely. It was round and large, there were shards of glass in it and the edges were ragged. He sniffed his fingers and gave a tight smile.

'Wine. He was stabbed with a smashed bottle of wine. Clever and opportunistic – Harry surprised someone in the wine cellar.'

Norman was watching from across the room. 'Why did he go down there?' he asked.

Marcus shrugged. 'Presumably, to check out the collection. He was a drinker. A greedy bastard.'

Norman pointed at the body. 'What was anyone doing in the cellar? Kelt must have known someone was there.'

Marcus snapped around as a thought occurred to him, a thought he didn't want to entertain. 'If you were in the cellar, racking wine, whatever, and someone comes in – someone you've never seen before – would you smash a wine bottle and kill him?'

'Maybe Harry attacked him and he killed in self-defence?'

Marcus shook his head. 'No sign of a struggle, no bottles broken, no skin under Harry's nails. He was surprised. That tells me that whoever killed him was waiting – and knew what had happened upstairs.'

Norman rose to his feet. 'What exactly could he have seen?' he asked, his voice ominously quiet.

Marcus shrugged again – he needed to be vigilant with his father. 'Lenny's gun jammed. I shot Kelt and then I shot Lenny.

But there was no one else there. It was a closed room, a dining room. How could there be a witness?'

'Maybe he heard and didn't see. Any names?'

'Of course not, they always refer to me as Boss. The bodies were in the van, the house was clean, Dad. There's nothing to link it to us, nothing for them to find.'

'And Kelt's notebook?'

'It's in his office desk, at the club. The boys will turn the place over tomorrow. They'll find it and then I'll burn it. Problem solved.'

Norman turned his back on the scene and stared into the fireplace. A full moment passed. Marcus went to the body and touched the wound again. It was a deep, upward thrust, from under the ribcage right into the heart. Then a strong hand had pulled the bottle out.

'Use the Carter passport. South America would be best. Go to Colombia and check out the drug supply lines and reinforce our –'

Marcus started to cross the room. 'No, Dad please –'

'Don't contradict me!' Norman roared.

This was banishment, loss of status, punishment. 'But –'

'You're a hot-head. Time and again you put this operation at risk. I've tried to drum it into you: don't pull the trigger, and then you can't be held responsible for the consequences. Tom can take over in the interim. You weren't in the country and nobody will find you. I want you on a plane tomorrow at the latest. And get rid of that body!'

* * *

Marcus was so furious he hardly knew what he had thrown into a suitcase. Sleep had evaded him, and he had sat up all night writing directions to Tom and the others, who would be clawing at each other to take his place, even temporarily. Why had he gone into the Kelt house? Why hadn't he told them to bring the man in? There was this damn need to show off, to big-note, and this time it had been a stupid mistake. He had given that snivelling little manipulator a foot in the door, a hand on his power base. Well, he'd show Tom, he'd show his father, and all the rest − he'd make the most of this trip and set up some supply lines of his own. Time to start branching out.

A little after nine in the morning he sent the suitcase to the front door, donned his coat and gloves, and made his way downstairs. He lived by himself, with a handful of loyal and well-trained servants, not far from his parent's home. He stood in the entrance hall and ran a meticulous eye over the rooms he could see.

His housekeeper came to the door. 'Goodbye, Mr Lane. Have a good trip.'

He smiled stiffly. 'I will. I'll let you know when I have a return date.'

He nodded to her and walked out the door and down the steps to the waiting car. His chauffeur opened the rear door and he got in. *The Independent* lay folded on the seat, waiting to be read on the airport run. As they reached the main gate and swung out, a plain black car pulled across the road and stopped a few metres ahead of them.

Marcus leaned forward. 'What the hell?' he muttered.

Another black vehicle pulled in behind his car. Sudden fears swirled through Marcus's startled brain: dangerous possibilities, such as kidnap, rival gangs, revenge and contract killings − suppressed nightmares from his younger days.

The passenger door of the front car opened and a familiar figure climbed out. He lumbered over as Marcus pressed a button and the window slid down. Thank God, no one important.

'Morning, Mr Lane.' DCI Matthews grinned down at him. The man was as dishevelled as ever, but ominously cheerful.

'Detective Chief Inspector, what brings you here at this hour?'

'On your way to the office, sir?'

Marcus gave a small nod. 'Naturally.'

'Would you step out of the car, please, sir?'

'Why? I'm a bit pressed for time. Could you make an appointment to see –'

'Step out of the car … sir.' The voice was firmer this time.

Marcus felt an unease stirring in the pit of his stomach. There was another man, younger, also in a suit, standing between Matthews and the car, and Marcus didn't like the smile on his face either.

Slowly and deliberately, Marcus opened the car door and got out. He was at least six inches taller than Matthews.

The DCI looked up at him and sighed. 'I've waited a long time for this day, Mr Lane. I am arresting you for the murders of David Kelt and Lenny Kendell.'

He turned towards the other cop, who was walking towards them. 'Cuff him, Harper, and read him his rights.'

CHAPTER NINETEEN

GOODBYES

As Mary Whitney-Ross lifted two bags of groceries from the open boot of her car, Vinnie's Mercedes swung around the corner of the lane. She watched the car pull up and Vinnie and Anna sit for a moment before alighting, followed by Merlot.

'Vin, Anna, darlings! What a lovely surprise. Hello there, Merlot.'

Vinnie was carrying a plastic carrier bag. 'Hello, Mum. We've brought treats: wine and chocolates for our favourite lady.'

Mary put the groceries back into the boot, and they all hugged and kissed. She loved Vinnie's bear hugs. Today it felt as though he wanted to hug the daylights out of her.

'Hello, Mother,' said Anna quietly.

Mary patted Merlot as he circled around her and eyed Vinnie with a concerned frown. 'You look tired, both of you.'

Vinnie ran a hand through his curls. 'A bit. Not sleeping. Here, let me take these. I could murder a cuppa.'

Anna threw him a sharp glance, and he grimaced at her.

For the first time ever Mary could sense tension. She hesitated, then took the bag and peered inside as he picked up the groceries.

'Oh, doesn't that look terribly wicked! You do spoil me. Will you stay for lunch?'

Vinnie took a huge breath and smiled. 'Absolutely. We've got all day, and a big favour to ask.'

'How intriguing,' she said, as she held open the garden gate.

* * *

'So you identify him and testify at his trial, and then you both leave.'

Mary sat on the sofa beside Vinnie and he held her hand.

'Yes, that's the deal.'

'Why?'

'Because it's the right thing to do, and because, if I don't, there's a good chance they'll find me anyway.'

'How?'

'They're powerful and they just can.'

Mary looked at him closely. He returned her gaze without flinching, but he knew she could see the truth in his eyes.

'It's them, isn't it?' she asked softly.

For a long moment he didn't answer.

'Who?' Anna demanded sharply.

Still neither of them spoke.

'Excuse me, I *am* here and I *do* matter. *Who is them?*'

Vinnie shook his head, then turned and looked at his wife. When he saw her expression, he felt as though his heart would break in two.

'Of course you matter. Remember I told you how my dad was an accountant and got caught up with a dodgy client? Well, that man was Tobias Lane, a major crime boss and the head of a London gang. When Dad went to see Tobias, I went too, and I played with his grandson, Marcus. Then when I was ten, Dad … died … and the visits stopped.'

Anna was sitting on the edge of the chair, focusing very hard on what he was saying. He knew she would be hurt that he hadn't told her this at the beginning, and if his mother hadn't been in danger he probably would never have told her, but now he had no choice. Did he have any choice about anything anymore?

'For reasons best left unsaid, the Lanes paid for Vinnie's education,' Mary added.

Anna shook her head, her bewilderment obvious. 'What's that got to do with …' Her voice trailed off and she put her hand over her mouth. She had made the connection.

Vinnie nodded. 'The man I saw murder David? It was Marcus. I recognised him as soon as he –'

'Vinnie!' Her reaction was a mixture of shock, anger and fear.

He went over to her, pulled her to her feet and wrapped his arms around her. 'I know and I'm so sorry. I should have told you straightaway. I didn't know what to think or say.'

She was on the verge of tears, but something held her back.

He hugged her tight and stroked her hair. 'It'll be okay, my love, we'll start a new –'

Anna pulled back, her expression reflecting a sudden alarming thought. 'What about Mother?' Her voice was tight with stress.

'Yep.'

Vinnie gave a small nod and led Anna over to the sofa. Mary sat watching them, tears in her eyes.

'Mum,' he said, as he sat down beside her, 'I'm afraid you're not safe here. If they make the connection at any time, for any reason, you're the first place they'll come.'

Mary shivered.

'I only met Norman Lane at the time of your father's death, but if he's anything like Tobias, he's a nasty piece of work.'

'Anna thought we were coming here to leave Merlot with you until the DS can send him to us, but actually I have a far bigger plan. I need you both to listen very carefully.'

* * *

It was raining as they drove back to London. Anna sat very still, her face turned towards the passenger window. Vinnie stared straight ahead. The rhythmical swish of the wipers on the windscreen was almost like a lullaby. He was stressed and needed sleep badly, a dangerous combination.

'Would you like me to drive?' she asked suddenly.

He glanced at her. She was looking at him, and he could see the exhaustion in her face.

He smiled gently. 'I'm okay. How about you?'

She returned the smile. 'Hardest part over with. Do you really think she's going to agree to it?'

He shrugged. 'Don't know. It's a big risk for an elderly lady.'

'Not as big as losing her only child.'

He didn't answer. There was nothing to say.

Anna reached across and touched his leg. 'She'll be okay, whatever she decides to do. She's a strong woman.'

* * *

Mary's lounge was cluttered with ornaments and knick-knacks. She liked it that way; it made her feel as though her life was here in the room with her. On this rainy evening she sat in an armchair with a glass of red wine on the table beside her. Merlot lay in front of the roaring fire, happily chewing on his slipper toy.

The television was on, but she wasn't watching. Instead, she was looking at a group of four wedding photos on the wall, Vinnie and Anna on their special day. Tears rolled, unheeded, down her cheeks.

* * *

Anna was packing. She pulled clothes out of the wardrobe and threw them onto the bed, where two empty suitcases lay open.

Vinnie came as far as the door, leaned against the jamb and watched her. She didn't look at him.

'You're better at packing than me. Do you want to help?' she asked.

'Leave it – come and have a drink.'

She turned around, and her face was tear-stained. 'And how will that help? Will a drink make it any easier to fit our lives into two suitcases?'

He could hear the pain in her voice, and it tore at him and made it hard to breathe.

'We'll start new lives, buy new things –'

'I don't want new things! I want what I bought with my dad's money, things my mum gave me, our wedding presents.'

He went to her, took the clothes hanger from her hand and tried to put his arms around her. She burst into tears and beat against his chest with her fists in a vague attempt to push him away. He enveloped her and soothed her until she stopped fighting.

'I love you,' he said softly.

She hugged him back, and he buried his face in her hair.

'I am so, so sorry, Anna. This is my fault. It's impossibly hard and you shouldn't have to –'

She pulled back and put her finger on his lips. There were tears on her cheeks, and he brushed them away.

'I remember that when we met, in Italy, you were the first person I had ever wanted to belong to. When I got home I couldn't breathe, I couldn't sleep, I couldn't eat I was so excited. Then you found me again and I was so in love with you that it scared me.'

She was trembling. He wanted to hug her and never let go.

'And now?' he asked.

'Nothing's changed. I feel the same. You're doing the right thing and I love you for that. I'm proud of you. I'm okay, you're okay. We have each other and that's all we need. It's a great big adventure.'

He kissed her.

'I don't deserve you,' he said.

She kissed him back.

'No, you don't, but you're stuck with me.'

* * *

Once again the Lanes were forcing her to move. Mary's anger burned like a hot coal, and she couldn't wait to see Norman Lane suffer the loss of his only son to a jail cell. She took days to pack her two suitcases, changing her mind several times and swapping clothes for figurines, photos, mementoes and jewellery. Then she locked the door behind her, took Merlot and boarded a train for Cardiff. A young female constable picked her up at the station and drove her to a farmhouse in the Welsh countryside.

CHAPTER TWENTY

TRIAL BY JURY

Vinnie and DS Harper stood in front of a one-way window, looking through to another room. On the other side, six men, all dressed in coats, gloves and shoes, formed a line. All were tall, thin, dark-haired and looked reasonably alike. Number three was Marcus Lane. He looked fatigued and angry, and the sight of him made Vinnie step back slightly. Harper smiled reassuringly.

The young detective had an easy manner, especially when his boss wasn't around, and Vinnie had decided he liked the man.

'Take your time, Vinnie. Be sure.'

Vinnie studied them one at a time. When he got to number three, he looked Marcus up and down and moved on. Not a flicker crossed his face. What would Marcus say if he knew who it was on the other side of the window? Would he feel betrayed? Vinnie was struck by a sudden memory of two little boys racing ducklings off a bridge, but put it firmly to one side. This was the moment; after this, there was no turning back.

How long should he take? Is it better to be emphatic and quick, or measured and thorough?

Then he turned to Harper. 'He's number three.'

'Sure?'

'Absolutely. I'll never forget his face.'

Harper went to the intercom, and instructed the guard that the line-up was over. As the men in the line-up started to leave the room, Marcus raised his arm slowly and pointed his forefinger at the glass, his thumb in the air and the rest of the fingers curled back, to imitate a gun. He pointed it directly at Vinnie and jerked his arm up as if he was firing repeatedly. His eyes were cold and full of hatred.

Vinnie gave an involuntary shudder.

Harper put a hand on his shoulder and indicated the door. 'He can't see anything, and he's no idea it's you. He's just being a manipulative sodding bastard. That's his Achilles heel, his need to boast and be the big man, in charge. And that's why he's here.'

* * *

The throng of media milling around the wide concrete steps were there to see one man. Journalists, TV reporters, cameramen and photographers pushed and shoved for the best vantage points. Excited and eager chatter drifted on the chill spring air. Today was day one of the trial of Marcus Lane for double murder, and his conviction rested on the testimony of secret Witness A. Norman Lane was a powerful man on both sides of the law, and was known personally to many in the media. After all the legal manoeuvring, no one had expected the case to actually come to court. Now that it had, Lane would be apoplectic with rage.

Norman Lane strode down the steps, Tom beside him and flanked by four men wearing suits and carrying briefcases. His grey hair was slicked back, and his very tall, muscular frame made him look remarkably like his late father, Tobias. As always, he was dressed in a designer suit with expensive accessories. His movements were deliberate but not small; he liked to be expansive and charismatic.

The party stopped halfway down the steps, and the media rushed up to gather around him. He smiled grimly at a couple of them, then held his hand up to silence the babble. His voice sounded like the rumble of a truck over gravel.

'On the morning of my son's trial I have just one thing to say: Marcus was not in that house and I did not know David Kelt. This is not simply a case of mistaken identity; it's a serious miscarriage of justice. Whoever the star witness is, he's either blind or he's a liar in the pay of the police. My son is innocent and we will prove it. I believe in the British justice system.'

Lane turned away from the mass of thrashing arms and the buzz of questions.

One journalist on the edge of the group thrust her microphone into his face. 'Do you have a message for Witness A, Mr Lane?'

He paused, then turned towards the microphone. His eyes bored into her and she shrank back.

'Whoever you are, you are a liar and I hope you have made peace with your god.'

Lane took the rest of the stairs two at a time, and the other men held back the media pack trying to follow him.

* * *

Several men sat watching the Lane interview on a widescreen TV at one end of the open-plan CID office. A couple of them swore gently. Peter Harper sipped his coffee and shook his head. It was all bluff, intimidation, like a bull elephant stamping its foot and bellowing at a poacher's rifle. If Lane wasn't worried sick, he wouldn't have fronted the media. He had to do everything he could to discredit the concept of Witness A, because he didn't know the man's identity.

DCI Matthews burst through the double doors and pointed his finger at Harper, who almost overturned his coffee in his hurry to get to his feet.

'Make sure Anna hasn't seen that bastard! Tell the PC to keep the fucking radio and TV turned off!'

He stormed out and Harper grabbed the mobile lying on his desk.

* * *

Miles across the city, in a nondescript room in a nondescript apartment block down by the docks, Anna sat slumped in an armchair. She had lost weight, and her clothes swamped her. The curtains were drawn to the outside world and the room was chilly and damp. A print of a bullfight hung crookedly on a wall, but there were no personal possessions or photographs in the room. Anna was picking at the frayed corner of a cushion as she watched the TV screen in the corner of the room.

The woman who had asked Lane the question was speaking to camera. 'So, as you heard, Norman Lane has made it perfectly clear: he labelled Witness A a liar and called the trial a serious miscarriage of justice.'

A young uniformed policewoman, cell phone to her ear, walked rapidly through the doorway from the kitchen and stopped short when she saw the horrified expression on Anna's face.

'Too late, boss.'

Anna looked up at her, making no attempt to hide her distress. 'Did you *see* that man?'

The policewoman lowered the cell phone and smiled. 'Don't you worry about a thing, Mrs Whitney-Ross. Norman Lane is all bluster. DS Harper will keep your husband safe.'

* * *

In the lounge of her Welsh safe house, Mary also watched a widescreen TV, the cup of tea beside her forgotten. Merlot lay at her feet. Her tears spent, her expression had hardened into fury and hatred. At the sight of Norman Lane a hundred memories of his father flooded her consciousness.

'You murderous bastard! See how you like losing someone you love,' she muttered.

* * *

The courtroom at the Old Bailey was in session. The judge sat on the bench, the jury to one side of him, Marcus in the dock, the Queen's Counsel at his lectern and the defence team in their seats, and the police, the media, the public, Tom and Norman in the gallery. The room reeked of tradition and centuries of justice. The QC gestured towards the jury, his black silk gown swirling around him.

'Ladies and gentlemen of the jury, do we have two bodies? No. Do we have the murder weapon? No. So how do we know the murders occurred? Because someone saw them. We have an eyewitness who will testify that he saw Marcus Lane, the accused, murder two men in cold blood. First, well-respected businessman, David Kelt, and then fellow gangster, Lenny Kendell. We know why he shot Kelt – he believed the man had hidden something from him. But why Kendell? Because when Kendell attempted to shoot Kelt, under direct instruction from Lane, the gun jammed. That still makes no sense. Why murder his best enforcer? Marcus Lane killed Lenny Kendell because Marcus Lane is a psychopath. Murder is his answer to weakness.'

* * *

In the bowels of the building Vinnie sat on a bench. He wore a boiler suit and held a balaclava in his hand. The minutes ticked by excruciatingly slowly. He felt as though everything was happening in slow motion and he was wading through a puddle of waist-deep treacle. He had rehearsed the testimony with Harper, and now he repeated it over and over in his frazzled brain. All he had to do was explain that he was there, what he heard, what he saw, what he did, where he went. No embroidering the truth, just relate the events of the evening chronologically. He wouldn't mention the murder in the cellar, and the defence couldn't raise it without admitting that they knew more about the evening than they had indicated. He could hear Harper telling him: *If they accuse you of murder, they have to admit who the victim was – one of theirs. You're perfectly safe on that score.* With sightless eyes, Vinnie stared at the bare concrete wall and wished himself anywhere else in the world.

* * *

Upstairs, the QC was in full flight and the jury sat transfixed.

'Our witness is a respectable member of the general public who was in that house under a lawful pretext. To protect his safety he'll testify in closed court, from behind a screen and be referred to only as Witness A.'

The QC swung around slowly and pointed to Marcus, who sneered back at him from the dock. The jury followed the finger in unison and stared at the defendant.

'We take these precautions, ladies and gentlemen, because this man, Marcus Lane, is such a dangerous psychopath. But I assure you all, Witness A is no criminal. He's an honest man, doing the right thing, at huge personal cost.'

* * *

Back in the basement, the heavy door swung open and Vinnie turned to face DS Harper, who grinned happily as he held the door.

'They've cleared the court. Ready to rock'n'roll?'

Vinnie pulled the black balaclava over his face.

'No, not really. Actually I've booked a colonic irrigation, followed by a root canal ...'

His voice trailed off as Harper chuckled, checked his watch and waved him through the door.

'Maybe later. Just remember, only the judge, the jury and the lawyers are there – neither Marcus nor Norman Lane will hear you. His lawyers can't ask you what you do, why you were there or how you knew Kelt – anything that could identify you. If anything makes you feel uncomfortable, stay silent and the QC will object.'

Vinnie stood up straight and squared his shoulders.

'Take some deep breaths,' Harper suggested.

Vinnie shot him an exasperated glance. 'If I had a bucket list to complete before I died, this would not be on it.'

* * *

The QC waited at his podium. To the judge's left stood a tall, plain-coloured, multi-panelled screen, which was folded completely around the witness box. Every pair of eyes in the room was watching that screen. On the other side, Vinnie took his place. His foot tapped the floor in a nervous rhythm, and he licked his dry lips. *Just the truth, just what you saw and heard, nothing more.* It was a mantra that whirled inside his mind.

'Are you ready, sir?' asked the QC, his tone noticeably gentler.

'Yes.'

It was more of a dry croak than a word. Vinnie picked up the glass of water in front of him and took a gulp. It was cold and soothing.

'Then, in your own time, and without divulging any details that could lead to your identification, I would ask you to describe the events you witnessed in the house of David Kelt on the night in question.'

For a long moment, Vinnie sat in silence, his eyes closed.

'I'd gone down to the cellar, when I heard a noise from upstairs …'

* * *

The defence tried to rebut the testimony, called him a liar and accused him of being a police plant. He was expecting all of that and just stuck to his story, kept telling them that he was there and that was what he saw. The one question it never occurred to them to ask was whether he had ever seen the accused before. The defence called a psychiatrist who testified about why people sometimes come forward and claim knowledge of a crime when they were nowhere near the scene.

Suddenly and dramatically they provided a witness, a woman who testified that Marcus was with her on the night of the murders. But she was increasingly nervous under cross-examination, and the Crown's accusation of perjury obviously terrified her. They were grasping at straws and everyone knew it. The summing up came down to who the jury was prepared to believe.

The decision was quick, and the seven men and five women looked resolute when they filed back in. Marcus Lane stood in the dock, his head bowed and his anger well hidden.

'Have you come to a decision upon which you are all agreed?'

The foreman looked at the judge and then back at the clerk of the court. 'We have.'

'On the charge of first-degree murder number one, how do you find the defendant? Guilty or not guilty?'

There was a long pause.

'Guilty.'

An audible murmur from the gallery was hushed by a scowl from the judge.

'And on the charge of first-degree murder number two, how do you find the defendant? Guilty or not guilty?'

No pause this time.

'Guilty.'

* * *

Vinnie and Anna sat on the sofa, resting against each other. They both felt as exhausted and overwhelmed as they looked. Anna's hand rubbed Vinnie's arm rhythmically. Two suitcases waited by the open door to the bedroom.

Vinnie watched Harper. He stood at the lounge window, looking down on the people crossing the square to the doorway of the apartment building. He reminded Vinnie of some sort of zookeeper, waiting to send his charges off on an adventure. The conviction was a real feather in his cap, might even mean a promotion, and he couldn't hide his happiness.

Harper glanced at his watch, turned back to the room and smiled warmly at them. 'Right, let's get on with it.'

He opened the leather folder in his hand and took out a long brown envelope, which he handed to Vinnie. 'Itinerary, tickets, passports, birth certificates, UK driver's licences, EFTPOS and credit cards. All in your new names –'

Anna pulled a face. 'The new us.'

It wasn't phrased as a question. Harper seemed a bit thrown and then he smiled at her. 'Indeed. You're flying Emirates and you'll transit through Dubai. In Auckland we have organised a car to take you to a motel, discreet and anonymous, prepaid for a fortnight. There'll be a man to meet you at the airport, holding a sign. Just don't look for Whitney-Ross or you'll never find him. He'll only know you as ... Dominic and Ava Darcy.'

Vinnie and Anna exchanged glances, and he dug her in the ribs.

'You're married to Mr Darcy. You got lucky.'

'Really?' She stared pointedly at Vinnie. 'How exactly?'

Okay, that wasn't what he expected. He turned back to the detective. 'What about the bank account?' he asked.

Harper nodded. 'Everything's been deposited. Your resettlement, compensation for the house, the cottage and businesses, the money you gave me. It's a tidy sum, especially in New Zealand dollars. Twice as much –'

'And Mum and Merlot?' Anna asked anxiously.

'When you're ready, I'll take care of everything.'

Vinnie turned the envelope over in his hands. So far, so good. 'Thank you for doing that, Peter. It means a lot.'

Harper shrugged. 'Lane is away for life, and you did that.'

Vinnie could tell by the way Anna held herself so tightly that she didn't want to hear any more about Marcus Lane. And who could blame her? He didn't respond.

Harper was watching him cautiously. 'You were a very credible witness, Vinnie. They all believed you. The records have been expunged and sealed, so no one can trace you. From today you are Dominic and Ava Darcy. And soon you'll be able to add "vintners".'

Vinnie gave a small smile of satisfaction as he opened the envelope.

PART FOUR

WINE

CHAPTER TWENTY-ONE

MR AND MRS DARCY

The Mountain Lane Motel was typical of its kind: two-storeyed, U-shaped around a courtyard, with a small swimming pool, trampoline and barbecue area on the back lawn. Cars were parked in front of most of the downstairs units.

Inside unit three, Vinnie and Anna sat on the lounge floor with a map of New Zealand spread out between them. Magazines and brochures lay on the coffee table, and plastic bags of groceries had been dumped on the small kitchenette table in one corner.

Vinnie circled areas on the map with a black felt-tip pen. 'Time to make some final decisions, my lovely. Where are we going to look first?'

Anna frowned and pointed at the map. 'As I've said before, if they all make good wine, shouldn't we look at other things too? Like climate.'

He smiled at her. He needed to bring her with him, gently. 'All this and you want to be warm as well?'

'Lack of snow in winter would be very nice, close to the sea, good cafés and some nightlife.'

He ran his hand down the map from Auckland to Otago. 'Waiheke Island, Hawke's Bay, Martinborough, Marlborough, Central Otago. Pinot is definitely Otago, but they're hard grapes to grow and a complex wine to make, too complex for me at this stage. The Bordeaux blends that really float my boat, that's Waiheke Island or Hawke's Bay.'

'And what we can afford.'

Anna slumped back on her heels and looked out the ranch-slider door, which was covered by a frayed, thin curtain.

He watched her for a moment, then moved across to her. 'You've seen how many are listed on the internet and the prices they're selling for. We can afford a very good life.'

She smiled at him tenderly. 'I know.'

He stroked her cheek. The exhaustion and sadness in her eyes made him flinch inside. She was trying hard to be strong and positive, but for the moment her sparkle had gone.

'And I know you miss home – so do I. The sooner we find our new one, the sooner we can have Merlot back. Then it will feel more like we belong here.'

He took her hand and laid it across his chest, over his heart. 'With your hand upon my heart,' he said solemnly.

Anna smiled again, and the flash of appreciation of the familiar, of their connection, reassured him.

She took his hand and laid it across her chest, over her heart. It was their shorthand: whatever, wherever, whenever, they loved each other.

'You make me stronger than I thought I could be,' she replied.

He kissed her gently on the lips. She started to giggle.

'What do you find so amusing about my attempts to be romantic?' he demanded.

She grabbed him and started to laugh more loudly. 'No, sorry, love. It's not you, it's just I had a black thought. Oh Lord!

I wonder how our funeral went, and the will-reading. I wonder who came. What I wouldn't have given to be a fly on the wall.'

He straightened his back and drew himself up on his knees, his hands folded in prayer at his chest. 'Dearly beloved, we are gathered here today to witness –'

Anna punched him on the arm and giggled. 'Idiot! That's the wedding service.'

'Suitably morbid, I thought.'

* * *

The little stone church in Sussex was packed for the joint funerals of Vincent and Anna Whitney-Ross and Vinnie's mother, Mary, tragically killed together in a car accident. They had gone on a holiday, and Vinnie's Mercedes had rolled and caught on fire on a road made treacherous by a heavy rainstorm. The charred corpses were identified by dental records.

The three polished mahogany coffins, covered with long bouquets of bright flowers, lay on trollies at the foot of the altar. Many in the crowd were obviously upset. Anna's three brothers sat in the front pew with their wives, and her three half-sisters huddled together in the pew behind.

Half an hour later the crowd gathered in the church cemetery. The coffins were laid onto green straps above three open graves.

An elderly vicar, with a leather-bound Bible in his hands, surveyed the crowd. 'And so, dear friends and family, we gather here to say our last farewells to Mary, to Vincent and to Anna, taken so suddenly and tragically from us. And yet, their death is an illusion, for we know they live on.'

He paused for effect, and then continued. 'When I say that, what I mean is: when we keep our loved ones in our memories, in our hearts, they never really die. For we know that they are in the presence of God and we have not lost them. We should be comforted by the thought that they are, indeed, in a better place.'

Anna's brothers were approached at the simple wake by a lawyer, who told them he had acted for Mary Witney-Ross for years and asked them to attend the reading of the wills.

* * *

'What happens in this situation, when they all die together?'

The speaker was Anna's brother, Philip.

The lawyer looked from one to the other. He had seen the barely concealed avarice in their expressions so many times before.

'I could read each will separately, but the situation here is very clear. Vinnie and Anna had the same provision: everything was left to the other should they pre-decease each other, and then it was all left to Mary. So, legally, Mary's will is the only one that counts.'

'She left everything to her mother-in-law?' Philip's tone was incredulous.

'Yes, I understand they were very close. Unfortunately, Mary also died at the same time. She left everything to them, and then to a local animal charity, a dog's home. So that's where it will all go. But Anna did make one provision for the three of you.'

The men were all staring at each other. The lawyer knew that expression too: it was the dawning realisation of the meaning of 'cut out'. He rose and took the three small boxes that sat on the table. One by one he put them in front of the men.

'She wanted you to have these.'

Philip picked up his box. 'A golf ball?'

'Yes, I believe she said it was to go with your father's golf clubs? She said you'd understand.'

The Waiheke Island ferry sliced through the sparkling water of the Waitemata Harbour. Vinnie had read out the brochure description: 'It's a forty-five minute commute between downtown Auckland and Waiheke, and the population is increasingly working in the city and living the relaxed island life. It's home to boutique wineries, orchards, olive oil makers, painters and craftspeople, and each summer sees an influx of tourists to the wonderful surf beaches.' Anna had agreed it was definitely worth a trip to look at the three vineyards for sale on the island.

Passengers sat inside, drinking coffee, reading papers or working on their laptops. Those outside lounged on the chairs fixed to the decks and basked in the sunshine. Vinnie and Anna leaned against the rail and watched the boats and the seabirds. His arm was around her shoulders, and she leaned her head on him. After all the stress and horror, the secrecy and the very real fear, he could, at last, feel his body starting to relax.

New Zealand was a genuinely beautiful place – the people were welcoming and helpful and gave the impression that they enjoyed their surroundings. With every passing day in their new country it seemed more likely that they could be happy here.

A dolphin surfaced close to the boat and rode the bow wake. Anna saw it first and pointed excitedly.

'Look, darling – a dolphin!'

Vinnie took his camera from the pocket of his cargo pants and snapped a photo of it. 'Stand against the rail and I'll record your first venture onto Auckland harbour,' he instructed.

Anna leaned back and he moved the camera around until he got her, the dolphin and a passing yacht in the shot. She laughed with pleasure.

The first winery was in the middle of the island, with no real sense of proximity to the water. The vines were well established and the machinery was adequate. They both liked the house, with its Mediterranean feel, terracotta-tiled roof and fountain in Italian-style gardens.

Vinnie led Anna by the hand to a swinging seat, and they turned towards each other. 'It's very nice,' he said, watching for her reaction.

She nodded. 'Yes, it is. It's lovely.'

'But?'

She hesitated and then frowned. 'There is a "but". I don't know what it is, Vin, but both of us can feel it.'

He nodded slowly. 'Not the right place for us, then.'

He pulled a piece of crinkled paper from his pocket. 'So, on to the next one. On the coast, called Rocky Bay. Is that an omen?'

***

Rocky Bay Winery sat in a natural basin. On all sides the vines ran down gently sloping hills to the flat valley floor. Some of the vines were bare, and some still had red and golden leaves attached. Three buildings clustered around a concrete courtyard, and up on the rim sat a magnificent house, with views out to sea from the front and down to the vineyard from the back.

Anna and Vinnie walked hand in hand down a sloping row, touching the vines on both sides and smiling at each other with growing excitement. They stopped, and he squatted to examine the plants and scoop up a handful of soil, then let it run between his fingers. He looked up at her and nodded. Her eyes shone back at him.

At the foot of the row they wandered down to the courtyard. On one side was a storage shed, and on the other the top third of a building, with five square holes spaced evenly along it.

Vinnie pointed back to the vines. 'It's simple but effective. After harvest the grapes are brought into the courtyard and sorted on a conveyer belt. Then they go through one of those holes and into the vat in the room below. Come and see.'

He led her down concrete steps to the lower level, past the fermentation hall with its huge shiny silver vats and into the barrel hall. Round oak barrels lay stacked on their sides along both walls and down the middle, the whole length of the long hall.

A woman in her mid-twenties stood waiting for them. Gabby McLean was the epitome of a winemaker, her frizzy brown hair tied in a messy ponytail, her short fingernails stained dark red, and her clothing practical, from the gumboots to the sweatband.

When she saw them she broke into a wide smile. Nonetheless, Vinnie could see the anxiety, although she hid it well. It was a good operation, created with meticulous attention to detail, but the current owners had done all they could afford to do and it needed new capital. They had moved on and were keen for a quick sale and settlement. It was clear that Gabby's passion and skill had maintained the extraordinary standard, and other owners had started calling her, but apparently she desperately wanted to stay.

'So what do you think? Of the vines?' she asked.

Vinnie shook his head gently to show his respect. 'Amazing, beautiful, so well looked after.'

'Thank you! Now, the best bit: come and taste the result.' Gabby beckoned to them to follow her into the hall and led them to one of the nearest barrels.

'Almost ready to bottle,' she explained as she dipped the slender glass wine thief into the barrel, drew out some deep red liquid and let it drain into a small wine glass. She held it up and swirled it around.

'Mixed and left to settle again. A left-bank kind of Bordeaux, with a deep-press fraction of Cab Sav, Merlot, Cab Franc and Malbec.'

She handed the glass to Vinnie. He breathed in the heady aroma a couple of times and then took a sip before handing the glass to Anna so she could do the same. Closing his eyes, he imagined drinking it on the far side of the world, removed from the source. The initial tastes were what he was expecting – cocoa, blackberry, French vanilla, cedar, cloves – but then other flavours surprised him – roasted red pepper all the way to new oak and a strong finish of white pepper. It was as complex as any comparable French wine he had ever tasted, and still had a long, long way to go before it reached maturity.

His heart soared. 'It's beautiful, Gabby. A very, very fine wine.'

* * *

The semi-circular tasting room was at the front of the house. Its huge picture windows looked out over tall cliffs to a bright green sea that boiled as it pounded the rocks. There were tables and chairs in groups over by the windows and stools pulled up to the curved bar. Bottles of wine lined the shelves behind the bar and filled display stands. Vinnie and Anna sat at one of the tables and looked at the view as they sipped the wine.

'This house is gorgeous, so spacious. Imagine waking up to that view,' Anna said quietly.

Vinnie nodded. He could see excitement bubbling beneath her restraint, dreading to dream in case it was all in vain. The emptiness and pain of the past few weeks had melted away, though, and the sparkle was back in those green eyes.

'The winery needs some investment, new machinery … but the vines are in excellent condition, and the winemaker definitely knows what she's about.'

'We could grow vegetables and fruit trees!'

He laughed. 'Goodness me, do I see a domestic goddess in the making? Does chocolate go with vegetables?'

'Chocolate! Gabby said there's a wonderful Saturday market. I'll start with stuff I can make in the kitchen.'

'Oh, good Lord in heaven, do we have enough cash to pay danger money to the whole island?'

She glared at him in mock anger. 'I could never divorce you, Mr Darcy, but I'm seriously considering murder.'

His eyebrows shot up. The repartee was as solid as ever. It showed him that she knew him, she understood the need for verbal parry and thrust, for the humour to help him cope with the horror they'd left behind.

'Really? Do you want lessons? Sorry, too soon?'

She stifled a laugh and took a quick sip of the wine. He held his glass over towards hers. It was time to make a stand and start a new life – this place suddenly felt like the right environment in which to do that.

'We need to stay on the island for a few days, have a look around and do a serious trawl through the books, but in principle, is it a yes, Mrs Darcy?'

She touched her glass against his. 'Very much a yes, Mr Darcy.'

* * *

The next day started at the Saturday-morning Ostend market. It was a busy place; the concrete paths that snaked between lush patches of grass were crowded with families eating, drinking

189

and buying. The wooden tables were piled high with produce and handmade gifts.

Vinnie and Anna tasted olives, cheeses, preserves, breads and oysters, and sampled wine from some of the local wineries.

They were examining some handmade paper when a redhead approached them.

'Mr and Mrs Darcy?'

For a second they ignored her, and then they turned towards her in unison. She wore a long tie-dyed dress and lots of jewellery.

'Yes, sorry – miles away. I'm Dominic and this is Ava,' Vinnie said.

She shook their hands. 'I'm Louisa Logan. I do wine tours, and I'm a potter and I also run the market. I understand you want to talk to me about a stall?'

Anna took up the conversation. 'We're looking at buying here, a winery. We're recent arrivals from London. I'm a chocolatier and I had a market stall at Covent Garden. I make chocolate treats – dipped fruit, truffles, desserts, that sort of thing. I had a commercial kitchen, but I'd look at homemade small-scale, at least to start with.'

Louisa clasped her hands together. 'That would be wonderful, my dear! We'd be delighted to have you. The winter would give you time to get established before the next summer rush.'

Vinnie nodded at her. 'We've heard about this summer rush.'

'About eight thousand people live here year-round, but during the height of summer we can get around forty thousand extra bodies. The great thing is that most of them only come for the day.'

A golden Labrador stopped beside Anna, and she stooped to pat it. 'I see you're a dog person,' Louisa said to her.

The dog went from Anna to Vinnie and back again, its tail wagging furiously as they both stroked its head and body.

'We left our Lab, Merlot, behind,' Anna explained, still looking at the dog, 'but he'll join us when we're settled.'

'Oh you poor things, you must miss him!'

They exchanged glances, and Vinnie smiled at her. 'We do, very much.'

'We have two dogs and two cats. Come for a meal and you can spoil them to your heart's delight.'

'Thank you, that's very kind. We'd love to.'

* * *

After a seafood lunch on the veranda of a local restaurant, it was time to take in a beach. Onetangi was a long stretch of white sand, peopled by bodies on towels, children building sandcastles, and hardy souls taking a dip in the blue sea. It was mid-autumn and eventually the warmth in the sun would fade and the rain would come, so for now everyone was making the most of the Indian summer.

Anna was sitting on a towel, eating a huge peach. Vinnie had been for a walk, and he stopped a short distance away and watched her for a moment before joining her. She held a slice of peach out towards him, but he just opened his mouth, so she cut the slice in half and popped half in.

'God, I love the fruit in this country,' she said.

The juice ran down his chin, and she wiped it away.

'That's incredibly sexy. Can I have the other half, wench?'

Anna gave him the other half, and he lay down on his back and wiggled his toes.

She laughed.

'What's so funny?' he asked without opening his eyes.

'You.'

She lay down beside him and put a sticky finger to his lips. He licked it.

'You're funny and cute and *very* rich, and if I was Elizabeth Bennet I think I'd marry you,' she added.

He smiled. 'Is this happiness I hear, Mrs Darcy?'

'Yes, I do believe it is. I'm happy here, I love it here, and I want to live here. We made a damn good choice.'

They kissed.

'Rocky Bay, here we come,' he said softly.

* * *

Not quite two weeks later a large truck pulled up in the turning bay outside the house on Rocky Bay Winery. The front door was open, and Anna stood on the steps that led up from the drive. Two men got out of the truck and started to open the rear doors.

'Good morning, gentlemen,' she said as she walked down to the truck. It was packed to the doorway with furniture wrapped in plastic. The first piece was a large leather sofa.

'Good morning, Mrs Darcy. Where would you like us to start?'

She pointed at the sofa as they lifted it down. 'This goes in the door and up the four steps to the lounge, middle of the room, facing the window, thank you.'

One of the men grinned at her as he passed. 'Not often we unload a whole house of brand-new stuff. You guys bring nothing with you?'

She smiled to herself as she followed them. 'Not a single thing. Fresh start.'

CHAPTER TWENTY-TWO

DS DONNA CRAWFORD

Detective Sergeant Donna Crawford was born addicted to heroin and was orphaned young. Her unmarried parents both died of accidental overdoses. Her mother was an upper-middle class, high-achieving teenager who chose drugs over university and got herself pregnant to a dealer who lived on a council estate. Donna was found in a squat, cold and hungry, lying on a soiled mattress beside her mother's corpse. The body of the man assumed to be her father was in the same room.

Her maternal aunt and uncle had little choice but to take her in and add her to the three children and two dogs in their nice Cheshire home. When she was twelve, they sat her down and told her the truth: her three older siblings were, in fact, her cousins, and the people she thought of as her parents were her aunt and uncle.

She looked like her mother – dark hair, fair skin, blue eyes – and had never stood out as an obvious addition to the family. The news came as a complete shock. Each one of her siblings told her that they had always thought of her as a sister, and she knew she was loved.

What she didn't know was anything about her biological father – what he looked like, where he came from, what his name was, whether she had any other siblings. The official line was that he was dead, but how did they know that? Was it just wishful thinking? These thoughts plagued her, but she kept them to herself; instinct told her that her parents didn't want to be questioned any further. They had done their duty and there was an end to it.

After an uneventful upbringing, she left school and got a job in the local Sainsbury supermarket. Not what her parents had in mind for her, but she was happy enough. She was a pretty girl, and male staff and customers paid her flattering attention. One day she would get married, have children and probably still be a happy checkout operator when she was fifty.

One night, however, just before New Year's Eve 1999, she was having a drink in her local pub when a skinhead came in. Donna didn't notice him at first, then the fact that he was looking for someone registered with her. She watched as he walked up to a young woman who was standing not far away. The girl wasn't pleased to see him and turned away angrily. The skinhead pulled out a knife.

For a second everyone froze. Donna could see his arm going back and the weapon being driven into the young girl's belly as if it were happening in slow motion. The blood on the blade flashed in the harsh light as he withdrew it. The girl screamed and fell to the floor. The man turned on his heel and ran. Donna reached her before anyone else and gathered the girl into her arms.

'Someone call an ambulance!' she yelled up at the stunned onlookers. If Donna looked down, she could see stomach exposed and blood pouring out of the jagged wound. She grabbed a nearby bar towel and stuffed it over the hole, holding it there with as much pressure as she could muster.

'Hang on, honey, the ambulance is coming,' she said. Two terrified eyes looked up into hers, and she held the gaze until there was a final blink of resignation, the life seeped out of them, and the girl died. A dribble of blood ran out of the corner of the girl's mouth, and her head flopped against Donna's arm.

'Shit!'

It was a traumatic encounter with a lifestyle she had never known, and it galvanised her into action. The next working day she went to her local police station and told them she wanted to apply for a job. For the first time she had a purpose and a motivation to succeed. She was physically strong, articulate and intelligent, and she excelled from her first day of training.

* * *

By 2012 she had done her time, gained the rank of detective sergeant in CID and shifted down to London. The force was her life – all her friends were fellow officers and she adored the job. Somewhere in the back of her brain, though, was the idea that her work would bring her into contact with her biological father, and when that happened she would know him, she just would. However, the attack in the pub and the memory of the dying girl haunted her more than she cared to admit. When she was stressed she would wake at night, sweating and her heart racing, with those lifeless eyes staring out of the darkness at her.

Everyone in the force followed the Lane trial and the story of Witness A. DS Harper and DCI Matthews were heroes, and the story was the source of endless pub gossip.

Donna was listening to just such a conversation in her local when her mobile phone rang. 'Donna?' It was her adopted dad.

'Dad! I meant to come and visit last weekend.'

'Donna, I need you – it's your mum. Can you come?' He sounded upset.

'Now?'

'Can you?' It was a tone she wasn't used to hearing. He was usually such a calm man.

'Of course. I'll be about twenty minutes.'

'Thank you.'

The relief in his voice was obvious, and she drove quickly, avoiding the built-up areas and peak evening congestion.

When her parents had retired, they shifted down to London from Cheshire, to a quiet outer suburb, and downsized to a nice semi-detached cottage. She parked on the road and strode up the path to the door. It was opened by her father before she got to it.

'Donna – thank God.' As he embraced her, she could feel his heart pounding.

'Dad, what on earth is wrong?'

Her father stood aside to let her in.

'She's in the kitchen.'

Her mother was seated at the table, her hair dirty and in disarray, and her clothes smelling strongly of alcohol. A bottle and a glass both lay shattered on the floor, in the middle of a puddle of brown liquid.

'Donna! Darling! Have a drink with me. Get a glass and find another bottle.'

Donna went to her and gave her a hug.

'You're a good girl. We can celebrate you coming to see us,' her mother said as she patted Donna's back.

It was obvious that her mother hadn't showered or changed her clothes for some days.

'You've had enough, Mummy. Why don't you let me take you upstairs and you can have –'

Her mother pushed her away with surprising strength. 'Get off me! I don't want to go anywhere. I want another bloody drink.

Your bloody father has hidden all the bloody bottles. Go down to the off-licence and buy me some scotch, there's a good girl.'

There was a pleading, whining sound to her voice, and it made Donna flinch. She hadn't seen her parents for about a month, and things had obviously changed, and rapidly.

Suddenly her mother rose shakily to her feet, leaning against the table. 'I know what we should do! Donna, get your purse. We'll go to the casino! I want to play the tables and the pokies and have some decent quality scotch –' She lurched over sideways and steadied herself.

Donna felt her father pass as he approached his wife in a rush of energy.

'Now, now, come on, dear. Bed for you –'

With one enormous effort, her mother punched her fist as hard as she could into her father's groin. He cried out in pain and fell to his knees.

'Don't you come near me, you bastard! I told you I want a bloody drink.'

'Mum! Stop!'

The cry was full of shock and horror and genuine disgust. It pulled the older woman up, and she sat down at the table and glowered at Donna.

Her father crawled over to the bench and hauled himself up. He turned to his daughter, his distress plain to see. 'It's like this every day, sometimes before lunchtime. She's either drinking or she's gambling somewhere. She has debts, to loan sharks. I can't pay them, and any money she gets goes on drink.'

Donna shook her head in disbelief. 'You should have told me earlier. She needs rehab –'

'We can't afford anything like that, and she refuses to even talk about AA.'

She went to him and hugged him. He was trembling.

'Don't worry, Dad. I'll fix it.'

Donna rang her colleagues.

There was a great deal of shouting, cursing and fighting, but eventually her mother was sedated and admitted to a drug and alcohol ward at the local hospital. Donna stayed awake all night talking to her father about her mother's addictions. She couldn't help but remember the scathing way her mother had spoken about the sister who had given birth in a drug-induced haze and then died. If it hadn't been for her aunt and uncle … And now here was the judgemental sister, at the mercy of her own demons.

As she walked into the office in the morning, she was still weighing up her options – who else could she tell, who could she ask for help.

After a strong cup of coffee, she sat at her desk and opened up her emails. A subject line in the middle of the page leapt out at her. It said: *Your mother.* The cursor paused over the email for a second, and then she double-clicked on it.

I know about your mother and I can help. I also know who your biological father is. He is alive. Meet me at the Diana Memorial at midday. Come alone, Hyde Park, midday.

Donna glanced around the office but no one was looking at her. She clicked the email closed, moved it to the deleted folder, grabbed her coffee and got to her feet.

* * *

It was a damp autumn day, cloudy and bracing. The trees were losing their leaves, and dogs chased them as they drifted to the manicured grass beneath. Donna sat on the concrete side of the Diana Memorial and watched people strolling through the park. The water gushed behind her, and the noise made her feel strangely peaceful. Maybe he, or she, wouldn't even turn up –

'Detective Crawford?'

She could see a long coat and a Fedora in her peripheral vision. He sat down, but facing away from her.

'Yes.' She started to turn towards him.

'Stay facing the other way. I'll say what I've come to say and then I'll leave. It's better if we don't have a good look at each other.'

She nodded and turned away, her gaze roaming over the crowds going about their business. It felt as though she was meeting a snout in a dark alley. But this one was articulate.

'What do you want?' she asked, allowing the suspicion to be clear in her tone.

He hesitated for a moment. 'I have a proposition for you. I'll solve all the problems in your life. I'll pay off your mother's gambling debts.'

'How do you know about Mum's debts?'

'Don't interrupt, Detective, just listen. I'll organise for her to go into rehab, a place that will give her every opportunity to get clean and sober. And I'll give you the name and address of the man who fathered you.'

'How –'

'I said no questions!'

His voice was sharp and angry. She was dying to turn around and confront him, but her instinct told her that if she did so he would get up and walk away.

'Okay, sorry. What do you require from me?'

Again he hesitated. 'That's better. Just a favour.'

* * *

Marcus had remained impervious to all the taunts and stares during his first day. Only when he was alone in his cell did he allow the emotion to surface. He knew he had to have an outlet for it or the stress would kill him. Inside, he felt like a scared six-year-old locked in a cupboard full of monsters, but on the outside he had to maintain the tough-guy façade. If any of the inmates saw a glimpse of tenderness or vulnerability, his life would turn to hell faster than he could make it back to his cell. He had a choice: be broken or stay strong. To stay strong he needed protection, and that cost money. His father would arrange for the most powerful inmate to receive protection money, and that would keep him safe from the knives and fists, but what else would he have to endure at the hands of the 'prison boss'? The possibilities made him shudder.

He sat at a small table and kept his head bent low. Occasionally his eyes flicked towards the prison guards who stood around the walls of the room. His mother was watching him from across the table, and he knew her face was full of concern. The same scenario was being played out at most of the other tables.

'How's Dad?' he asked quietly.

She shifted. 'Busy. He sends his best.'

'And Tom?'

She hesitated. 'Doing well.'

He grimaced. 'Doing my job. Has he made it plain? What we expect?'

His voice had a touch of urgency, and he hated that.

'Tom's made it crystal clear. Debts have been paid, and now there is a very clear obligation to us.'

Marcus glanced at the nearest guard who scowled back. 'Well get them to tell the cop not to waste time. They'll expect curiosity.'

His mother shook her head. 'Nothing too fast, nothing to raise suspicion. Just be patient – your father will solve it.'

Marcus felt something surge inside, and he wanted to slam his fist down on the table, but he clenched it instead.

He looked Melissa in the eyes. 'There are worse things than dying. Imagine your worst nightmare: that's this place, with real monsters. They're all the same – filth. Give Harper a chance and he'll boast.'

* * *

It was a busy time of year for DI Peter Harper. Successfully convicting Marcus Lane had topped off a very good twelve months and seen him promoted from Detective Sergeant to Detective Inspector. Now he had to interview his replacement and incorporate her into a tightly knit team. There were a couple of high-profile burglary charges and a vicious sexual assault to deal with, but first he had to travel to Wales to pick up a dog and take it to a transportation company.

He hadn't met Mary Whitney-Ross, although he had spoken to her on the phone. He understood why she was noticeably reserved towards him, but now he could tell her that everyone who lived where Merlot was going was well and happy.

'I'm very glad to hear that,' she said stiffly, as she handed over the collar, lead and well-chewed slipper. As he closed the car door on the confused and energetic young dog, Harper turned back towards Mary. She was watching him with very sad eyes. He was reminded of his own mother, widowed young and remarried to a frontline policeman, a woman who knew what it was to live with grief and stress.

'It won't be long now, Mrs Whitney-Ross – the waiting is nearly over.'

She smiled and gave him a slight nod of acknowledgement.

* * *

Later that day, DI Harper sat behind his desk, fiddling with a ballpoint pen and scrutinising the newest member of his team, Detective Sergeant Donna Crawford. The young woman was reading the documents before her with a fierce frown of concentration. Harper remembered his first day, determined to make a good impression and not quite sure how to do that. Crawford was good-looking in that innocent sort of way – late twenties, slender and fresh-faced. She looked, as he was sure she was, like a woman who still felt uncomfortable in a suit and high heels. His boss had informed Harper that his CID greenhorn came with a warm recommendation from 'on high'. Crawford was tagged for a fast track, but Harper was determined to make sure she worked for her promotion and learned the reality of CID.

He glanced at his watch and dropped the pen onto the desk. 'That's quite enough for a first day. There's an excellent pub around the corner. Fancy a bite and a glass of wine?'

Crawford looked up. 'Oh, I don't drink, sir. But I wouldn't say no to a sandwich.'

Harper's eyebrow shot up in surprise. 'A teetotal detective? Not often we come across one of those.'

Crawford gave a sheepish smile and put the documents onto the desk. 'Bad example at home, sir.'

Harper nodded and got to his feet. 'Fair enough. At least I won't need to worry about you having a hangover. Me, I'd miss my red wine too much.'

* * *

The Half Crown was a typical London pub, with a mix of business people, tourists and locals. In one corner Crawford and Harper shared a plate of sandwiches. Harper drank a half pint of lager, and Crawford lemonade.

Harper pointed to the glass in the woman's hand. 'So, is your old man still around?'

Crawford paused and took a sip before answering. 'How do you know it's my dad, sir?'

'Sorry, just assumed.'

'Actually, my mum's in a rehab clinic. Best place for her. Can't run up any more gambling debts while she's under the influence.'

Harper nodded his understanding. 'Was a time when a family history like that would have made you too much of a risk.'

As he drank his beer he thought he saw a momentary expression of disgust cross the young woman's face, but as quickly as he registered it, the look was gone.

'Congratulations on the promotion, sir. Was it tied to a result?' she asked.

'Thanks. Not really, just too much hard graft. Lesson number one: if you're not careful, this job becomes your life.'

They both ate, and the silence hung between them. Harper felt suddenly old and weary: would you look at him, passing on tips to the eager DS. Yet, in a way, it confirmed his progress, that he had knowledge worth sharing. Past colleagues would take the piss, good and proper, if they could see him now.

'So, what's the case you're most proud of, sir?' she asked suddenly. 'If you had to choose your most satisfying day in the job so far.'

Harper put his sandwich down and smiled with satisfaction. That one was easy to answer. 'The day that bastard Lane went down was a very good day.'

Crawford leaned in, interest written all over her face and her food forgotten. He was used to this reaction.

She nodded. 'Everyone in the force heard about that one! What are the chances, someone witnessing the crime.'

He couldn't help but feel proud, not that it was right to let it show. 'We got a very lucky break, happens sometimes. And he was a reliable witness. A great guy.'

Crawford frowned, as though something had just occurred to her. 'Huge thing to do, though, sir, an ordinary member of the public testifying against a mob boss in a murder case. Must have changed his whole life –'

'Oh yeah, and some.'

'How does a family react? Having to relocate, I mean it's not just him –'

'Brave people. Now, enough of the past! What do you do when you're not working?'

* * *

The car park was nearly empty and the police headquarters sat in darkness, apart from a few windows of warm yellow light. Up on the seventh floor DS Crawford sat down in her boss's chair and turned on his hard drive. She took a small black box out of her jacket pocket and plugged it into the USB port on the side of the computer monitor. When the screen prompted her she typed in *DI HARPER*, then pushed a button on the box. A line of dots scrolled in the password prompt until there was a tiny bell sound and the screen opened to reveal a desktop of files. She pulled the box out and put it back in her pocket.

The corridor outside the room was empty, apart from a cleaner, who wandered out of an office and put a plastic rubbish bag onto his trolley. His earphones were connected to an iPod strapped to his upper arm, and he hummed in time to the music as he pushed the trolley along the corridor before stopping outside a closed door. He checked his watch and opened the door.

Crawford looked up, startled at the interruption. 'Hello?'

'Oh! So sorry, ma'am. I didn't know you was still here,' he said as he ripped the earphones from his ears.

She smiled broadly at him. 'No problem. Catching up. Do next door and then come back. I'll only be a few more minutes.'

'There's no hurry, ma'am. So sorry.'

He shut the door, and she got up, moved to the printer and retrieved a coloured picture of Merlot.

CHAPTER TWENTY-THREE

ROCKY BAY

Vinnie was making his way back to the house on a quad bike. In the middle distance he could see Anna hard at work in her new vegetable patch, weeding between rows of beetroot, carrots, silverbeet, broccoli and potato plants. It was December, early summer, and the weather on the island was a few degrees warmer than on the mainland.

Out of the corner of his eye he saw a small Holden ute climbing the hill towards his gate. Who was it this time? Occasionally people turned up and asked to taste the wine, and, although they didn't sell from the winery gate anymore, he always took them to the tasting room and laid out the range available. More often than not they joined the mailing list and ordered a case or two.

As his quad bike left the path and drove onto the crushed-shell turning circle, the ute turned in the gate and headed towards him.

He stopped the bike and stayed astride it, watching. There was something on the back, a crate.

The vehicle stopped a few metres away, facing him. He dismounted and walked towards it.

A pretty young blonde climbed out of the cabin. 'Mr Darcy?' she asked.

'Guilty as charged. What can I do for you?'

She shook his hand. 'I'm Paula from Pet Quarantine. We spoke on the phone? I've got someone here who belongs to you. He passed all his vet checks this morning with flying colours, so I thought I'd pop over to the island, deliver him and stock up on some grog.'

At that moment there was a loud bark from the back of the ute.

'Merlot!' Vinnie ran towards the crate.

The young woman followed him, unbolted the tray and opened the crate. The dog bounded out and onto the ground. He had grown more than Vinnie had expected, and his body had become sleeker, more streamlined.

Merlot barked and jumped up on him, licking furiously, and Vinnie rubbed his head and ears.

'Hello, my gorgeous boy! How are you?'

Paula stood to one side, smiling and watching.

'Merlot?' Anna came around the corner, running towards them, gloves still on her hands, her eyes shining. 'Did I hear my beautiful puppy?'

Vinnie pointed towards her. 'Look, Merlot. It's Mummy.'

The dog bounded over to Anna and jumped up, licking her face.

'Oh, my God! Look how much you've grown! And how beautiful you are!'

Vinnie turned to Paula. 'Thank you. I guess you're used to these reunions.'

She nodded. 'But you never get sick of them. It's great to see pets and owners reunited.'

Merlot barked and circled them, and they both squatted and fussed over him.

Anna smiled up at Paula, tears in her eyes. 'We've waited a long time for this. Thank you so much.'

'My pleasure, Mrs Darcy. He's been really good, but there's no place like home and I can see how well he'll be looked after here.'

* * *

Summer was the time for barbecues on Waiheke Island, and the dinner invitations were as regular as the hot, sunny days. Tonight's was held at a home which Vinnie and Anna had become very comfortable visiting. It belonged to the potter Louisa and her husband, Andrew, the local vet. They lived on a block not far from Rocky Bay, grew grapes and made wine as a hobby. Several of Louisa's works had made their way into Vinnie and Anna's growing art collection.

The group sat on the wide veranda and watched the gulls circling over the sea in the distance.

'How's Merlot?' Louisa asked as she refilled Anna's glass.

'You make Merlot?' One of the other winemakers looked over at her, the surprise obvious in his voice.

Anna grinned sheepishly. 'We do grow Merlot, yes, as part of the blend. But the Merlot Louisa is referring to is our dog, a chocolate Lab. He arrived the other day from England and he's fine. Just loves the vineyard. Races around like a lunatic, chasing birds.'

'It's wonderful that you brought your dog out,' Louisa said as she touched Vinnie's shoulder and refilled his glass.

He smiled up at her and nodded. 'Couldn't leave him behind, he's our baby.'

Louisa sat down. 'So are your families coming to visit? Now that you're settled here. I would miss my mum tremend—'

Anna cut across her firmly. 'My parents are dead, Dominic's mum is elderly. He has no brothers or sisters, and mine are all busy with their lives. We do miss friends' – she raised her glass to them all – 'but we've made such good ones here already.'

Vinnie nodded.

'I'll second that. This is such a civilised way to dine. That marinade was stupendous, Louisa – you should bottle and sell it.'

Andrew pointed to him. 'That's *my* secret family recipe. I could share it with you, but then I'd have to kill you, and we wouldn't want that.'

Vinnie took a sip of the wine. 'Indeed we wouldn't,' he murmured.

***

February 2013

The Waiheke Wine and Food Festival was an annual mid-summer event, held at one of the island's most popular vineyards. A broad rectangle of mown grass was covered in temporary accommodation. A white marquee stood in the centre, and smaller coloured tents were dotted down the side of a gently rolling hill between bays of vines. Crowds milled around, drinking, eating, chatting and laughing. Tired patrons flopped onto shiny metal chairs, around white plastic tables under green sun umbrellas, to rest and regroup.

The summer air was heavy with the smell of food cooking – skewered garlic prawns sizzling on barbecue hotplates, pizzas fresh from a wood-fired oven, huge piles of smoky pork ribs, herb-crusted racks of pink lamb chops, enormous mussel fritters, plump venison sausages smothered with caramelised onions and served in soft white buns … All of the tents were full of sweaty bodies queuing to get to the laden trestle tables. On the other side of the tables stood the enthusiastic winemakers, pouring, talking, listening and selling.

At one end of the rectangle of lawn was a raised stage. People gravitated towards it, glasses in hand, to sway to the music of a seven-piece jazz band.

Vinnie stood on the stage and sang 'For Once in My Life' in his rich baritone voice. Some of the women blew him kisses, and he winked back at them.

At the far end of the row of smaller tents, Vinnie's singing echoed faintly over the buzz of conversation. A banner reading 'Rocky Bay Winery' was pinned to the back wall of the tent. Two trestle tables stood at an angle to each other, creating a semicircle area in which people congregated.

Gabby and two young women stood behind a table with open bottles of red wine and jugs of water in front of them. They filled a continuous stream of glasses while they talked about the wine.

Anna stood behind the other table, which was spread with single-bowl servings of chocolate mousse topped with a chocolate-dipped strawberry, platters piled with truffles, chocolates and pieces of chocolate-dipped fruit, and a stand of small chocolate bars wrapped in gold foil. Merlot lay on the grass under Anna's table and chewed on a rawhide bone.

Louisa contemplated the array of chocolate goodies and sighed. 'It all looks just too delicious! We were saying only the other night, Ava, what a blessing you and Dominic are to island life. How dull it was before you rescued us! Dominic really should join the Waiheke Winemakers committee.'

Louisa was a touch ostentatious, but she meant well and she offered very genuine hospitality tinged with more than a little genuine curiosity. Anna smiled warmly at her. 'Thank you, Lou. Everyone has made us feel so welcome.'

Louisa picked up a flat chocolate shape and turned it over in her hand. 'What's this little masterpiece?' she asked.

'A dried apricot, soaked overnight in Grand Marnier, then dipped in dark chocolate, and those are vodka cherries in milk chocolate.'

Louisa gave a little giggle. 'Dear Lord! As if the chocolate wasn't enough, the alcohol makes it feel ever so slightly sinful,' she said in a half-whisper.

Anna ate a cherry, slowly and with relish, the juice trickling down her chin.

Louisa almost bit into the apricot, then frowned and put it down.

Anna suppressed a smile. 'You know, when I first met Dominic he insisted that chocolate could absorb alcohol in the bloodstream. He made it sound so convincing, I fell in love on the spot,' Anna said in what she hoped sounded like a conspiratorial tone.

Louisa looked at Vinnie in the distance as he bowed to an appreciative audience. 'Oh, and I can understand why,' she murmured to herself.

* * *

On the stage, the band struck up a new song and Vinnie clicked his fingers. It was a day to stand back and look at how far he had come, singing on stage at a festival while people sampled their wine and Anna's chocolate. Safe and warm and living the dream.

'Oh, yeah! Great choice, boys! Here's one for all our talented winemakers. We love you all!'

The people on the grass started to clap and sway to the gentle melody as the soulful strains of 'Red Red Wine' rang out.

CHAPTER TWENTY-FOUR

HERMAN D GRANGER

An enormous man in an exquisitely cut pale-blue linen suit, a striped shirt, a silk cravat and a Panama hat stepped into the Rocky Bay tent. Herman D Granger was six foot five and weighed two-seventy pounds. He dressed in custom-made suits and carried a black walking stick with a solid silver wine glass as the grip. He was an American, a wine judge, and a critic with a widely read online blog – and a keen sense of his own importance.

'Ah, Rocky Bay! Now, I've heard about you.'

His southern drawl carried through the small space, and heads turned as bodies stepped aside to make room for him.

He tipped his hat as he passed. 'Much obliged, I'm sure. Bordeaux blend.'

He extended his hand towards Gabby. 'Herman D Granger, wine critic.'

She shook it. 'Gabby McLean, winemaker. And that,' she said as she pointed towards Anna, 'is Mrs Ava Darcy, co-owner of the winery. Yes, indeed, Bordeaux blend. What can I get you, sir?'

He bowed slightly in Anna's direction, and she returned the gesture with a nod and a smile. Then he balanced his stick against the table and looked over at the bottles.

'I was told you're a must-try, m'dear. What's your blend?'

Gabby picked up the bottles one by one and handed them to him. He examined each one in turn, and then put it down to receive the next.

'Three blends. This is Decoro, a beautiful mix of second-press and free-run Cabernet Sauvignon and Merlot. This is Gravitas, deep-press fractions of Cabernet Sauvignon, Merlot, Cabernet Franc and Malbec. It's a left-bank kind of Bordeaux, very, very popular. And this is our star, Celo.'

He turned the last bottle in his hands and looked up at her, enquiringly. The pride ran deep in her voice and was reflected in her smile and the sparkle in her eyes.

'All five of our grape varieties: Cabernet Sauvignon, Merlot, Cabernet Franc, Malbec and a little Petit Verdot. Deep-press, beautifully rich, dense tannins. Would you like to try all three, sir?'

'I surely would! What a treat.'

She picked up a tasting glass and poured a swig of Decoro into it. He swirled the glass, put his nose into it, breathed deeply, then took a sip and drew in air over his tongue. He let it linger for a moment before swallowing.

'Very nice.'

She took another glass and poured some of the Gravitas. He didn't try any more of the Decoro, and they exchanged glasses.

'I'm interested in the names,' he said, before trying the wine. 'Latin names?'

Gabby nodded. 'The current owners, Dominic and Ava Darcy, are about to bring in their first harvest. But they have renamed the wines in the barrels. "Decoro" means to adorn or beautify.'

He repeated the process with the Gravitas wine and his face broke into a slow smile. 'Now that's a lovely wine. Soft and smooth, and a very clean after-taste. Tobacco and chocolate.'

Gabby beamed. 'Thank you! I love Gravitas. It's supposed to mean something serious and important, and I think it's so well named.'

He took another long sip. 'My, it certainly is.'

She poured some ruby red liquid from the bottle of Celo into a third glass. He exchanged glasses with her and held it up to the light.

'Exquisite colour, m'dear. And Celo? If I'm not mistaken it means to hide something, to keep it a secret. So what is the great secret about this wine?'

She looked confused and straightened the bottles on the table to give herself a moment to collect her thoughts.

'The power and complexity of the wine is a secret, until people taste it for the first time,' Vinnie said, as he held out his hand towards Granger. 'How do you do? I'm Dominic Darcy, and I own Rocky Bay with my wife, Ava.'

Ganger swapped the glass to his left hand and shook Vinnie's hand. 'Herman D Granger. English?'

Vinnie nodded. 'Fresh from London.'

Granger swirled the wine, breathed it in then took a deep sip. He closed his eyes and stood very still. Eventually he swallowed, paused and took another sip. Then he opened his eyes and shook his head gently. 'Magnificent! Absolutely magnificent.'

Vinnie acknowledged the praise with a slight nod. He was aware that Gabby was squirming with delight beside him.

'Thank you. It's Gabby's philosophy and attention to detail, from the grape to the bottle: near enough is not good enough.'

Granger picked up an unopened bottle and looked at Vinnie. 'Corks? Interesting choice, and relatively rare here.'

Vinnie smiled at him. 'I'll change to screw caps when Mouton Rothschild does.'

Granger put the bottle down. 'Well said, sir. Are you selling it?'

'We're taking orders for case lots,' Gabby said.

'Most of it goes by mail order. We're a small winery,' Vinnie added.

'Then I would like two cases of this and a case of Gravitas. If I may.'

He took a business card from his pocket and handed it to Vinnie. 'I'm here on a working holiday, always looking for grand stories. You probably know my blog, *Fruit of the Vine*. Modesty forbids me sharing the numbers, but I do believe it is one of the most widely read wine sites on the whole of the internet.'

Vinnie looked at the card, ran his hand through his curls and said nothing.

'Could I be so bold as to ask if I may come visit your very fine establishment? If you're not too busy, could I impose on you tomorrow? Only take an hour or so. I'm due back on the mainland tomorrow evening.'

Gabby's eyes shone with excitement. 'I'm sure that'd be fine, wouldn't it, Dom?'

'Absolutely. Gabby will show you around – she's the star. And you can taste the vintages in the barrel. They're going to be even better.'

Granger took another sip.

'I'll take your word for that, Mr Darcy, but this little beauty will take some beating. It would give second-growth Bordeaux a run for its money.'

* * *

215

The next day dawned clear and warm. Gabby was bubbling with an anticipation she hadn't felt since the new machinery had arrived.

Herman Granger was prompt and as charming as ever. She met him in the driveway and escorted him to the tasting room. He gave her a running commentary on the wines he had tasted since arriving in the country, and she was delighted to hear that Rocky Bay was right up with the very best. She had done her homework on his blog and the awards he had won, and her flattery made him blush with pleasure.

Using a wine thief, she drew some liquid from the pre-selected barrel and let it drain into the glass. 'This was blended last year. It'll become Gravitas.'

A young photographer took photographs of Granger as he swirled the contents of the glass, breathed in the aroma and then tasted the wine.

Gabby tried to hide her anxiety as she fiddled with the wine-thief.

'Oh, m'dear! It's remarkably complex already! It'll age magnificently,' he pronounced.

She grinned with relief. 'I think so, too. Dom's not kidding when he says our wine in barrel is going to be even better.'

The photographer turned away and started snapping the hall, close-ups of the glasses on top of the barrel and the stacks of barrels down the wall.

Granger pulled a dictaphone from his pocket and read aloud from the card attached to the barrel. 'I need to get my thoughts down at the moment of taste, while it's still fresh in my mouth,' he explained, and Gabby nodded her understanding.

* * *

An hour later they stood on the edge of the turning circle outside the house, the vineyard spread out below them. The photographer roamed the area, using a long lens to take shots of the vines, the buildings in the bowl of the natural amphitheatre and the view out to sea on the other side of the house. Granger pointed into the middle distance. Halfway down a row of vines Vinnie and Merlot were together.

'You're on the brink of harvest,' he said.

'Yes. It's a tense time for the vineyard, waiting for the levels to be right, hoping the weather holds.'

He nodded thoughtfully. 'Tell me, m'dear, Dominic Darcy doesn't strike me as a shy man.'

'He's not, he's an extrovert. Knowledgeable and witty and totally devoted to the vineyard.'

'And yet he leaves the publicity to you. With all due respect, he's not on your website or your Facebook page. He doesn't tweet. Why not?'

Gabby scuffed her shoe against the crushed shell and looked out towards the vines. She had wondered how she was going to answer this question and how to make sure it didn't become the focus of the article. While she suspected she should resent Dom for putting her in this position, she was far too fond of him to harbour any grudge.

'I'm not sure. He's a passionate winemaker and he's made so many wonderful improvements. But that's the way he wants it to be, and he's the boss. I tell him he's hiding his light under a vine leaf.'

Granger tapped her foot with his cane. 'Well, you're the expert and very talented, if I may say so.'

She smiled shyly, and was about to respond when her cell phone rang. 'Excuse me a moment,' she apologised as she turned away. 'I have to take this.'

'Not at all, take your time.'

217

As Gabby turned and walked away, Granger beckoned to the photographer and pointed towards Vinnie. 'There's a story here. Something smells to me like rat stew. Get some shots of him – zoom in – and the dog,' he muttered.

CHAPTER TWENTY-FIVE

NORMAN LANE

Norman Lane still lived in the big brick house in Richmond. He took great pride in his perfectly groomed gardens and his huge vegetable patch, and he kept a close eye on whatever the gardeners did. The house was just as immaculately presented and, as it had been for his father before him, was his showcase for exquisite antiques and original art. He liked to demonstrate the proceeds of his career, almost daring anyone to question the source of his considerable wealth.

His study was a masculine room, with a black Chesterfield sofa and chairs, antique fishing rods and guns mounted on the walls, Persian rugs on the polished wooden floor and a vast mahogany desk. In one corner stood an oversized card table covered in a half-finished jigsaw puzzle.

He sat in an armchair, smoked a cigar and watched Crawford squirm uncomfortably on the edge of the sofa. He disliked coppers. He disliked bent ones even more.

'I've checked it out, twice.' Crawford's tone was apologetic. 'The records are there. The car crash, coroner's report, death certificates, obituaries. Car burnt out. They were all identified by dental records.'

Lane didn't answer, and then he sighed. 'So there's absolutely nothing to link the death of Vincent Whitney-Ross to my son's case?'

Crawford shook her head decisively. 'Absolutely nothing, sir.'

'Not even the fact that he worked for Kelt and could have been in the cellar?'

'Coincidence.'

'Nor the fact that his father worked for us, and he knew Marcus as a youngster?'

'Another coincidence.'

'And Harper gave the dog away? A chocolate Lab?'

'Apparently. It was called Merlot.'

Lane got to his feet and walked stiffly across the rug. His gut told him that something wasn't right. He took his cigar from his mouth and pointed it at Crawford. 'I don't believe in coincidences, young lady.'

Crawford shrugged. Lane knew she was going to stop trying and he silently cursed the young woman's inexperience. She might be bright, but she sure as hell didn't have a copper's nose. Why couldn't Tom have found him someone a bit older?

'What more do you want me to do, sir?' she asked.

Lane paused by the card table and with one hand swept all the jigsaw pieces onto the floor.

'Find me fucking Witness A!'

The outburst hung in the air, and Crawford didn't react. Lane swung around and faced her, his fury now clear in his contorted face. 'I want my son out of that damn prison.'

'I understand that, but it's not as easy as you appear to think. The file is sealed, and the only person with that information in writing is DCI Matth—'

'You're the detective, do some detecting. Find me Witness A. Or I'd venture to say your career is over, your mother will be required to pay back her debts and that piece of information you want so badly will die with me.'

Crawford jerked as if the words hit her like a fist. 'Are you … are you threatening a policewoman, sir?'

Lane sneered at her. Stupid bloody greenhorn. 'I don't waste time with threats. I just act.'

* * *

Later that night Norman and Melissa hosted a dinner party in the dining room. Eight people were seated around a three-pedestal Queen Anne table and the air was filled with conversation, laughter and the clink of silver cutlery on fine china. Lane's booming voice cut across the others and held everyone's attention. When he thumped the table to emphasise a point, everyone and everything jumped.

They were halfway through a main course of roast beef when a uniformed butler leaned over his shoulder with a bottle of 1978 Romanée-Conti in his hand. 'The next bottle on the table, sir,' he murmured quietly. 'I thought I should check with you first.'

Lane nodded, took it from him, gave the label a cursory glance and turned the bottle over as he handed it back.

'Wait a moment,' he ordered briskly. Doing a double-take, he pulled the bottle to him and peered at the back more closely. Finally, he looked up at his silent guests. They were watching him with obvious interest. Melissa looked menacing, but this had to be dealt with now.

'If you'll just excuse me, only for a moment.'

He got to his feet and strode out, bottle in hand.

The study was on the other side of the hall, and he went straight to the desk, took out a magnifying glass and studied the reverse side of the bottle closely. Then he put it down on the desk and took his cell phone from his jacket pocket.

The number was on speed dial, and he scowled at the bottle as he waited for the other phone to be picked up. The high-pitched voice on the other end was stressed, and there was traffic noise in the background. Brian Davis was a wine dealer who could get anything, for a price.

'Mr Lane, what can I do for you?'

'I've got a bottle of '78 Romanée-Conti here and it came from you.'

'Only the best for my regul–'

He could hear both pride and anxiety in the voice.

'Where did you get it?'

'You know the deal, Mr Lane: sometimes the source wants to remain anonymous.'

Lane's expression darkened. *Not this time, you little weasel.* 'Bullshit, Davis. Did you get it from David Kelt?'

'What? No way! What makes you ask that?'

Davis sounded genuinely surprised, so it must have come through a middle man. A flash of frustration crossed Lane's face.

'Because he marked his very best wine with a tiny K in a circle and the date he bought it. This one was purchased in 1991. And he never, ever sold that wine. So if he didn't sell it to you, who did?'

A loud crackling surged through the phone.

'I gotta go, Mr Lane. Sorry, the line's breaking –'

Lane thumped the desk so hard that the bottle jumped in the air. 'Shall I send someone around to ask you in person? If I do, he'll bring a fucking knife. Do I make myself clear?'

There was a pause and the crackle ceased.

'Perfectly. He's no use to you, though: he's dead. Died in a car crash a few months ago. He was a small-time wine merchant, used to deliver wine to Kelt. Guy called Vinnie, Vinnie Whitney-Ross.'

Lane smiled slowly. A connection. At last. Another piece of the puzzle fell into place.

'He may still be of a great deal of use. Thank you, Davis.'

Lane snapped the cell phone shut and picked up the bottle, much more gently this time.

CHAPTER TWENTY-SIX

HARVEST

Vinnie was doing what he called a 'hands-on' job: he and Gabby were capping the fermenting grape juice. He rested against the vat and breathed deeply. He was proud of the fermentation room at Rocky Bay. It was a rectangle with roller doors at either end, which were raised to allow ventilation when the room was in use. Five shiny stainless-steel vats stood close to one long wall, with metal stepladders attached to each vat and metal gantries running above them. The wall was punctured by a line of five square holes, closed by a sheet of wood, and each vat was lined up beneath a hole. The purpose of the gantries was to allow a winemaker to stand there and plunge the grape skins back into the fermenting juice. This was called capping. It was a job with some considerable risk: the air above the skins was almost pure CO_2 and that made breathing impossible.

Once more Vinnie grabbed the metal plunger in his hands and pushed the skins deep into the juice with strong, rhythmical strokes. There was a fair amount of resistance, and he could feel the dull ache in his arms and the sweat running down his back.

It was a nice feeling, though, a satisfying feeling, a connection to the physical process of winemaking that he doubted anyone other than Gabby would fully understand. She stood above the next tank, doing the same thing, and her timing matched his.

All of a sudden he reached out a fraction too far and his rubber boots slipped sideways on the mess of skins and water. He felt himself starting to topple towards the sea of red. He let go of the plunger and grabbed the side of the tank.

'Shit! I have to stop doing that.'

Gabby stopped and moved carefully to the end of her gantry, as close to him as she could get. 'Careful, boss. You okay?' she asked.

He grinned sheepishly at her. 'By vintage number ten I'll have the hang of this. Be like a mountain goat.'

He reached out for the plunger. 'Or maybe not.'

It bobbed away from his fingers. He missed it and his momentum carried him forward. This time his other hand hit the rim of the gantry so hard he couldn't get a grip and he fell in, shoulder-first. His body made a loud splash.

'Dominic!' Gabby threw her plunger away and ran along the gantry to the steps.

In the tank Vinnie raised his arms above his head and twisted his body sideways. The sheer viscosity of the grapes kept him from sinking, but it also made moving very difficult. The aroma of grape juice was almost overpowering.

'Hold your breath,' Gabby called out from the floor of the room. 'Don't breathe in the CO_2.'

She grabbed a ladder from the wall and dragged it to his tank.

'The side. Try and get to the side, Dom. Hold onto the side!'

Vinnie pulled himself through the thick custard-like red must. It had started to act like quicksand and suck him down.

He could feel a searing pain as his lungs screamed for oxygen in the dense cloud of CO_2 gas, and his head began to spin.

Gabby climbed the metal steps, dragging the ladder behind her. It banged against the side of the vat. She moved gingerly along the gantry, lowered the ladder into the tank and hooked the top over the rim.

Vinnie was trying to hold on, but the must was dragging him down, and he kept letting go and then reaching up again. As he started to sink below the level of the caps, she thrust his plunger out towards him.

'Take it! Grab hold and I'll pull you to the ladder.'

The plunger hit his shoulder and he wrapped one arm around it. His body moved slowly through the swirling must towards the ladder. He was close to losing consciousness, and the scene above the tank was a blur of light. The plunger reached the ladder and his fingers grabbed the metal rails.

'Pull yourself up. Come on … that's right … just a bit more.'

Vinnie raised his hands up, and his scrambling feet found the bottom rung of the ladder. He used his strength to push himself into a standing position, above the CO_2 and into fresh air. Gabby latched onto his shirt and hauled him upwards with both hands. He gulped in mouthfuls of air, filling his lungs. Slowly he climbed over the rim of the tank and sank to his knees on the gantry. Red juice ran off him in streams and pooled around his body. He was stained red from head to toe.

'Damn CO_2,' he gasped.

She bent down beside him. 'Just breathe.'

He gave her a weak smile. 'Thank you. Quick thinking.'

She drew her finger along his cheek, then licked the fingertip. 'Impressive amount of effort to check the sugar level. Next time, use the saccharometer.'

He laughed. 'Ha! At least I know the cooling rings are working.'

She helped him to his feet. 'It's a sort of initiation. *Now* you're a winemaker. Joking aside, please don't do it again.'

'Believe me, Gabby, I now know how dangerous wine can be to your health.'

* * *

Anna was dipping fruit in her kitchen. A chocolate tempering machine stood in one corner, and the bench was covered in stacks of moulds. She carefully lifted apricots from a bowl of dark liquid, drained them on paper towels and dipped them into a pot of melted chocolate, before lowering them onto a tray lined with baking paper. At the sound of footsteps she looked up to see Vinnie coming through the exterior door. He was soaked through and stained red. The excess juice had been hosed off, but it was obvious what had happened.

She burst out laughing.

'Oh, thank you. No sympathy here, then?' He tried unsuccessfully to hide his smile.

'I could ask what in God's name happened to you, but I think I can see.'

'We were capping. I slipped and went for a swim.'

'Good Lord! How did it feel?'

'Most unpleasant. Lots of CO_2, not much oxygen, and the consistency of porridge. Gabby hauled me out. I think I was drowning.'

She bit her lip. 'My poor darling. Sorry I laughed.'

He went to her and took her in his arms. She pulled back.

'Not that sorry! You're all wet and sticky.'

He dipped his finger into the pot of melted chocolate and licked it.

'Yummy chocolate. You really should do a line of alcoholic body paint. We could do test runs. Call it Paint and Lick.'

She picked up an apricot and popped it in his mouth. They exchanged a fond glance of remembrance.

'Wish we could pay the pickers in extremely good chocolate,' he said as he reached for another.

'Stop eating all the profits and go and have a shower. I'm popping to the shops. Do you want anything?'

He shook his head as he wandered towards the hall. 'Nope. Herman sent me a text. His blog goes live in an hour. You can have a read when you get home.'

* * *

Two hours later Anna's car pulled into the turning circle behind the house and screeched to a halt. She leapt out and ran across the crushed shell, up the steps and into the house. Vinnie was standing at the window in his study, his cell phone at his ear, staring at the picture-postcard view out to sea. His laptop was open on his desk, beside a stack of magazines, some unlabelled bottles and some tasting glasses.

'I'm under no obligation to give you a reason, Herman. I want that picture replaced with a shot of the vineyard, and I want it to happen now – immediately.'

Vinnie turned and extended his free arm towards Anna. She went to him. She knew her rising panic was clearly evident on her face.

He hugged her close and kissed the top of her head.

'Surely you had to ask my permission to use a photographic representation of me? That's just responsible journalism.'

Anna could hear the American's honeyed voice, slightly raised, from the cell phone.

Vinnie frowned. 'Not at all, I would've decline–'

Anna moved away, leaned against the windowsill and watched. 'If I have to threaten legal action, I will, and believe me, it won't be an empty threat. If you really want to go to all that trouble … Thank you. I'll check again in five minutes. Thank you.'

Vinnie clicked the phone shut. He looked angry and afraid. 'That fucking arsehole! Excuse my language. He said the photo adds to the mystique of the story, so changing it will diminish the piece. He never gives away editorial control … all bullshit.'

'What I want to know is how Gabby could let the photographer take the photo in the first place?' she asked.

Vinnie shrugged and then let out a deep sigh. 'She says she didn't know. She doesn't understand why it upsets me. Sorry I called you. I just suddenly felt alone.'

Anna went to the desk and swung the laptop around. It was a close-up of Vinnie and Merlot beside a vine, with Vinnie's face clearly visible. The headline of the post was 'The Secret of Rocky Bay'.

'It's a bloody good article,' he said as he ran his hand through his curls. 'Says Gabby McLean and Dominic Darcy make a sensational team and the wine is world class. Anyway, he's removing the picture as we speak.'

She glanced up at him, and the strain evident on his face made her heart surge. 'He'd better, or he'll have me to deal with.'

Vinnie gave a gentle laugh. 'Danger averted. It wasn't up for long, and it is the middle of the night in the UK. Odds are –'

'Only one man matters. But your old customers are wine buffs, and you're supposed to be dead!'

CHAPTER TWENTY-SEVEN

RUMBLED

Norman Lane was asleep. The enormous master bedroom contained two king-sized four-poster beds. Moonlight shone through a gap in the heavy brocade drapes and threw a shadow on to the carpet. Lane snored loudly in his bed, and his spread-eagled body barely moved. Melissa slept lightly and tossed frequently in hers.

Lane's cell phone rested on the nightstand beside him. When it started to ring and move around on the wood, the noise woke Melissa first. She rolled over and lifted her head from the pillow.

'Norman!'

There was no response from the other bed.

'Norman. For God's sake, your phone's ringing!'

He grunted. One hand came out from under the covers and groped around the table until it landed on the phone. He opened it and pulled it to his ear.

'This better be bloody life-threatening,' he snarled.

'It's Tom. You told me to call you the minute I had any news.'

Lane sat bolt upright. 'Go on.'

'I've been keeping an eye on wine blogs. And I've just read one called *Fruit of the –*'

'Herman Granger. A Yank. I know him.'

'Well, he's just written about a vineyard in New Zealand called Rocky Bay. The first version featured a candid photo of the owner, an Englishman called Dominic Darcy. Taken from a distance with a zoom, I'll bet my life on it. He has a chocolate Lab with him. Second version, minutes later, that photo's gone. The whole blog is about how the winemaker takes all the credit, while the relatively new owner stays out of sight.'

A slow smiled spread over Lane's tired face. 'Well done, Tom.'

He clicked the phone shut and sat for a moment, deep in thought.

'Who was that?' Melissa asked. She was resting on her elbow, watching him. Lane turned to her.

'Tom, with a get-out-of-jail card for Marcus.'

He swung his feet over the side of the bed and thrust them into slippers, pulled himself upright and reached for his robe.

'I've got some calls to make, loose ends. I'll go to the study. You go back to sleep.'

* * *

Rain lashed Mary's Welsh cottage, wind tore at the plants in the garden, and huge drops splashed into the puddles. She watched out of her front window as a car came up the drive towards the house. Her suitcase stood by the door, and her handbag was over her arm. This was the beginning; this was what she had been waiting for.

The early morning mist rose off the Thames and the river reflected the steel grey cloud above. Peter Harper walked briskly down some dirty concrete steps and out onto the bank at the edge of the water. A group of men was standing around something lying on the mud, and one was crouched down beside it. Harper's stride checked momentarily when the man moved and he caught a glimpse of the object.

Then he walked over to them and stared down at the body of DS Crawford. There were rope marks on her wrists and ankles, her shoes were missing and her clothes were water-logged and caked in mud. There was a single bullet hole through the centre of her forehead.

'Who found her?' Harper asked.

'Kids. About thirty minutes ago, sir.'

He followed the officer's gaze to two young boys talking to a uniformed policeman about twenty metres away. The pathologist stood up and removed his rubber gloves.

'Not dead long – sometime early this morning. Before she entered the water, by the look of the bullet hole, but the post-mortem will tell us. Body was weighted down, judging by those marks.'

Harper leaned over and examined the face. 'Looks like a hit. Report on my desk, quick as you can on this one.'

* * *

Mary Whitney-Ross stepped up to the check-in counter and handed her ticket wallet to the smiling girl in uniform.

'Hello, dear.'

'Hello, Mrs Darcy. You have one stopover, in Madrid.'

Detective Chief Inspector Ron Matthews glanced up as a sharp knock on his closed door broke his concentration.

'Come.'

Peter Harper was carrying a laptop. He put it on the desk, opened it and swung it around to face his boss. 'Have a look at this, sir.'

'Why?'

'It's Donna Crawford's. The last search she did was for this wine blog, out of the USA. And then look at this.'

He hit a couple of buttons and a Word document filled the screen.

'It's a cut and paste she did of the same blog, an earlier version. Scroll down and look at the third photo.'

Matthews did as his junior officer suggested and then sat up in his chair with a start.

'Jesus Christ, Peter! That's Vinnie Whitney-Ross and his bloody dog.'

Harper nodded.

'I've had a call from Vinnie's mother, she's about to board a flight to Chile. She'll buy a return ticket to New Zealand in Santiago.'

'Have you got Crawford's cell?' Matthews asked sharply.

Harper shook his head as he closed the laptop and picked it up. 'It wasn't on her body or in her desk. Uniform is searching her home.'

'Pull the call records. Why would she be searching a bloody wine blog? Can you find a link between Crawford and Norman Lane?'

Harper's body language mirrored his boss's confusion. 'No, not at all, sir. She asked a couple of questions about the case, but everyone does that.'

Matthews nodded slowly. 'The recommendation to move her to your unit came from top brass and they said she showed huge promise.'

Harper hesitated. 'Nothing out of the ordinary, but she was a good copper. Thorough, honest, inquisitive and ambitious. She didn't even bloody drink, said her mum was in some sort of rehab for alcohol and gambling ...' His voice trailed off and he looked like he had seen a ghost. 'Oh sweet Jesus, Mary and Joseph,' Harper murmured. 'Donna, what have you done?'

Matthews thumped his desk. 'Are you saying ...? Christ, Peter, why didn't you see this?'

Harper shrugged. It was clear from his expression that his nightmares were materialising in front of him. 'Coppers have families, sir. Sometimes there's a weakness that makes them vulnerable. People like Lane exploit that. But why kill her? Why risk alerting us?'

'We weren't supposed to find her. Her body slipped the weights – the current is very strong there. Lane had got what he wanted, and Crawford was always going to be a loose end.'

'Why would Vinnie do an interview like that? And allow that photo to be taken?'

Matthews shook his head in amazement. 'That one makes no sense. I thought he understood the damn rules.'

Harper came back to the desk and Matthews could see that the confusion was gone. 'Lane will demand that Vinnie recant, sir, and apply whatever pressure he needs to. We've got to help, we owe him that.'

Matthews thought for a moment, then came to a decision and nodded at his DI. 'You go. You can get local back-up, but he trusts you. He'll listen to you. Pull them out if you have to.'

* * *

Marcus hesitated at the doorway to the visiting room. He knew the state of his face would shock his mother. He had cuts and bruises around his eyes from a fight.

Melissa half-rose as he sat down. 'What's happened?'

He touched her hand. 'It's okay. You should see the other guy.'

'Marcus! What have –'

'No really, you should. He's in the infirmary. Nothing important, just a disagreement with one of the Clerkenwell Gang.'

She took a piece of paper from her handbag and gave it to him. 'This is Witness A.'

The face in the photo had matured and aged, but the blue eyes were the same, and the curls. Memories danced across his brain, happy thoughts, long buried under the crap of his adult life.

'Vinnie,' he said softly.

His mother nodded. 'He recognised you and he betrayed you. No wonder the prosecution were so certain Witness A's testimony was rock solid. He didn't pick you out from a mug shot. He knew you.'

Marcus sucked in his bottom lip and chewed it. 'His mother blamed us for his father's death. I remember wanting to tell him it wasn't my fault.'

'It doesn't matter now, darling. Your dad knows where he is and he'll get Vinnie to recant his evidence. He'll come back, and then you'll be free.'

'I wonder if he remembers the warehouse.'

'What warehouse?' Her voice was sharp.

'He was a petty hustler, back in the day, on the markets. He stumbled across one of our Colombian shipments, and Tom was going to put a bullet in his kneecap. I stopped him. It was obvious he had nothing to do with the theft …' His voice trailed off.

Melissa reached across and took his hand in hers. The guard by the door took a step forward, and she let go and pulled her arm back.

'Don't fret. Have you ever known your dad to fail at anything important? He's tracked Vinnie down, and now he'll fix it. Just you wait and see.'

CHAPTER TWENTY-EIGHT

REUNION

It was late summer 2013, and all the grapes had been harvested and most of the vines were still covered in nets. A tractor drove slowly down the middle of a bay of five rows. Two men walked down the outsides of the bay and fed the net back towards the machine. A woman stood in the box mounted on the back of the tractor and pushed the net down with her feet as it came swirling off the vines. The four winery dogs, including Merlot, raced up and down, tails wagging and noses to the earth.

In the fermentation hall all the tanks were empty apart from one. Gabby stood on the gantry and carefully plunged the caps back into the dark red must. Over to one side, a woman used a high-pressure hose to clean the chute down into the pressing machine.

On the other side of the hill, others were preparing the garden for the end-of-harvest party. Long trestle tables were covered in white tablecloths and piled with plates and cutlery rolled in napkins. At another table a woman was arranging wine glasses. A colourful banner along the brick wall read: 'I survived the vintage at Rocky Bay!'

Vinnie was up a stepladder hanging a string of fairy lights from a tree to a wooden pergola. As he worked he sang a loud, happy song about wine and women.

Anna came down the steps from the kitchen carrying a box of decorations. 'Do you know the words to "I Married an Angel"?' she asked.

He stopped, looked down at her and frowned. 'No, I don't think so. Should I?'

She put the box on the ground and exchanged a smile with the women working at the tables. 'Good, sing that.'

He gestured towards the women. 'Very funny. Meet my wife, the stand-up comic.'

Anna tickled Vinnie's leg. 'Want another one? I spent time at my husband's grave this morning. He isn't dead – he thinks I'm digging a pond.'

Vinnie and the women couldn't help but laugh.

'It'll be the best harvest party this vineyard's ever seen,' Anna exclaimed happily as she climbed the steps again. 'But you'd better get a move on. There are more decorations to come.'

He shook a fistful of lights at her disappearing back. 'What did your last slave die of?'

She didn't look back as she reached the door. 'You know that, husband: insubordination.'

* * *

Louisa stood beside her minivan and waited for the ferry from Auckland. She had a wine tour client, booked by phone this morning. The woman said she was looking for something very specific, and would say more when she arrived. Louisa's

238

curiosity was piqued, but then you never knew what tourists were going to want. Some even came to Waiheke looking for world-class Sauvignon Blanc, and she had to explain that they were in the wrong part of the country.

The ferry docked and people started to disembark; tall, short, thin, fat, young, old, visitors and locals.

Louisa watched until she was sure the elderly woman was looking out for someone to meet her. She strolled over. 'Are you looking for me? I'm Louisa Logan from Waiheke Wonderful Wine Tours.'

A smile of relief reached the tired grey eyes. 'Yes, I am. How do you do, Louisa? Thank you so much for meeting me.'

Louisa shook the extended hand. 'No problem, but it's a bit late in the day to do an extensive tour. Are you staying over? Can I take you somewhere and we'll tour the wineries tomorrow?'

The woman looked past Louisa at the van.

'I know exactly where I want you to take me, my dear, if you don't mind. It's a winery run by an English couple. I believe their name is Darcy.'

Louisa was surprised and intrigued. The woman's accent was English – was it a surprise reunion

'Dominic and Ava? I'm going there myself. They're having an end-of-harvest party tonight.'

Mary nodded firmly. 'Very good. Shall we be on our way?'

* * *

Louisa tried a couple of subtle questions during the journey, but Mary batted them away with vague answers and seemed intent on taking in the scenery. Eventually, they turned into the gate and drove along the rim of the basin to the turning circle in front of the house. Louisa leapt from the driver's seat and opened the sliding door of the van. Mary stepped out and went to the edge to look down into the valley.

'Oh my, it is so beautiful!'

Louisa joined her. 'It's a gorgeous place, and they've done so much with it.'

Merlot came bounding around the corner of the house barking, and ran straight to the woman, his tail wagging. She dropped her handbag and rubbed his ears.

'Hello, my pretty boy. Look at how you've grown!'

Before Louisa could ask her another question, she picked up her suitcase and walked up the steps to the open door, Merlot running after her. Louisa followed, but Mary turned around with her hand on the doorknob.

'Thank you, my dear, I'm fine from here.' She stepped inside and closed the door.

* * *

Anna was making a salad at the kitchen bench when she looked up and saw her mother-in-law standing in the doorframe, watching her. She dropped the knife in shock, opened her mouth and shut it again. Mary extended her arms and Anna ran to her. Their embrace was tight, long and silent. When they pulled back, they were both crying softly.

'Oh, we've missed you so much,' Anna said as she brushed the tears from her face.

'Where is he?' Mary asked in a small voice.

'In the garden.'

Anna gestured to her. 'Come with me. He'll be beyond thrilled.'

Mary took her hand, and they walked across the kitchen together and out the door to the path.

'Let me check, first. He was up a ladder before, and I don't want him to fall.'

Mary nodded and stepped inside the doorway. Anna walked slowly and steadily down the path. Vinnie was still perched on the ladder hanging red paper lanterns. She stopped beside him and touched his leg.

'Vinnie.'

He looked down at her, saw the tear streaks and frowned. 'What's up?' he asked.

'I want you to come down. I have a surprise, and I think you'd better be on the ground.'

He smiled suspiciously. 'Is this one of your pranks?'

She bit her bottom lip and shook her head. 'I promise you you'll like it, just climb down.'

'Okay, boss.'

He came down the ladder and took her in his arms. 'What's my surprise?'

She pointed towards the steps where Mary was coming down. Vinnie dropped the lantern. He started to say something, then swallowed it and ran towards his mother. She reached the bottom and looked up just in time to raise her arms as he arrived.

'My boy!'

They hugged tightly for nearly a minute. Anna joined them as Vinnie let his mother go.

CHAPTER TWENTY-NINE

SHOWDOWN

Three hours after Mary's flight from Santiago, another two planes landed at Auckland International Airport within fifteen minutes of each other. The first was a Singapore Airlines A380 Airbus from London via Singapore. Norman Lane was a first-class passenger with a small, but very comfortable, suite. He had been trying to distract himself with a magazine, but as the plane taxied to the terminal, he let it drop to the floor and watched the view outside one of the three windows of his suite.

The second plane was also an airbus, but this one was an Emirates plane from Dubai. Peter Harper had flown economy and enjoyed the flight – the service had been excellent, and he had watched several movies.

Inside the terminal he retrieved his bag from the luggage carousel and wheeled it towards the baggage x-ray queue. He was a patient man and had a healthy respect for people in uniform doing their job.

Lane was further through the arrival process. He walked past the immigration queues and into a priority area.

A female immigration officer was waiting to receive his documents. 'Morning, sir. What's the nature of your visit?'

He smiled at her. 'Holiday and some wine tasting.'

She glanced at the photo and put the passport into a scanner. 'And how long do you plan on staying, Mr Carter?'

'Not long enough, I'm afraid. Work calls me back. Ten days.'

She read his forms, glanced up at him again, stamped the passport, marked the forms and handed them all back to him.

'Thank you, sir. Enjoy your wine.'

He smiled as he took back his documentation. 'Oh, I'm sure I will.'

At the x-ray machine, Harper pushed the extendable handle into the top of his bag and lifted it onto the conveyer belt. He handed his form to the official.

'Thank you, sir.'

Lane came through the doors and paused to scan the waiting crowd. They created a tunnel in front of him and then fanned out into the wider terminal space. A row of men and women stood slightly behind each other down one side, each holding a printed sign. About halfway down he spotted a sign with 'Carter' on it and strode over to the woman.

She extended her hand. 'Mr Carter? I'm from the Langham, your courtesy car to the hotel.'

'Excellent!' He beamed at her. 'Thank you so much.'

He left the trolley in front of her and strode off towards the door. She watched him for a second, raised an eyebrow and then pushed the trolley after him.

Five minutes later, Harper came through the doors and also scanned the crowd, before walking up to a man holding a sign with 'Harper' printed on it. The man was young, Maori, slender.

Harper held out his hand as he approached. 'Are you looking for me? DI Harper?'

The man shook his hand, a smile of relief on his face. 'Yes, sir. DC Ruwhiu. Welcome to New Zealand.'

'Thanks. If we could drop by the hotel, I'd like a shower and a change of clothes. And then I'll brief your boss.'

'Of course, sir. This way.'

Harper stood beside DC Ruwhiu as the young policeman opened the car door. They were on the edge of the car park, with only a stretch of sidewalk between them and the internal road out of the airport complex. A black Lexus, with 'The Langham Hotel Courtesy Car' written in curly gold script on the side, glided past them. Harper caught a glimpse of the profile of the backseat passenger in his peripheral vision. He did a double-take, but the car was disappearing down the road. When he turned back, his companion was watching him.

'Sir?' he asked anxiously.

Harper shook his head. 'Nothing. Just jetlag shadows.'

* * *

Norman wasn't sure what to expect, but the pub was more like an American bar. It was a low-slung modern building that looked like a warehouse from the outside. The interior was noisy and bathed in bright lights, with a jukebox, a busy pool table and large TVs showing the local horse racing.

He went straight to the bar and ordered a neat scotch. It was early afternoon and he was jetlagged. This was something he wanted to get over and done with as quickly as possible.

A bearded and tattooed Maori man moved down the bar to stand beside him.

Lane glanced at the man and nodded.

'Afternoon,' the man said.

'Afternoon. I heard this was the place to come for some hunting. Someone called Mick?'

The man nodded slowly. 'Could be me. You the one who called?'

The barman put a glass down in front of Lane and poured the scotch.

'Thank you. Could be.'

Norman downed the drink in one.

'Follow me,' the man said as he turned on his heel and walked towards the door.

Norman raised an eyebrow, took a banknote from his wallet and put it on the bar. 'Nice house scotch.'

The barman watched him leave. 'Thank you, sir. You take care.'

* * *

Norman followed the man across the car park to a large black SUV. The man held his hand out. 'Money.'

Norman shook his head. 'Merchandise.'

The man opened the car door. He took out a padded parcel from the front seat, and put it down on the bonnet.

'It's a bloody good piece,' he said.

Norman grunted and pulled a gun from the bag. 'Should be, for the price.'

The man shrugged. 'It's clean and unregistered, and the only prints on it now are yours.'

Norman cocked the gun, examined it and clicked the trigger. Then he sighed. 'The last man who spoke to me like that ended up dying a slow and painful death,' he said.

The corners of the man's mouth twitched with humour. 'You trying to frighten me?'

'If you had any brains. I need ammunition and I need some muscle, armed and trained. Someone not afraid to kill.'

The man hesitated for a second and then shook his head. 'It's not that easy. He'll have to bugger off to Oz. Small country, all the muscle knows where to find –'

'Double whatever you usually charge. I need him today.'

'Okay, time and place and he'll be there.'

'Waiheke ferry, five o'clock.'

* * *

As twilight turned to evening, the guests started to arrive at the winery. Some cars were parked on the turning circle; others pulled in alongside the driveway and stopped. The front door was open and people walked up the slate steps, chattering and laughing.

Out in the garden the tables were groaning with food and bottles of wine. Decorations hung from every structure, and red Chinese lanterns swung from the trees that lined the path down to the buildings in the basin below.

An eclectic group of people stood talking, glasses in hand. Vinnie watched them with a deep sense of satisfaction. They were good people and they had accepted the English immigrants without a moment's hesitation. He tried not to feel guilty about the deception. As Anna had pointed out, this was their new life, their new names, and they weren't lying.

Over in one corner his mother was in deep conversation with the proprietor of one of the most famous wineries on the island. Everyone had been delighted to meet Mary. Her excitement at being reunited with her 'darlings' was palpable, and she was, so far, managing to remember their new names.

Out of the corner of his eye, he could see Louisa trying to casually sidle towards him. She fancied him, which was flattering, but it was also important that Anna didn't feel threatened by it.

'Dominic, what a gorgeous setting. And congrats on your very first harvest. You've done wonders with this place.'

He kissed her on each cheek. 'Thank you, Lou. It certainly feels good.'

'And your mother is such a gem. I don't know why she didn't tell me who she was.'

Vinnie smiled and sipped his wine. There was something about this situation that was genuinely farcical. 'She's eccentric.'

Louisa brushed her hair from her face and smiled into his eyes. 'Are you pleased with the press?'

He nodded enthusiastically. 'Absolutely! It was a hot summer and I'm confident it'll be a superb vintage. All the readings were excellent.'

She leaned in towards him and placed her hand on his chest. 'Would it be too cheeky of me to ask? I'd love to try a little from the barrel. It gives me so much more to say to my clients when I bring them here.' Her voice was barely above a whisper.

He hesitated. Could she be more obvious?

'Before it gets really busy. Only if you have time,' she continued.

He extended his arm towards the path. 'Why not? But I can't take long.'

* * *

The barrel hall was dimly lit – only the lights on the outside rows were on. The barrels were stacked three high along the length of each wall, and there was another double row down the middle of the long room. Each barrel had a white label, with writing in black ink, stuck to it.

Vinnie dipped a wine thief into a barrel, drew out some liquid and then dropped it into two tasting glasses. He held one out to Louisa. Their hands touched as she took it.

'Cheers,' she said.

She tasted the wine and smiled. 'You can taste what it will become. The depth of flavour is there already. It's lovely, Dom.'

He nodded, swirled the glass and took a sip.

'It's part of the next blend of –'

A frown of concern crossed his face, and he bent down to look at the label. No way should it taste that raw. 'But that's wrong!'

He moved a couple of barrels along and read the label. Wrong barrel, wrong row and wrong blend.

'What the –?' he muttered under his breath as he strode over to the row against the right-hand wall. He checked the labels on three barrels in quick succession, all completely in the wrong place. A sick feeling started to swirl in the pit of his stomach. Gabby had assured him that the label system worked well.

'Is everything okay, Dom?' Louisa asked uncertainly.

Was she still here? He needed to fix this and fast.

He returned to her and took the glass from her hand. 'Everything's just fine. You'll have to excuse me, though. I'm sure you can find your own way back.'

'Of course,' she said. She paused.

She needed to leave; surely she would take the hint. He put her glass down, picked up the wine-thief and went to other side of the hall, squatted on his haunches and read the label on a barrel.

'Thanks so much for the sneak peek, Dom. I'll just –' She turned and left.

Vinnie opened the barrel, drew out some wine and let it drain into the glass. He swirled the wine around, breathed in the aroma and then tasted it. It was a new press. 'Shit!' He spat it out onto the concrete.

A sudden sound down the back of the hall caught his attention. He wasn't alone.

'Who's there?' he called out, as he straightened up and peered into the gloom. No response.

'Gabby? What the fuck's up with all these barrels? What have you done?'

Suddenly he could hear steps on the concrete floor, heavy steps, a man's step. He closed the barrel and walked around the front of the middle row to stand just inside the entrance way. His anger blinded him to any danger.

A very tall figure moved out of the shadows at the other end of the hall. His left hand held Merlot by the collar and his right hand held a gun.

A hot jolt of shock stabbed through Vinnie's chest, and he grabbed a barrel to steady himself.

'You!'

'Come now, Mr Whitney-Ross,' Lane's voice rumbled in the enclosed space. 'I'd have been very disappointed if you hadn't recognised me, even after all these years. Do I look that unlike my son?'

He smiled and moved to one side. Another man, bald and with tattoos on his neck, muscles bulging under his tight-fitting shirt and a gun in hand, stepped up beside him. Lane had brought local muscle.

Vinnie moved backwards towards the door and pulled his cell phone from his pocket. 'I've no idea who you mean, but I do have my phone –'

Lane pointed the gun at Merlot's head. 'But *I* have my gun, and I will kill your dog without a moment's hesitation.'

Vinnie gave a slight nod and put the phone away. 'What do you want?' he asked. He knew the answer, but dialogue was better than bullets.

'That's better. You're Witness A, and you testified at my son's trial. You betrayed your childhood friend. Don't bother deny–'

'How did you find me?'

Lane gave him a smile that was almost a taunt. 'You've been lazy. You made two big mistakes: stealing Kelt's wine and reselling it, and keeping this dog.'

Shit! How on earth did he know about Kelt's wine? *Stall for time – someone will come looking.* 'And you've mixed up the labels on my barrels.'

Lane shrugged.

'We were bored while we waited for you. It was fun. Plus I knew it would annoy you. A lot.'

As he spoke, Lane and the other man walked slowly forward until they stood only a metre in front of Vinnie. The height difference was very apparent, and Lane was in great physical shape for a man who must have been in his seventies by now.

'I want you to recant your evidence,' Lane continued, 'make it perfectly clear that you lied about seeing my son in that house. You were mistaken. The man you saw was not Marcus.'

'Or? I take it there is an "or".'

Lane nodded. 'Oh, most definitely. *Or* I'll find a way to poison your wine. *Or* I'll kill your dog and then your beautiful wife.'

Time to play the card. 'Did it not occur to you that I might have a little insurance?' Vinnie asked.

Lane frowned with impatience and pointed the gun down at Merlot again. 'Don't play with me, Vinnie. I don't like dogs and I'm a bit short-tempered where my son is –'

'I have Kelt's notebook.'

Lane looked at him in genuine surprise, and the gun jerked away from the dog's head. 'He showed me where it was really hidden, in case anything ever happened at the club. He didn't expect your men to come to the house. I took it with me that night. Never told the police.'

Lane was looking at him with new interest. It would buy some time. 'And it's here?'

'Of course. My lawyer has a photocopy, to be handed to the police if anything happens to me, or to Anna.'

Lane scoffed at him, but it wasn't convincing. 'Without Kelt, it means –'

Vinnie held up his hands, palms towards Lane. 'Fine. The bank account numbers and names and dates are very clear. It's a detailed record of fraud and money-laundering on a massive scale, through his club and others. Very clever, too. Of course, you don't have to believe me. You could just take the risk.'

Lane scowled and indicated the doorway to the courtyard with the gun. 'Give me both copies of the notebook, change your testimony, and you and your family will be left in peace. You have my word.'

'Very comforting thought.' Vinnie pointed to the rapidly fading light outside. 'It's buried in the vineyard. Not a lot of daylight left.'

Lane turned to the thug standing beside him. 'Take him and get it. If he tries anything, wing him – *don't* kill him. Understand?'

The thug nodded, and Lane turned back to Vinnie. 'Give me your cell phone.'

Vinnie handed it over reluctantly, and Lane pocketed it.

'If I hear shots, I'll kill your dog or your wife. Or both.'

* * *

The evening was drawing in fast. Vinnie and the thug rode two quad bikes up the steepest row of vines, to the rim of the basin. As he rode, Vinnie's mind raced ahead. There would be only one chance, and he had to make it work.

He stopped, dismounted, took a heavy metal torch and a trowel out of the box on the back of the bike, walked to a rose bush at the end of a row and looked up at the pine trees planted across the road. The thug sat astride the bike, gun drawn, and watched. Vinnie made a show of counting the trees carefully, then looked back at the rows and nodded. As he bent down, the thug got off the bike and walked over to him.

'Dig!'

Vinnie switched on the torch and laid it on the ground. Then he took the trowel and began to dig. After four small handfuls of dirt, he stopped and looked up. *Are you as dumb as you look?* 'Must be deeper than I thought,' he said.

The thug grunted, pushed him out of the way and grabbed the trowel. 'Give it here.'

Vinnie picked up the torch and shone it into the hole. The man dug one-handed at a much faster pace. As he touched something solid with the tip of the trowel, Vinnie raised the torch in a high arc and hit him, hard.

The man let out a loud, surprised roar and fell backwards, blood gushing from a deep cut. Then he rolled over and started to pull himself up to his knees.

Vinnie hit him a second time. The torch glanced off his bald head. 'Christ, your head's hard!'

Vinnie whipped it upwards across the thug's face and blood spurted from his nose as he fell. The thug roared again: 'Fuck!'

Vinnie grabbed the gun, pulled the notebook from the hole and ran to the bike, leapt on and fired up the engine. The thug pulled himself to his feet, his hands still grasping at his face.

Vinnie raced down the narrow row back towards the buildings. He wasn't sure what to do next, but he still had his bargaining chip and now he had a gun.

The thug leapt onto the other bike and followed him, blood streaming from the cut in his head and his broken nose.

As they burst from the end of the row, Vinnie glanced over his shoulder. His bike was older and he was only just ahead.

As the bikes drew level, the thug launched himself sideways. The momentum knocked them both off the bikes and they wrestled to the ground, the machines skidding away on the grass. Their arms were locked and the gun was held between their bodies. Vinnie clawed at the man's face with his free hand. The thug was trying to turn the barrel towards Vinnie. Suddenly a muffled shot rang out and the thug relaxed his grip on the gun barrel as he slumped back against a rose bush, a gaping hole through his stomach.

Vinnie scrambled to his feet and staggered backwards. The man's blood was all over his shirt. How on earth did that happen? Once again, kill or be killed. He bent down and felt for a pulse. Nothing.

'Jesus Christ! Why can't you people leave me alone?'

CHAPTER THIRTY

THE VAT

Vinnie ducked behind a stack of empty bins as he reached the edge of the courtyard. Lane was just outside the entrance to the barrel hall. Anna stood in front of him, and he had a hand around the top of her arm and his gun to her temple. Shit! She must have come to see what was keeping him. The terror on her face made his stomach churn. His plan had been to get across the courtyard and up to the house to phone the police, but he couldn't leave her like that.

Merlot stopped circling them and stood directly in front, his ears forward and his tail rigid, his weight on his front legs. He was snarling and giving them his best guttural growl.

'Go get 'em, boy,' Vinnie whispered as he watched his dog preparing to attack. Suddenly Merlot lunged at Lane's leg with an open mouth and sharp teeth snapping.

'Shit!' Lane yelled as he kicked out at Merlot. He let Anna go, then shot the dog in his rear hind quarter.

Merlot let out a loud yelp and limped away.

'You fucking bastard!'

Anna's voice was shrill with fury. Her devotion to the dog overrode everything, and Vinnie felt as though his heart would break. He broke cover and walked rapidly towards them, the thug's gun pointing straight ahead in one hand and the notebook raised in the other. A strange calm descended upon him. He could do this; he could outwit an old man.

'No! Vinnie, no!' Anna cried out.

Lane grabbed her, and the gun went back to her temple.

'Shot the dog. The beautiful wife is next.'

Vinnie shook the notebook.

'Not if you want this. Here it is, Lane. The original. Let her go.'

'Where's my muscle?' Lane asked.

'He sprang a leak. He's fertilising my Cab Sav.'

Lane shook his head. 'You clever arsehole. I've clearly underestimated you, Vinnie. You take after your father. You could have a great career as a criminal, and I could make you very rich.'

Vinnie glared at him. He could taste years of resentment and betrayal – it tasted like acid.

'You've no beef with her. Let her go. I'll do whatever you want. Just let her go.'

Lane frowned and shook his head again. He was playing for time. 'You know I can't do that. It's time for your family to pay –'

The rage had started to build inside Vinnie from his first sight of Lane and now it boiled over. 'Pay? Fuck you, you bastard! We lost our whole lives because of you and your murdering son. Well, not anymore. It's time to fight.'

As he yelled he walked forward, clenched his fist around the notebook and drew his elbow back into his stomach. He knew Anna was watching, and he knew she would understand. She read the gesture instantly, and jerked her elbows backwards into Lane's gut.

The double blow winded him, and he dropped the gun.

She spun around, stomped on his instep and thrust her knee hard up into his groin. 'From beautiful wife!' she screamed at him.

He bent over double in agony. 'Ahh! You bitch!'

Vinnie sprang forward and grabbed a wine bottle by the neck. He hit Lane over the head with the bottle, then punched him on the side of the face with his closed fist.

'That's for my father!' he yelled.

Lane dropped to his knees.

'Run!' Vinnie called to Anna. 'Call the police. Get Gabby and as many of the pickers as you can. Fermentation room.'

He ran across the courtyard and up the three steps to the fermentation room. Anna tore her gaze from Lane's straightening figure and sprinted in the opposite direction towards the house. As she passed Lane's gun, she kicked it away under a pallet of bottles.

* * *

The natural light in the fermentation room was almost gone. Vinnie hit the switch as he entered, and harsh, artificial light flooded the scene. He crossed the wet floor, put the gun in his belt and started to climb the steel steps to the one vat that still contained must. This was a highly dangerous option, but it was the only one that offered revenge.

Lane reached the foot of the steps as Vinnie moved off onto the gantry. Vinnie took the notebook from his pocket and held it out over the liquid.

'Come on you sick, murdering bastard,' he called down. 'You want us, you come and get us.'

Lane pulled himself up the steps and, as he reached the top, Vinnie flicked the notebook over his head and onto the floor as he kicked Lane in the face. Lane's head jerked back, but he grasped Vinnie's ankle in one hand and pulled him towards the ladder. Vinnie fell backwards, seized the side of the tank on the way down and battled back to his feet. Lane hauled himself onto the gantry and the two bodies met, fists flying.

Lane was six inches taller and was punching from above, but he was older and nowhere near as muscular as Vinnie, and his blows glanced off Vinnie's shoulders. Both men grunted with the effort. Try as he might, though, Vinnie couldn't land a substantial hit – Lane was just too tall.

The metal floor was slippery and they both lost their balance and hit the tank as they slid down. For a moment they stared at each other, naked loathing on both faces. Lane snatched at the gun in Vinnie's belt, but Vinnie countered and bashed Lane's forearm against the metal. The gun flew from his grasp and into the must.

'Contaminate my wine?' Vinnie panted. 'I don't think so.'

He pushed himself off Lane's chest and stood up. As Lane started to rise, Vinnie swung for him, but Lane blocked the punch and twisted his arm, wrenching his shoulder.

Lane hissed in his ear: 'Fuck your vinegar piss! There's something I haven't told you –'

Vinnie jerked himself away, breathing deeply to combat the rising CO_2 and the pain in his body.

'What would I want to know from *you*?' He spat out the last word.

Lane smiled slowly and wiped the blood and juice from his own face. 'I saw your stupid father die, before I put the gun in his hand.'

'But –'

Again Lane snorted.

'All these years you thought he killed himself. All that shame and betrayal. You even came to my father and apologised! I made Bert write the note, and then I –'

Vinnie let out a primeval scream and launched himself at Lane's waist. The momentum drove both men sideways. They teetered for a moment against the rim of the tank. Lane resisted and tried to push Vinnie away, but both sets of feet gave way and they toppled in, still clinging to each other.

* * *

They were sensations he recognised, cold, wet and sticky, followed by the overpowering smell and lack of oxygen. Lane grasped at him and hung on, not in anger now, in desperation. Vinnie landed a weak punch, peeled Lane's clawing fingers off his arms and kicked off the big man's flailing body. He flung himself at the smooth steel side, reached up with his hands and gripped the rim. *Take a deep breath and hold on.* The voice came from somewhere inside.

Out in the middle of the tank Lane fought against the viscous liquid and choked as the CO_2 enveloped him. 'Help me! Vinnie!' The more he writhed, the more rapidly he sank.

Vinnie tried to pull himself above the cloud of gas, but his hands slipped and he had to scramble to get his hold back. The pain in his lungs was agonising, and he tried again to gasp some air. *Hold on, they won't be long.* They better not be; he didn't have long.

* * *

At the same moment that Anna and Gabby reached the entrance to the fermentation room, Peter Harper sprinted up the steps, followed by DC Ruwhiu.

'Anna!' Harper exclaimed.

She stopped in her tracks. 'Good God! Peter!'

Gabby looked from one to the other in complete bewilderment.

'What are you –' Anna asked.

'Lane, he knows about –'

She pointed inside. 'He's here. Vinnie ran, Lane's chasing him.'

Gabby looked towards the tank. 'Get the ladder!'

As she indicated the ladder against the wall, Ruwhiu reached it. Gabby ran to the tank and started to climb, Harper just behind her. Ruwhiu handed the ladder to Anna, who handed it to Harper, who handed it up to Gabby, who hooked it over the rim of the tank.

'Get me that plunger,' Gabby barked.

The desperation in her voice was clear. She pointed to a metal plunger hanging from a hook on the wall. Ruwhiu retrieved it and handed it up the chain to her.

'Dom, can you hear me?' Gabby called out. 'I've got the plunger. Reach out, grab the plunger.'

* * *

Vinnie was losing consciousness. His body felt numb and his mind was wandering. The bitter juice splashed into his mouth and stung his eyes. He could see the metal rod coming towards him, a silver shape amidst all the red must – there and then gone, there and then gone. Something else shimmered in the distance – two blue eyes and brown curly hair. Where was Anna? Wasn't she the last thing he was supposed to see as he died? All he could hear was a line from *Jesus Christ Superstar* about sinking in a puddle, or was it a pool, of wine?

Gabby clambered over the edge and held onto the side of the ladder. She stretched the plunger out until it just bumped Vinnie on the shoulder.

His fingers slipped off the rim and he clutched the rod, almost an involuntary gesture.

'Yes, that's right. Come on, Dom. Nearly there!' Gabby called.

He wrapped his arm around the plunger, and she pulled him through the must to the ladder. He could see her now, the eyes, the freckles, the ponytail, the vision swimming in front of his eyes. Was it the Angel of Death or were they coming to rescue him?

She looked back at Harper and Ruwhiu, who stood on the gantry above her. 'He can't climb. He's got nothing left. Help me haul him up.'

Harper leaned past her and seized Vinnie's shirt. He rose up out of the must, his hands running along, but not gripping, the sides of the ladder. As soon as the men could get a decent grip on him, Gabby ducked sideways and they hoisted him up and over the rim. He fell onto the gantry, sucking in deep breaths of oxygen and coughing up must.

Harper knelt down beside him. 'Where's Lane?' he asked gently.

Vinnie pointed towards the tank and spat out skins. Gabby clambered over the edge and back onto the framework. Like Vinnie, she dripped with red juice.

'He's gone under,' she panted. 'Only hope would be to drain the must. But he won't have survived this long …' Her voice trailed off, and she looked up at them.

Harper nodded, and he and Ruwhiu helped Vinnie to his feet.

'Do it,' he ordered. 'Make sure.'

* * *

As Vinnie and Anna walked slowly across the courtyard, his arm around her shoulders, a dog whimpered somewhere close in the darkness. They stopped.

'Merlot,' Vinnie called urgently. 'Come here, boy. Come to Daddy.'

Merlot limped out from the vehicle shed, his tail wagging slowly. Vinnie went down on one knee and the dog wobbled over to him.

'There, there, boy. Let me see. Good boy.'

He cradled the dog and gently examined the hole in his hindquarter. Merlot turned and tried to lick him. Anna knelt and stroked his head, and Merlot licked her fingers.

'That's my good boy,' she said softly.

Vinnie looked up at her. 'It's a flesh wound, more of a graze.'

Anna put her face down and kissed the dog and rubbed his ears. 'Oh, thank God! You were such a brave boy, growling at the bad man. Yes, you were.'

She looked up at Vinnie. 'Well, the vet's up there, drinking our wine, so he may as well patch Merlot up while he's here,' she said.

Vinnie grinned at her and wiped juice from his face with his hand. 'A house call! Let me take a shower before you tell him. I don't really want everyone to know I've taken a swim in the Malbec.'

* * *

Twenty minutes later, Anna was standing in the kitchen, staring out the window at the party in full swing in the illuminated garden below. She turned as Vinnie came into the room. He had showered and changed. As they embraced, he enveloped her and held her tight.

'I could have lost you,' she murmured.

He kissed the top of her head and buried his face in her hair. 'No chance. I'm not that easy to misplace.'

So much had changed in a matter of moments and she felt overwhelmed, but still his humour could make her smile.

She waited a moment, then pulled back and grinned up at him. 'Dear Lord in heaven, we've got some explaining to do to Gabby!' she said.

'You think?'

Harper appeared in the doorway. As Vinnie turned towards him he felt a tickle of dread in the back of his exhausted mind. Peter wasn't just there to warn them, to save them from Norman. Marcus would find out where his father had died, and how and why. Their beloved Rocky Bay was no longer safe.

'Come in, Peter. Nice to see you again.'

Harper walked across to join them. 'Just wanted to tell you the ambulance is here. They'll take the bodies away. I've called CID –'

'But they'll accept self-defence, won't they?'

The sudden fear in Anna's voice was plain to both men.

Harper smiled reassuringly. 'Absolutely. I just wish I'd got here earlier,' he said. 'We'll all need to go across to the Auckland station –'

Anna touched his arm. 'Tonight? He's been through so much, and we have a garden full of confused, but unsuspecting, guests. And Mary's here.'

Harper nodded. He and Vinnie exchanged a glance loaded with understanding.

'Tomorrow will be fine; we'll face it all tomorrow. I, for one, want to taste this famous wine of yours!'

Vinnie broke into a relieved grin. 'Wouldn't mind a drop myself.'

PART FIVE

CHOCOLATE

CHAPTER THIRTY-ONE

MELISSA LANE

Eventually two undertakers presented the correct documentation and were allowed to collect Steven Carter's body. The mortuary workers asked no questions and helped them load the corpse into their hearse.

Melissa Lane waited for the arrival of her husband's remains. She was tense and filled with a diffused anger that swung from Vinnie to Marcus to Norman and back to the bloody justice system. Then the practical details took over from her grief and she became determined to give her husband a good funeral. He hadn't been an easy man to live with, but he had provided well and kept his business life away from their home – except, she had to admit, for the last months. Her daughter was long dead, now her husband was dead and her son was in prison: the 'business' had all but destroyed her family.

When she faced the world it would be as the widow of an important man who had died of a heart attack while gardening at home. No one but she, Marcus, Tom and the 'family' undertakers knew about the trip to New Zealand, and that was the way it would stay.

They put the coffin in the front room and opened the lid for her to take a look, then suggested it be closed again as he had been in storage for some time. His travelling under an alias had meant there had been a delay in finding him. She touched his forehead. His skin was hard and waxy, his body looked smaller and his face was shrunken. She leaned closer and clipped a lock of his hair, then whispered: 'Goodbye, my sweet.' Then she straightened up and nodded to the men standing over by the wall.

* * *

Marcus Lane sat in his cell and wrote a letter to his mother. He'd had a phone conversation with her, during which she had told him what had happened to his father. All she knew was what the police had said about Steven Carter: he had gone swimming at a surf beach on Waiheke Island and had drowned. She knew that was untrue. Norman wasn't there for a holiday, and he would never have gone swimming – he hated beaches.

Marcus felt as though someone had stuck a knife in his heart and twisted it. They had had a tumultuous relationship, but Marcus had secretly adored and respected his father. As soon as he had heard about his father's death, he had made an immediate request for compassionate leave to attend the funeral. Now his mind was a fierce mêlée of emotions: fury, guilt, grief and frustration. He should be there for her, and he should be running the family business …

'Lane.'

He looked up. The deputy governor and a senior guard stood on the other side of his cell door.

He got to his feet and dropped the pen. 'Yes, sir.'

The deputy governor nodded and the cell door slid back.

'I have some news for you.'

'About my request?'

Marcus hated how hopeful his voice sounded, how dependant he was on these men for his happiness. It was a clear indication of how much of his edge he had lost.

The men stepped inside the cell. 'You have been a model prisoner, and it is your father. Request granted. You will be escorted by two guards and will have to wear handcuffs.'

Marcus closed his eyes for a moment. 'Thank you, sir.'

* * *

The funeral was at All Hallows Church in Twickenham. It was a big service, with lots of flowers and mourners, a choir and speeches from friends and family. Marcus spoke on behalf of his mother and thanked everyone for coming.

'My father was acutely aware of the injustice of my conviction and worked tirelessly to secure my freedom.' There was a murmur around the church. Marcus stared hard at them and the sound died. 'I loved him for that. The fact that he never gave up. I know my mother will continue the fight, and when I am a free man I'll raise a toast to Dad.'

As they walked away from the graveside service, the guards were about to direct Marcus back to the prison van when a short, middle-aged man approached them.

'Melissa, may I offer my condolences?'

She shook his extended hand. 'Thank you, Stephen.'

'Marcus, how are you?' he asked.

'Quite well, considering.'

It was Stephen Scott, Norman's senior lawyer. The two men hadn't met since the end of the trial, and Marcus was polite but distant.

'Good, good, glad to hear that. Melissa, can I come and see you? I want to discuss relevant issues.'

Melissa nodded. 'Of course. Give me a couple of days and then call.'

* * *

A week later Melissa sat at her dining room table and read her husband's will. Everything was left to her, and then to Marcus on her death. Norman had changed his will when his son went to prison, appointing Tom McGregor as his successor until Marcus was released, and leaving the house and his fortune to Melissa if he predeceased her.

'I have one question before we go any further, Melissa,' Stephen Scott said, his tone quiet and reassuring.

She looked at him. For some reason she found him repulsive, reptilian and smug. 'Which is?'

'Where did Norman die and what was he actually doing?'

She didn't answer him. Instead, she folded the will in half and laid it on the table. They gazed at each other.

'What makes you think he didn't die of a heart attack in the garden?' she asked.

He shrugged. 'Instinct. And I knew Norman.'

She stared into the middle distance for a full minute. What would it take to make him disappear and never come back? Can you kill someone simply because they are odious? She was quite sure Norman would, and had.

'Why do you want to know? Does it change anything?' she asked.

'It might do. If he was on business connected with Marcus it might change a great deal.'

'How?' Her voice was sharp.

'Was it to do with Marcus?'

'Yes.'

'Did he find out the identity and location of Witness A?'

'He … might have done.'

'Tell me about him. Did he kill Norman?'

Melissa hesitated again. This was not a conversation she had expected to have so soon, if at all. She hadn't worked out what to do next, and now this lawyer was forcing her into a corner.

'I don't know who or what killed Norman. Witness A was Vinnie Whitney-Ross, a wine merchant. He delivered wine to Kelt, which was why he was in the cellar.'

'And they put him in witness protection. In New Zealand. That's very unusual.'

'Yes. The odd thing is that we knew his father. Bert Whitney-Ross was Tobias's accountant, and Vinnie and Marcus used to play together as children.'

Scott sat up very straight, and then leaned forward towards her. Something had caught his interest. 'They *knew* each other?'

'Yes, that's why the defence were so sure of their witness.'

Scott opened his briefcase and took out a legal pad. He began writing notes.

'How did it end? His father's relationship with Tobias?' he asked.

'That's another reason: Bert shot himself. It was almost forty years ago, but I remember his wife, Vinnie's mother, was very angry with us.'

'That's it! That's what we need.'

His sudden outburst startled her and she pulled back.

'What do you mean, Stephen?'

He was scribbling on his pad. 'It was an unsound conviction. Based on the evidence of a witness with reason to be biased, a reason to lie. They would have told him that they were keeping his identity secret to keep him safe – really it was because no jury would convict on the word of a man with that much bias against your family.'

'So what do we do now?'

There was hint of rising hope in her voice, and she fought against the emotion.

'I apply for the Royal prerogative of mercy and challenge the verdict, because we know that Witness A was known to the family and was biased against them, due to his father's suicide.'

She was staring at him. 'Really?'

He nodded empathically. 'Yes. There is precedent. I want you to go and see Marcus and talk to him about this Vinnie. Find out anything that we can use to show bias. I'll try and talk to Don to find out what happened, why Bert shot himself. His memory is intermittent, but when he's lucid he has a font of knowledge. And you talk to Tom about anything Marcus can give up as information – a gun cache or drugs, something belonging to another gang, a gem we can use as leverage.'

'I'll see him as soon as I can organise it.'

He stopped writing and looked up at her. She could see her excitement mirrored in his eyes. There was no denying it, for the first time in many months she felt a sense of hope.

He gave her a smug smile. 'If Norman had come to me with this information I might have been able to stop him rushing off to New Zealand and getting himself killed.'

She smiled back ruefully.

'I married into a family of hotheads.'

CHAPTER THIRTY-TWO

NEW BEGINNINGS, AGAIN

May 2013

The clouds were touched with pink and gold. The winter predawn darkness receded quickly, and the scene from the veranda sparkled with the promise of a new day. In the paddock to the left, two horses grazed on grass that was stiff with frost, and chickens scratched in the cold earth over by the barn. Tall trees swayed, and the wind in their leaves sounded like the sea. Vinnie missed the way the ocean broke on the rocks at the bottom of the cliffs in Rocky Bay.

He sat in a wicker chair and watched the rural world around him coming to life. Merlot was off exploring somewhere, following a thousand new scents. Anna was sound asleep in their warm bed. He could feel her tossing and turning at night, and it was good when she slept on in the mornings. Vinnie liked this time of day because his mind was clear and the stress was stilled by the quiet. Piece by piece he went over the past few months, the good, the bad, the stupid, the careless, the things he couldn't change. When he had talked to the police psychiatrist, she had told him to accept what had happened, the mistakes he had made and what it had nearly cost him, and let it go. He was to tell himself that Anna had forgiven him, his mother had forgiven him, and so he needed to forgive himself.

Still, he sometimes woke in the middle of the night and, in those seconds between dreaming and understanding, he saw the faces of the men he'd killed. In each situation it'd been a 'kill or be killed' scenario and he could honestly say he didn't regret his actions, but never in his wildest imaginings had he seen himself taking another human life. It was one thing to forgive himself and another to live with the consequences.

They had been truly happy at Rocky Bay, and he missed the routine and the people deeply. Once again everything had been sold up by the police and the money banked. The three of them were hiding in an isolated safe house deep in the farming province of the Waikato, about two hours south of Auckland. They were in limbo. They didn't shop or socialise, and the house felt like a gilded prison.

But today Peter Harper was coming to see them to discuss the future. They had to tell him what they wanted. Vinnie grimaced. What did they want? It was all too raw and too important to resolve in one day. Every time they started to discuss it, someone got upset and everyone went quiet and the whole conversation died. All he wanted was to go back to the beginning – whether that was working for David in London, or making wine with Gabby on Waiheke Island, was something he couldn't decipher right now – both were equally impractical.

Vinnie leaned back and closed his eyes. *Let it go … Start again … Forgive yourself … Take your time …* All the clichés swirled through his tired brain, and not for the first time he raised his forefinger to his temple and pretended to shoot himself in the head.

'So, how are we all?' Peter asked. He smiled at the three people sitting and looking expectantly at him. He could see the exhaustion in their faces. There was tension in the air.

'Fine and dandy,' said Vinnie. His voice was deadpan and his expression didn't change.

'Good. I've been thinking about what to say, and I've decided that you don't want me to sugar-coat anything.'

'Good grief, no. Tell it like it is,' said Anna.

Peter felt a trickle of concern; they had become impossible to read.

'Okay, I'm going to be blunt. You have some decisions to make. If you want to stay in wine, you'll need to relocate to another country. You will also need to accept that there will always be a significant element of danger. Herman Granger knows what you look like – if you make great wine using another alias his wine blog will track you down. And he won't let the story rest.'

He paused, but no one said anything.

'If you stay in New Zealand, but not in wine, we can find you somewhere to live and something to do, but you need to lead … smaller lives.'

'What does that mean?' asked Vinnie.

'Lives that don't attract attention, lives that don't show the talents that you have.'

Vinnie shrugged. Peter could see his frustration.

'What do you want me to be? A labourer? An accountant?' Vinnie asked.

'Not necessarily –'

'Who are we?' Mary asked suddenly.

The other two turned and looked at her.

'We are who we have always been,' Vinnie said firmly. 'No one can take your identity away from you.'

'But new names will help us to feel as though we belong somewhere. You have both done this before, but I haven't. I still feel as though I am on holiday, and any moment it's going to be time to go home and weed my garden.'

Anna took her hand and squeezed it. 'That feeling gets better, I promise.'

Peter opened his briefcase. It was time to move them along. 'Actually, I have your new identities here. They were created in England because you're obviously migrants.' He lifted out a large brown envelope.

'Aha, another one of those,' Vinnie said, his face betraying nothing.

Peter smiled at him. 'Yes. Hopefully the last one. In here I have passports, birth certificates, driver's licences, credit cards and bank cards for your new accounts.'

'Let me guess: Heathcliff,' Vinnie said.

'Or Copperfield? Shakespeare, perhaps?' Anna added.

Peter laughed, but it sounded strangely hollow. 'No, no more literary allusions. You are Michael and Charlotte Wilson, and this is your Aunt Muriel – Muriel Wilson.'

There was silence.

'I'm not going to leave you in the wind this time, Vinnie. We should have helped you to settle more last time. You tell me the kind of life you want and we will find it, and you will have a New Zealand handler who will look after you.'

Vinnie ran his hand through his curls. Peter knew that tic; there was an internal battle going on.

'To be honest, Peter, I have no idea. Last time I knew as soon as your boss asked me to testify.'

Peter nodded. 'You've had a deeply traumatic time.'

'I know what I want.'

Everyone turned to look at Anna. She was very composed, and she had spoken quietly and firmly.

'What?'

Vinnie sounded genuinely surprised. They haven't talked about this, Peter thought, as he looked from one to the other.

'I want to live in a warm place, where it doesn't ever snow, close to the sea, in a small community. I want to start a company that we can all work in, a company that makes very exclusive chocolates.'

'Do you want a shop?' Peter asked.

She shook her head. 'No. Mail order only, supplying speciality shops. We infuse the chocolate with flavours – sea salt, lemon oil, black pepper and cardamom – and then we fill them with alcohol – wine, lemoncello, Baileys, port, brandy, gin, vodka, rum. Pure ingredients and the best-quality handmade chocolates and truffles.'

Peter nodded slowly and looked at Vinnie.

'Vinnie?'

Vinnie smiled at Anna. 'Brilliant idea. Can I come?'

She smiled back. 'If you work hard and you taste everything for me.'

'Deal.'

Vinnie looked at Mary.

'Mum?'

She put her hand to her mouth and shook her head in amazement. 'It sounds wonderful. Can I come, too?'

Anna smiled at her. 'You most certainly can. You're our cover. As far as the world knows you make the chocolates and Aunt Muriel's Masterpieces has to have a real-life Aunt Muriel behind it.'

CHAPTER THIRTY-THREE

MERCY AND CRACKPOTS

March 2014

The Right Honourable David McNaughton had had only one other appeal for the Royal prerogative of mercy in his three-year term as Lord High Chancellor. By the time the Lane appeal file got to him, it had been the source of considerable comment and he had much to read. He did this very carefully, his lawyer's brain assessing each opinion and weighing up the likely public response.

Marcus Lane sounded like a particularly nasty individual, but had he had a fair trial, and was it possible that Witness A had had a vendetta against him? Was the conviction unsound? The prerogative was that of the monarch, but the Queen would be guided by his decision. As an added sweetener, Lane had offered to turn 'grass' on some of the other London gangs and give up information on guns, drugs and extortion. This was very tempting, and the police comments made it clear that the information would be extremely useful.

Still, the man was undoubtedly a hardened criminal and probably guilty of the crime. His father was not long dead, and he obviously wanted to reclaim his position as head of the Lane gang. Would the streets be safer if he was granted a retrial? McNaughton doubted it.

As the evening drew in, he packed his work away and asked his PA to order his car and driver. His constituency was in Wiltshire and he kept a London flat. The nights were still cold and he shivered, despite the heavy coat, as he walked down the steps towards the car.

His driver stood by the open rear door, an A4 white envelope in his hand.

'Evening, John.'

'Evening, sir. This was under the wipers of the car. It's addressed to you and marked private and confidential.'

McNaughton hesitated and then took the envelope. 'Thank you.'

He knew the rules – it could contain white powder, and he should leave it for his PA to open. But curiosity got the better of him. As the car lumbered through the crowded streets, he pulled the top tab off and reached inside. Three photos and a piece of paper slid into his hand. The photos were black-and-white candid shots of four children playing in the snow. His grandchildren. They were completely unaware that they were being photographed, and the laughing faces made his heart leap. Then he read the note: *You know what to decide. Their safety is in your hands.*

It was typewritten in Times Roman on a rectangular slip of paper from a notepad.

A strong visceral reflex hit him mid-chest, and his mouth seemed to fill with something sour. He swallowed the nausea down and thrust everything back into the envelope.

'John?'

The driver turned his head and looked over his shoulder. 'Yes, sir?'

'Change of direction: take me to the Met.'

Stephen Scott was incandescent with rage. He stood in his office and faced Melissa Lane. She sat very still and read the report in her hands. Finally, she looked up at him.

'This is a lie. This has nothing to do with Marcus.'

Stephen struggled to contain his emotion. 'I don't think you quite understand. I've seen the evidence, Melissa. Someone sent pictures of the Lord High Chancellor's grandchildren to him with a threatening note.'

'And I'm telling you that that someone had nothing to do with Marcus!'

'Maybe not, but it has almost certainly ruined any possibility we had of convincing the Lord High Chancellor that Marcus was unjustly convicted.'

She stood up. 'Which is why Marcus would never condone such a thing. Someone has sabotaged us. I suggest you find another legal avenue to get my son released.'

She turned on her heel and walked to the door. With her hand on the knob, she looked back at him. 'And don't ever address me in that tone again. Save your anger for the justice system.'

* * *

Melissa Lane called Tom McGregor and demanded that he find out who sent the photographs. The lawyer said they'd had a good case, a realistic chance of a retrial, and now that had gone. Someone had sabotaged the plan, and she wanted to know who. Someone was going to pay.

Tom reassured her that he was as devastated as she was and would put his best men onto it. Then he hung up and gave a small smile of satisfaction as he went back to his work.

Marcus had considered setting fire to his mattress or using the toothbrush he had been secretly sharpening to stab a guard. Eventually he had decided on a much bigger plan. The first step was a telephone call.

'Marcus, good to hear from you. How are you?'

It was Tom McGregor. The sound of his voice brought a hundred memories flooding back into Marcus's brain, and the inevitable questions: Why hadn't he sent Tom to deal to Kelt? Why had he been so stupid?

'Haven't got a lot of time, Tom. Just thought I'd let you know it's time to let my crackpot uncle loose. Soon as you can. Can you manage that?' Marcus asked.

There was a pause on the line.

It occurred to Marcus that this was a call Tom had never expected to get. He wondered how comfortable his childhood friend had become.

'Of course, give me a few days and I'll let you know when we're ready for him.'

'Mum's due here tomorrow week. She can confirm.'

'Done.'

The line went dead. Marcus stood holding the receiver in his hand. It was audacious and complicated and exquisitely dangerous. He needed very good men, and he needed them to have nerves of steel. It would take a great deal of the family money –

'Come on, motherfucker. Hang up if you're done.'

The gruff voice cut across his thoughts, and he hung up the phone and swung around to face the inmate. No brains but lots of brawn. He nodded briefly and walked away.

Melissa Lane was on her way to visit her son. She sat in the back of the car and silently rehearsed what she had to say. What would Norman have thought of this? It was going to take a frightening amount of money, almost all of the fortune Norman had amassed, and it depended on precise timing and detailed organisation. Even then, there was a very good chance it might not work. But Marcus had to try, that she understood. He trusted Tom McGregor completely, so she had to, too.

An hour later she was sitting opposite her son. He was watching her, and his dark eyes were glowing with hope and anxiety. His hair was quite grey at the temples now, and he had distinctive lines on his face. Prison was ageing him.

'Your crackpot uncle is on the loose again,' she said.

He smiled. 'Needs to be somewhere more secure.'

'We think so. Apparently the doctor said they'll move him Friday.'

He nodded at her. 'Friday sounds like a good day.'

* * *

Friday started like any other day in Belmarsh Prison. Inmates were unlocked at 8.15 and made their way to the dining area for breakfast. Except for cell 2034. Marcus had a wash, got changed, and then started a slow and methodical process of banging his forehead against the cell wall and yelling. Only the first few hurt; once the blood started to flow, it went numb.

After twenty minutes of continuous noise, two inmates came to see what was happening. As soon as one was near enough, Marcus grabbed him and put him in a choke-hold.

The man was small and light, and his feet dangled off the ground. He gave a squeal of rage before the arm around his throat severely restricted his oxygen supply. As his companion fled to raise the alarm, Marcus whipped out the toothbrush

280

he'd sharpened to a blade and cut the flailing arm to the bone. Blood spurted out.

When the guards arrived two minutes later, Marcus opened his eyes wide at them. 'Don't come in! You come in and I'll cut his fucking throat!'

The guards retreated and a siren blasted out.

* * *

'What is it you want, Marcus?'

He recognised the governor's voice and supressed a satisfied smile. The system was so predictable.

He gave a loud sob. 'I have to hurt him. The voices in my head, they won't fucking stop. If I kill him, they'll leave me alone!'

The voice from outside was calm and reassuring. 'We can make them stop, Marcus. Just let him go and let us help you.'

Marcus had relaxed his grip so that the terrified man didn't actually die. Now he poked the face with the knife to make him squeal again.

'I cut off a man's ear once, Governor. Did you know that?'

The man squealed again. It was an exquisite sound, a sound Marcus had missed.

The governor coughed. 'Don't do anything stupid, Marcus! Let me come inside and talk to you.'

Marcus waited for nearly a minute. 'Okay. Just you.'

The suited middle-aged man stepped into the cell. Marcus saw his reaction to the blood – there was a lot of blood, everywhere.

He raised the knife to the struggling man's eye. 'An eye for an eye, Governor.'

'No!' The governor's voice was a shocked cry. So much for calm and reassuring.

'But the voices –'

'I can make the voices go away, really, I can. Trust me, Marcus. You've been a model prisoner. We can fix this. We can send you to a place where they will make you well.'

Marcus glared at him and pressed the knife close to his prisoner's eye. 'Where?'

'A hospital, a special hospital. Broadmoor. Your mother can still visit.'

'I want to go now. Today. I want them to make the voices stop *now*.'

The governor nodded emphatically. 'Yes. Yes, I promise you: if you put him down, you can go today.'

Marcus hesitated again. Could he trust the governor? Better to make certain of it. He thrust the knife into the unprotected eye and then threw the screaming inmate across the room. Both men scrambled out and the cell door slammed shut.

* * *

Four hours later Marcus was bundled into a prison van. He was the only occupant, and they put him in the rear inside compartment, the one closest to the back door. His hands and feet were shackled, his head was bandaged and the painkiller had taken away the ache. He leaned against the wall and smiled. Nothing to do now, but wait. Trust Tom, and wait.

CHAPTER THIRTY-FOUR

WHAKAMARIA BAY

'Vinnie?'

Anna walked rapidly through the lounge towards the bedroom. 'Vin, are you here?'

No response. She stuck her head around the door and glanced at the empty room. He wasn't in the house. With quick, determined steps she went to the kitchen, out the back door and down the path towards the shed. The roller door was up and a truck was parked on the concrete apron. As she approached the entrance, she could see two men loading cardboard boxes onto the long table. Vinnie was checking their labels against a sheet in his hand. He looked up and smiled.

'Hello, lovely. Nearly done.'

'I need to talk to you, now.' She kept her expression as composed as she could, but she knew her eyes were giving her away.

He frowned. 'Okay, mystery woman.'

He followed her out of the shed and onto the lawn that led up to the house.

'I've just had a call from Peter Harper.'

He pulled up abruptly. 'Why? What's happened?'

She could hear the immediate fear, and her heart rejoiced at what she was about to do to his life.

'He had news, wonderful news.'

'About?'

'Marcus Lane. The bastard is dead.'

He stared at her for a moment, frowning, seemingly digesting the information.

'How?'

'All Peter could say was that he'd had some sort of breakdown and attacked a fellow inmate. They were transferring him to a psychiatric hospital, and the van blew up on the way. Two guards were killed as well.'

Vinnie nodded slowly. 'And they're sure? That it was his body?'

'Well, they've announced his death, so you have to think they've checked. I don't know how much of him was left, though, if it blew up.'

He pulled her to him and hugged her.

'So maybe the running is over,' she said.

She knew the excitement in her voice was obvious, and perhaps he thought that was inappropriate, but she felt dizzy with hope.

'Maybe it is. What else did Peter say?'

'Nothing, just to tell you and that he'll be in touch again soon. He was on a burner cell phone.'

* * *

Vinnie, Anna and Mary had moved to a remote bay at the end of a long coastal road. Many of the houses were holiday homes and only occupied during the summer months. There was a pub, a general store with a post office counter, a petrol station and a primary school. The land around the bay was sheep country, softly rolling and prone to drought during the dry months.

They had bought a big rambling house made of native wood, with a veranda all around it and lots of windows that folded back to let in the sea breeze. The front lawn ran down to the beach, and they could lie in bed at night and listen to the waves breaking on the sand.

For a month they did nothing but walk Merlot on the beach, get to know others in the community and help Mary adjust to her new identity. Peter had suggested they buy a boat, and all three of them had discovered an instant love of fishing. It was a good way to blend in, and their neighbours were more than happy to provide instruction. The trauma of the confrontation with Norman Lane and the hasty exit from Rocky Bay started to melt away and, after yet another night of sitting outside and watching a sky aflame with stars, they all agreed that it was time to get to work.

The first project was to build a shed with a commercial-grade kitchen, cool storage and a packaging area for preparing boxes for transport. Vinnie and Anna searched the country and the internet for all the machinery they needed and the best sources of flavourings and fillings. It was still a work in progress, what with all the planning permissions and red-tape, and so Anna had limited the first release to four chocolates and three truffles, sold in boxes of four, seven, fourteen and twenty-eight pieces. She had researched a range of possibilities and fiddled in the kitchen for days, tweaking and experimenting. Vinnie and Mary had hung around watching, tasting and looking things up on the internet when required.

'Ishpink.'

Vinnie looked up from the laptop and smiled. Anna stood in the doorway, latex gloves on her hands and a chocolate-smeared apron around her waist.

'Same to you. Is this a new language known only to chocolatiers?' he asked.

She smiled back. 'It's a spice, from Ecuador. Sort of a bit like nutmeg and cinnamon. See if we can get any.'

'Yes, ma'am. Anything else?'

'Try for combava, it's a fruit. Apparently it smells like citronella and tastes like lemongrass.'

He shook his head in amazement. 'Seriously?'

'Of course. I thought of a white frankincense ganache, but it's horrendously expensive.'

* * *

Eventually, she sat them down at the kitchen table in front of two plates. Five chocolates and five truffles sat in two neat rows on each plate.

'Here they are. I want you to try the same one at the same time. Eat it slowly and then tell me what you can taste and give it a mark out of ten. At the end I want them ranked from one to ten. I need a final choice of seven.'

Both Vinnie and Mary nodded. Vinnie picked up a white chocolate.

'I wish someone would create a distilled spirit and call it "Kindred". Then we could make a chocolate filled with kindred spirit.'

Anna smiled at him. 'Very droll. Get on with it, clever clogs.'

'Let's start with this one, then.'

Mary and Vinnie both popped the chocolate in their mouths and let it roll around.

'Ginger,' said Mary.

'Chilli!' Vinnie exclaimed.

'And coconut. It tastes like … what does it taste like, Vin?'

Vinnie swallowed. 'Warm and spicy, with a hit at the end. It sounds silly, but it tastes to me like a curry.'

Anna nodded. 'And the rating?' she asked anxiously.

'Around a seven for me, I think it's a chocolate you'd eat on its own. It's quite strong,' Mary said.

'I agree. Let's try this one next.'

Vinnie picked up a milk chocolate with grains of sea salt on it. Mary picked up the same one, and they grinned happily at each other as they put the chocolate in their mouths.

'Oh, this is gorgeous!'

Vinnie looked up at Anna and nodded. 'It is – definitely a ten. This is really brilliant, darling. Tequila and lemon and salt.'

Anna smiled. 'Top of the class. A tequila ganache in lemon oil–infused chocolate and topped with sea salt. Would you prefer lime? It's sharper.'

'I think so, the lemon might get a little lost … I just had a black thought.'

'Really? How unusual. Spit it out before it gets lonely.'

Mary laughed. 'You two are as funny as ever,' she said.

'Wait until you hear my black thought, you might not think we're so hilarious.'

'Go on, then,' Anna said, as she picked up a chocolate and put it in her mouth.

'I've used a bottle, a gun and a tank of must as murder weapons, quite successfully I might add.'

'Vinnie!'

Mary tried hard to look shocked, but Vinnie could see she was suppressing her amusement.

'So, how could you kill someone – in self-defence, naturally – using chocolate? Any ideas?'

* * *

Eventually Anna settled on her Secret Boozy Seven for Aunt Muriel's Magnificent Chocolate Masterpieces. They were: a cognac, coffee bean and coffee powder very dark chocolate; a tequila ganache in lime-infused milk chocolate with sea salt on top; a white chocolate infused with coconut oil and filled with a blend of ginger, cardamom and chilli; a mulled wine truffle with red wine, lemon, cloves and cinnamon; a truffle made from a bourbon-infused ganache rolled in finely chopped peanuts; a salted caramel and whisky dark chocolate; and a piña-colada truffle with pineapple, coconut and white rum.

The truffles and chocolates looked incredible in their silver paper baskets, nestled in soft silver tissue and lined up in black boxes tied with a silver ribbon. They had employed a graphics company to create a cartoon image of a grey-haired, plump woman with a chocolate in her hand and a twinkle in her eye. This was 'Aunt Muriel', and the banner around her read: 'Aunt Muriel's Magnificent Chocolate Masterpieces'.

The three of them stood looking at the boxes on the table. Vinnie picked up a four-piece box.

'They look so professional.'

Anna laughed. 'I should hope so, the amount of money we've sunk into packaging and design!'

He nodded. 'So now we send them out and see what happens.'

'We do – to shops, media, chefs, hotels. Aunt Muriel will invade them all.' She turned to Mary. 'Are you ready, Aunt Muriel?'

Mary picked up a box and smiled at her. 'I'll capture every tastebud in the land and hold them to ransom.'

* * *

That drive for recognition had brought them more initial success than they could handle. Big orders meant more machinery, and Anna took on some of the local women and taught them the skills she could share. She still tasted a sample from every batch and set very strict rules about how the temperamental ingredients were handled.

Summer heat caused transport issues, so they started packing the consignments in cold store boxes. By the autumn the business had become a well-oiled machine. Anna was in charge of the creative side, Vinnie handled sales and orders, and Mary was Aunt Muriel, a chocolatier of many years standing who had recently emigrated from London and brought her love of mixing quality chocolate and wonderful flavourings with her. It was a performance role, which suited Mary's love of amateur dramatics, and she happily did telephone interviews. When people requested a photograph, however, they were sent a high-resolution image of the logo, because that was how Aunt Muriel wanted to be known.

* * *

That evening the three of them sat on the veranda, sipping a glass of Rocky Bay Gravitas and talking about the news.

'His protection in jail must have cost a fortune, and maybe the well ran dry, with Norman dead,' Vinnie said.

'I feel very sorry for the families of the guards,' Mary said quietly.

Anna sipped her wine and looked up at the star-filled sky. 'I wonder how they got the bomb onto the van,' she said, 'Do you think the van was stopped en route or did it leave prison with the bomb on board?'

Vinnie shrugged. 'No way of knowing.'

'So, he's dead. Gone. We can stop looking over our shoulders.' There was no excitement in Anna's voice, only resignation.

Suddenly Vinnie sat up and put his drink down. 'The teeth-mould trick,' he said, almost under his breath.

'The what?' Anna asked, her curiosity aroused.

'Nothing … just something I remember from my misspent youth. I met a rather shady dentist once, and his job was making replicas of teeth for mobsters, using real human teeth, so that if they needed to fake their own death they could put a few teeth in the wreckage. When there's nothing left, dental records can then give a positive ID.'

Anna put her glass down and looked at him carefully. 'Are you telling me that you think Marcus faked his own death?'

He shook his head. 'No, I'm not. I'm sure he'd had death threats from other prisoners. Mob rivalry makes it a dangerous place.'

Anna shivered. 'Still, it's a horrendous thought.'

Mary hadn't reacted to their conversation at all. Now she turned her head towards Vinnie. 'Does this mean we could go home for a visit, Vinnie?'

Anna and Vinnie exchanged glances.

'We're dead, remember?' Anna said.

'But we could go as the Wilsons, on our new passports,' Vinnie added.

'Why? If we can't go near home, see family and friends, why would we go?' Her tone was a mixture of sadness and frustration.

Vinnie leaned over and touched her hand with his. 'I'll ask Peter.'

CHAPTER THIRTY-FIVE

MILLICENT MORRISON

Melissa Lane badly needed to recover from the tragedies that had piled upon her of late, as grief and stress and anger were taking a toll. So she announced to her friends that she had come to a decision: she was going to take a holiday, in New Zealand.

All the way through the twenty-four hour flight she kept thinking of Norman and how he must have felt. He was on a mission to free his son, and now she wanted to do her best to find out what had happened to him and where Vinnie was.

* * *

'Mrs Morrison? Millicent Morrison?'

Melissa wasn't as used to travelling under a false passport as the rest of her family were, and it took her a while to register the name and turn around. She had been enjoying the calm harbour and the boats.

'Yes.'

The redhead advanced towards her with hand outstretched. 'Louisa Logan. You've booked a wine tour with me?'

Melissa regained her composure and smiled. 'Yes. I love red wine, and I've researched a couple of wineries I want to visit.'

Louisa nodded and held open the door to her minivan.

'Which ones?' she asked.

'Stonyridge, Mudbrick, Kennedy Point and Rocky Bay.'

Melissa settled into a seat and did up her seatbelt, as Louisa swung herself into the driver's seat.

'Excellent examples, all of them. Rocky Bay has changed hands and been renamed Waitemata Wines, which means "sparkling water" in Maori.'

Melissa was a good judge of people, and she knew within a few moments that this woman liked to talk, liked to demonstrate how much she knew. This was the personality type that detectives described as 'gold' and others as 'insatiably curious'. It was simple enough to rearrange the schedule so that they visited Waitemata Wines just before lunch. She met the winemaker, a woman called Gabby, and noticed that she closed down as soon as she heard Melissa's English accent, which meant either she knew something about what had happened or was still hurting and was suspicious of foreigners and what they could cost. They had a taste of the wine and a small tour around the winery, then Melissa suggested she buy Louisa lunch at the nicest café her guide could recommend.

'I read an article about Rocky Bay and that winemaker, the girl we met,' Melissa said casually as she refilled Louisa's large glass with Stonyridge Larose.

'Thank you. The blog on the internet? It was very good. They were great, the owners, Dominic and Ava.'

'Do you miss them?'

Louisa nodded. 'Very much. Especially Dom, he was gorgeous.'

Aha, a torch was carried. That could be useful.

'They were recent immigrants, American or –?'

'English. Londoners, I believe. And right before they left they were joined by Dom's mother. I picked her up from the ferry and took her there – she wanted to surprise them.'

'And did she?'

'They were thrilled.'

Melissa ate her fish, and waited until she could see that the woman was bursting to say more but wasn't sure she should.

'So, wasn't it a bit strange that they left?'

Louisa nodded. 'It was all very strange. Apparently someone came to the house the night of the harvest party and there was an argument. The police arrived and ambulances, and then Dominic and Ava and a man, also English – called Peter, from memory – came and joined the party as though nothing had happened. The next day they were gone.'

'*The next day?*' Melissa leaned forward as though she were sharing a confidence. 'How bizarre. What on earth could have happened to make them leave so quickly?' she asked, her voice full of concern.

'No one knows. Everything was picked up by a truck – furniture and clothes –and the place was sold. Good price they got for it, too; it makes beautiful wine.' Louisa hesitated, and seemed to be deciding something.

'I'm very discreet,' Melissa said. 'I only came to see the place because I love their wine.'

'I don't actually *know* anything, and I don't want you to think that I gossip … but I have been told that there was a physical fight and someone died in one of those big vats we saw, a vat of must!'

'Must?'

'Fermenting grape juice and skins. There's carbon dioxide on the surface and breathing is very difficult. If you fall in, you need to be rescued quickly to have any chance. You suffocate and then you drown.'

'Goodness me!'

Melissa sat back and digested the news, her expression impassive, her heart screaming. What a horrible way to die.

'What were they like, Dominic and Ava?' she asked.

'Lovely people. Dom was funny and outgoing, and he sang and was passionate about wine. Ava was quieter and a wee bit reserved at times. But she had a wicked sense of humour. She made chocolates and sold them at the market. Her chocolates earned her a reputation. They were exotic flavours and just so moreish!'

Melissa took a sip of her wine. 'Do you think they've bought another vineyard? Be lovely to find out where and try their new wine.'

Louisa shook her head. 'If they were still making wine we'd know. It's a relatively small community, and everyone knows where the good owners and winemakers are. No, they've moved on.'

'Maybe they've moved to chocolate?' Melissa suggested.

Louisa beamed at her. 'I thought of that, too. It would be the obvious path if they wanted to try something new.'

'Well, let's hope the chocolate is as good as the wine, and then I might be able to find some of it.'

* * *

Melissa sat in her hotel room and surfed the internet on her laptop. There were chocolatiers from the northernmost towns to the southernmost towns, some had retail shops and some had an online presence only. She researched all the likely contenders, family businesses and small operations, and ones that looked new, and compiled a list of phone numbers.

'Hello, Death by Chocolate. Maria speaking.'

'Oh, hello. Can you tell me how long you've been in business?'

'Five years in these premises and four in our old building.'

'And you haven't recently changed hands?'

'No, ma'am, we're still owned by the original owners. My dad is the chocolatier.'

'Thank you. Sorry to have bothered you.'

'No problem.'

Eventually, Melissa decided she might have more luck talking to chocolate retailers. Her second stop was the Chocolate Box, a chocolate boutique in the upmarket suburb of Parnell. The shop was a treasure trove, with bars and boxes on every shelf and a counter display-case filled with trays of individual chocolates and truffles. A middle-aged woman was unpacking a box of bars.

'Good morning. Can I help you?'

Melissa took a moment to survey the wares. 'What a wonderful display!'

'Why, thank you. Looking for anything special?'

'I suspect you get this all the time, but I'm looking for some chocolate I've tasted and I can't remember who made it.'

The woman smiled. 'Can you remember what the flavour was?'

'Exotic, different, an unusual combination.'

'Well, that's knocks out a few —'

'And it was quite new, hasn't been around long.'

'That helps. Here, try these.' The woman leaned down and brought out a tasting tray.

Melissa looked at the chocolates and truffles. They were exquisitely made.

'Do you like raspberries?' the woman asked.

Melissa nodded.

'Then try this. It's filled with dried berries.'

Melissa accepted the half-chocolate and nibbled at it. It was delicious. 'Who makes these?' she asked.

'Chocalicious. They're in Dunedin, bottom of the South Island. They've only been going a couple of years. They make a beer truffle, too, with local ale.'

'No, I don't think that's it. Anything from a newer maker, maybe with wine in it?'

The woman pointed to the tray. 'That one is a mulled-wine truffle, and that one is my favourite – tequila, lime and salt.'

Melissa tried the half-truffle. 'That's lovely! Who makes that?'

'Aunt Muriel. They're marketed as Aunt Muriel's Magnificent Masterpieces.'

'Where?'

'From Whakamaria Bay – remote and beautiful. They import fantastic ingredients and the chocolatier is superb. We haven't stocked them very long, but they've proved really popular. Unusual combinations, but they work.'

'Do they have a shop anywhere?'

The woman shook her head. 'No, no. They only make about half a dozen different chocolates at the moment. They supply retail shops and restaurants, but the demand is growing. The salesman is English, Michael Wilson. He's lovely, really charming. I believe his aunt is the chocolatier.'

Melissa smiled at her. 'Thank you so much. Can I have five of whatever you have of Aunt Muriel's, please?'

The woman took a box and filled it, using small tongs to pick the chocolates off the tray. Then she laid a piece of paper over the top.

'I've put a guide to the flavours in there for you. Do you think it's the brand you were looking for?' she asked.

'Very possibly. Does it have contact details on it?'

The woman shook her head. 'No, they don't sell from their factory. You have to purchase through shops like ours. But I will tell Michael how much you liked them when next he calls in.'

* * *

It was almost a dilemma. Melissa's job was done. She had looked up Whakamaria Bay, and knew where it was and how to get there. She was certain that the Whitney-Ross family had relocated there and set up Aunt Muriel's Chocolates. It was time for her to go home and report to Tom. Except she was not a machine, she was a human being. Vinnie Whitney-Ross had identified her son and sent him to jail, and ultimately to a fiery death in the back of a prison van. And he'd drowned her husband in a vat of fermenting must.

Every fibre of her being ached with the desire to buy a gun and hire a car, then drive to this bloody remote little township. She could be judge, jury and executioner, execute all three of them, bullet in the back of the head, then drive straight to the airport and fly home. The knowledge that stopped her was not that she might get caught and never see home again – what did she have to go home to? It was that the wrath of Tom McGregor would descend upon her like the fires of hell. She wasn't frightened of the police but she was terrified of Tom. The man was a psychopath, and he was all that stood between the Lane gang and oblivion. He had promised her that he had a plan, and whatever vengeance he had for these people, it was his to execute and his alone.

CHAPTER THIRTY-SIX

MITCHELL DAWSON

December 2014

It was early summer and the ocean sparkled beneath a sky the colour of lapis lazuli. Anna walked barefoot through the sand, Merlot running ahead of her and careening in and out of the waves. She felt a deep sense of contentment, and it made her smile. This would have been unthinkable months earlier. Vinnie's actions had turned her life upside down. She loved him, she always would, but their path had taken so many twists and turns that sometimes it was hard to remember why they were still together.

At one end of the beach was a large bleached tree trunk, driftwood that had floated in on a high tide and become marooned above the water mark. It was weathered by windblown salt and sand, and she loved to sit on one of its branches and rest her head against the smooth wood. The sea breeze kept her cool, and the rhythmical sound of the waves made her sleepy.

'Mind if I join you, ma'am?'

The accent was American. She opened one eye and couldn't see much at all. He was standing with the sun behind him.

She sat up. 'Be my guest.'

He was wearing a cotton shirt and long shorts. As he sat down beside her, she tried to register what she could see without obviously staring. Short blond hair, blue eyes, strong chin, blond eyebrows and eyelashes. He had a muscular body, filled out, in proportion but barrel-chested, and with obvious muscles in his arms and long legs. His age was hard to ascertain – anything from early forties to a very well-maintained late forties.

'I'm new to the bay, only been here a few days.'

'We're relatively new ourselves.'

He extended his hand. 'I'm so sorry, I should have introduced myself. My name is Mitchell Dawson.'

She smiled and shook the extended hand. 'Charlotte Wilson.'

'An immigrant too, I hear. What part of England are you from?'

'London. Most of my life. What part of the States are you from?'

'I was born in Texas, but I've lived in New York, Boston, LA, London, Paris and Capetown. I like to think of myself as a citizen of the world.'

She nodded. 'For work?' she asked.

'I was a food critic, restaurant reviews, newspaper columns, book reviews. Now I'm a writer. I've taken a house here so I can write a book.'

'How interesting! What's your book about?'

He flashed what looked like a slightly embarrassed smile, and shook his head. 'Well, that's the thing. I knew I wanted to research the history of some of our most ancient foods. Things we take for granted and so don't think about where they came from or the part they've played in history. I thought I'd cover everything from cheese to 'erbs and spices. But I've found myself totally obsessed with a small number of fascinating tales.'

He looked at her with his bright blue eyes and she could see his passion for what he did. She felt a touch guilty about how attractive she found him. Merlot came running up to her, a wet stick in his mouth, and shook his coat. Seawater sprayed everywhere.

'Oh, Merlot, you idiot!'

She picked up the stick and threw it down the beach. The dog raced off after it.

'Sorry about that.'

He waved his hand to dismiss her apology. 'No need. Real beautiful dog.'

'Big heart, no brains. I'd love to know what the foods are. I think I could guess some of them.'

'Now that's a challenge I can't resist. Go ahead.'

She thought for a moment.

'Chocolate.'

'Correct.'

'Salt.'

'Correct again.'

He waited while she sat frowning at the ocean.

Suddenly she turned towards him. 'Rice!'

'Oh, you're real good. I bet you're a phenomenal cook.'

She smiled and made no attempt to conceal her delight. 'Actually, I'm a chocolatier.'

His expression went from surprise to obvious pleasure. 'For real? In a place like this?'

'It's a wonderful place for being creative. It's as peaceful a little town as you'll find anywhere, and the stillness and the beauty are inspiring.'

'Well, it certainly is quiet. I haven't really met a single soul yet, apart from the lady in the general store and the realtor who rented me my house.'

'Are you on the beach?' she asked.

'Yes, ma'am. About two hundred yards that way.' He pointed up the beach.

She stood up. 'We're the last house before the cliffs at the far end. Number sixteen. Would you like to come to dinner tonight? My husband is away on business, but his aunt is here.'

'I'd just love to, thank you. That's very kind.'

'Let's say I know what it's like to be the newcomer. See you at seven, Mr Mitchell Dawson.'

* * *

Mary was astonished that her daughter-in-law had invited a complete stranger to dinner, especially given that Vinnie was away and they were meant to be keeping a low profile.

'What do you know about him?'

'He's American and he's a foodie. He's here to write a book, and part of it is about chocolate, which might be useful. And he's nice. What more do I need to know?'

'What are you going to cook?'

'Chicken in a Mexican mole sauce with wild rice, followed by cinnamon churros with a chocolate and Kahlua dipping sauce.'

Mary smiled at her and shook her head. 'He must be very nice.'

* * *

Mitchell sat back and sighed. 'Lovely combination of different chillies and that hint of bitter chocolate. That sauce was just extraordinary, and you are far too kind, Mrs Charlotte Wilson.'

Anna felt a slight blush rising, and busied herself picking up the dishes on the table. 'Just basic home cooking.'

'Well, I'm looking forward to meeting Mr Wilson, because he is one lucky man if that is your basic home cooking.'

Mary sipped her sherry. 'He's in Wellington, visiting shops,' she said. 'He'll be back on Friday.'

Mitchell thumped the table.

'Well, I'd like to have you all over to my house on Saturday. Return the hospitality. What do you say, Charlotte and Aunt Muriel?'

Anna stood in the doorway, a coffee pot in her hand.

'I'll check with Michael when I speak to him next, but for now, that would be lovely, thank you.'

* * *

Vinnie enjoyed his time on the road. He sang along with his CDs and composed songs in his head. On long trips, he enjoyed audio books. The chocolates were kept at a constant temperature by a battery-operated cooler that he could charge through the car's cigarette-lighter or off a mains plug at night. He planned his route in a circular direction to the furthest point and back to the bay. The shop assistants and chefs were always pleased to see him, and took great pleasure in telling him how well the stock had sold and how much they needed the new supplies. Mostly they received the chocolates by truck, but he made sure he visited every shop or restaurant every few weeks.

The journey home was scenic and coastal, and he sang his heart out as the miles flew by. At long last the shadows of the past had been laid to rest. He knew the truth about his father, and the chains that had bound them to the Lanes for so many years had been broken. There were compromises – he missed winemaking more than he would admit – but they lived in a glorious spot, and Anna was truly happy. She could indulge in her passion all day long, and they were well rewarded for her skill. His mother was reunited with her family and loved her role as the face of the business. Things could be so much worse.

* * *

'I met him on the beach.'

'He approached you?' Vinnie asked.

She could see the concern, the suspicion, in his eyes. He looked tired, and she wanted to hug him and tell him that everything was finally okay.

'Yes, but he was just being friendly. He's new and doesn't know anyone. He came to dinner and he invited us back, tomorrow.'

Vinnie nodded. 'Have you checked him out? On the net?' he asked.

'No! Vinnie, relax. You know as well as I do that Marcus is dead. The time to be frightened of new people is over. I think Mitchell will make a good friend. I think you'll like him.'

Vinnie smiled at her. 'I'm sure I will. Shall we take one of the last bottles of Gravitas?'

'Yes, let's. He's a food critic. See what he thinks of the wine and don't tell him about our connection.'

CHAPTER THIRTY-SEVEN

A TESTING TIME

Every summer evening the air was heavy with the scent of barbecues. It seemed the only way the inhabitants of Whakamaria Bay cooked at that time of the year. On his second evening there, Mitchell had gone for a stroll along the beach and breathed in the smell of meat cooking over an open flame. As soon as he could, he had purchased a barbecue at the general store and charmed the lady behind the counter into showing him how to use it.

His bottle of wine was decanting, his salad was tossed and the steak was ready to put on the hotplate. He stood on his deck and looked out to sea. This was a truly glorious place to live, the absolute antithesis of his previous abodes. Shame he wouldn't be able to stay …

The sight of three people clambering over the sand towards his house alerted him to impending visitors, and he turned and walked inside. He felt strangely calm, considering how important tonight was. Maybe the role of jovial, easy-going Yank had become second nature, or maybe it was because he was in control at last. He was pouring wine into glasses when they knocked on the open sliding doors.

'Charlotte, Aunt Muriel, how lovely to see you!'

He walked towards them, his hand extended. They shook it in turn.

Anna turned to the man standing behind her. 'And this is my husband, Michael.'

Mitchell smiled broadly and extended his hand. 'Welcome to my house, Michael. Mitchell Dawson. May I say, your wife is one fine cook.'

Vinnie took his hand and their eyes met.

Not a flicker, not that he had expected one.

Vinnie handed over a bottle of wine. 'Nice to meet you, Mitchell. We brought some wine.'

Mitchell took it and looked at the label. 'Rocky Bay. Where's that?' he asked.

'On Waiheke Island, off Auckland. It's a wine called Gravitas.'

Mitchell nodded. 'Well, that's the next bottle off the rank. Take a glass and come sit on the deck with me.'

* * *

After dinner they went back onto the deck and sat watching the sun set.

Anna started the conversation. 'Have you settled on the foods for your book, Mitchell?'

He nodded slowly. 'Almost. Chocolate, salt, rice, chilli and bread, and then I'll see whether I add anything more.'

'Why not add wine?' Vinnie asked.

Mitchell smiled. 'It's a thought, I'll grant you.'

'People have been making wine for centuries, and not just for drinking. In biblical and medieval times it was a disinfectant, it was mixed with myrrh and used as a pain reliever, and it purified almost undrinkable water,' Vinnie said.

'That's mighty impressive. You seem to know a lot about wine, Michael.'

Vinnie hesitated. 'It was a large part of my life, but now we concentrate on chocolate. A much sweeter option.'

Mitchell turned to Anna. 'Tell me, Charlotte, do you use chilli in your chocolate?'

She nodded. 'Only one so far. It's a very small quantity and is combined with ginger and cardamom, in a white chocolate infused with coconut oil. The effect is warmth and a flavour vaguely reminiscent of curry.'

'How clever!'

Vinnie beamed. 'All her combinations are clever, exotic and delicious.'

'Spoken like a true salesman,' Mitchell said, as he got up and refilled all their glasses.

Anna laughed. 'He is very good at it: we have more orders than we can keep up with at times, and he still keeps selling. Why did you ask me if I use chilli?'

'It's such a fascinating food. People know about the Scotch Bonnet, and they think that's the hottest chilli. The Scotch Bonnet is around three hundred thousand on the Scoville heat unit scale, whereas the Carolina Reaper is over a million and a half, and there's one grown in Trinidad, called the Moruga Scorpion of all things, and it measures two million!'

'My goodness,' exclaimed Mary. 'Can you eat them?'

Mitchell shook his head. 'No, ma'am. Just a little ittie bit would kill you. Or so I understand.'

* * *

As they walked home down the beach, Anna took Vinnie's hand in hers. 'Well, did you like him?'

'He's nice enough. He certainly seems very "American", if you know what I mean.'

She frowned. 'He's a Yank. So, no, I don't really know what you mean.'

Vinnie looked out at the moonlit water. 'No, neither do I. He just seems like something ... so old-fashioned. Almost a caricature, like an extra from *Gone With the Wind*.'

She squeezed his hand. 'Herman Granger was like that.'

Vinnie nodded. 'Yes, he was.'

* * *

Mitchell waited for a week until he knew that Vinnie was away, then he called on Anna again. She was working in the commercial kitchen in the shed.

'Hello there!'

'Forgive the intrusion.'

'Not at all. Just let me finish this batch and we'll go into the house and have a coffee.'

He stood beside her and watched her rolling truffles in chopped nuts. 'Actually, I was wondering if I could ask a favour.'

She stopped and looked at him. 'Go ahead.'

'It would help my research if I could learn about your processes. Could you show me how you create these wonderfully tasty little morsels, from beginning to end?'

She grinned with obvious delight. 'It would be my pleasure.'

'I'll give you a credit and rave about how delicious they are.'

'Even better! Is this something you want to do now?'

He nodded. 'If you have time.'

'We need to get you kitted out. You need a cap, and these extremely attractive latex gloves and this special apron.'

He stood there while she dressed him appropriately, and shot her a smile full of humour as she reached up to put the hat on his head.

'Do I look fetching?' he asked.

'Stop fishing for compliments. Now, come over here.'

She showed him the raw Belgian chocolate that arrived in bulk, took him through the tempering process, explained how the ganache was made, how all the different oils and flavourings were added, and how the chocolates were filled and the truffles were rolled. He paid close attention and asked a series of relevant questions.

'It's just amazing! They take so much labour, so much love and care!'

She smiled at him. 'That's why they're expensive. Each one is a masterpiece.'

He raised one eyebrow. 'Now who's fishing for compliments?'

At the end she laid out the seven chocolates and truffles on a tray, and he cut them in half, examined and tasted them.

'The tequila, lime and sea salt is sheer brilliance,' he said as he let it roll around in his mouth.

'Thank you! That's Michael's favourite, too, and it's very popular with restaurants. Mind you, so is the cognac one and the salted caramel with whisky. Great with a post-dinner coffee.'

'Do you sample each batch?' he asked.

She nodded. 'Yes, before they're boxed. Once they're packaged they don't get opened again.'

Mitchell pointed to the storage room. 'Is that where you store the finished product?'

She nodded again. 'Storage is very important. Michael has a special portable storage box in the car. It has to be between fifteen and seventeen degrees Celsius, between sixty and sixty-four degrees Fahrenheit, and with a relative humidity of less than fifty per cent. If you don't look after chocolate, it gets bloom, which is perfectly safe to eat, but customers won't buy chocolate with bloom on it. And it has to be kept away from other foods because it absorbs odours.'

'Sounds very high-tech. Can I take a look?'

Anna went to the large, heavy door, and pulled it open. 'It's kept dark but there's a light that comes on when the door is opened – only for three minutes, though. If you leave the door open, the light stays on.'

He followed her in. The boxes were stacked against the wall, different piles for each type of chocolate, clearly labelled. The room felt pleasantly cool and dry.

'I could spend the summer in here,' he said.

'Don't you like the heat?' she asked.

'I prefer to be cool, and just think of all the chocolate I could eat!'

She laughed and ushered him out. 'I'm afraid Michael would scold me if he knew I'd shown you in here. He's very protective of the product.'

Mitchell gave her a polite bow. 'And he has a real good reason to be so. Thank you so much for the guided tour. I shall go home and make notes.'

* * *

When Vinnie rang, Anna didn't tell him about Mitchell's visit, and that made her feel vaguely guilty. Was she keeping secrets or being efficient? She couldn't tell him every little thing that happened while he was away. But they had agreed that there would never be anything important held back between them ever again. It had taken her time to forgive Vinnie for the things he had omitted to tell her, and trust was vital to their survival. Was she now guilty of a sin of omission? What was it about Mitchell that made her keep him to herself? Mary made

309

no comment, but Anna could see the tiny seeds of concern in her expression.

* * *

'Charlotte?' His voice was rich and buttery, like toffee, and he sounded like he was smiling.

She gripped the phone slightly tighter. 'Mitchell, how are you?'

'Just fine. I need to take a break from making notes, and I thought I'd go for a picnic. Can I seduce you away from the kitchen?'

She hesitated. All the batches were packed and she wasn't planning on starting another run until tomorrow.

'You might be able to. Where were you thinking of going?'

'I'm told there's another bay around the point, where there are dolphins.'

'There is, and the slope is gentler so it's a great swimming beach.'

'You bring the chocolates and flowers and I'll bring the food and the wine.'

* * *

Mary came into the kitchen as Anna was packing a box of chocolates into an insulated bag.

'Where are you off to?' she asked.

Anna hesitated. 'Mitchell rang and invited me on a picnic. We're going just around the point, to Te Kura Bay. Want to come?'

Mary shook her head. 'Do you think you need a chaperone?'

Anna laughed out loud. 'Hardly! But you're welcome to join us if you think I need chaperoning.'

Mary smiled. 'It's not me you have to think about.'

Anna picked up the bag and kissed Mary on the cheek before walking towards the door out to the beach. 'Very sweet. I promise I'll think about Vinnie all day.'

* * *

Mitchell poured Anna a glass of wine. 'I found some more of that wine you brought. Apparently it's in short supply because the winery has changed hands and they've renamed it.'

She took a sip. 'Really? This is nice.'

'It's a lighter blend than the one we had the other night.'

He showed her the bottle. It was Decoro. Their baby.

'How's the research going?' she asked.

He pointed towards the sea. 'I find I'm easily distracted, as you can see today.'

Oh yes, she thought, *aren't we all?* 'This place does that to you. Before we started the chocolate business we spent months doing nothing, just relaxing.'

'Where did you come from?' he asked.

She smiled. 'I guess you could call us citizens of the world, too, but we've found our home here. Sometimes I think I could die here.'

'That's a morbid thought!'

'Well, maybe stay here until I die.'

He nodded. 'Do you ever think about death?' he asked.

For a moment she didn't answer, then she looked away, up the empty beach. So much she could tell him, and somehow she felt strangely inclined to, but that was a dangerous path.

'I didn't used to. My parents are both dead and I'm not frightened of it. One way or another it becomes part of life as you reach middle age, but you can have too much of it.'

'True. There are worse things than dying.'

She looked back at him. He was watching sand trickle through his fingers.

'Are there?' she asked.

'Oh, yes.'

Something in his voice sounded empty, as though life had sucked the goodness out of him. It unnerved her.

'Let's go for a paddle' she suggested.

She put the wine glass down and got to her feet. He didn't move, so she turned her back and started walking towards the sea. The water was cool after the hot sand, and she kicked a spray in front of her. Then he was beside her and she could smell his aftershave.

* * *

Mary stood in the kitchen and stared at the phone. She wanted to ring Vinnie. And tell him what? That the American is flirting with your wife and she's letting him? You're away too much. Come home and talk to Anna. This behaviour is more dangerous than she seems to realise. Make it clear to Mitchell Dawson that Anna – Charlotte – is not available.

When she tried to put her fears into words they sounded ridiculous and like shadows of nothing. And yet something deep inside told her that all was not right. The American was not what, or who, he pretended to be. He was more, or less, and his motives were suspect. She just had no idea what they were.

CHAPTER THIRTY-EIGHT

SABOTAGE

The shed was silent, dark and vacant. A figure, dressed head to toe in black and wearing a balaclava, stood in the shadow cast by Vinnie and Anna's house and breathed deeply while he studied the closed door. There was no moon and his only light was a tiny white pinprick from a miniature torch hidden in the palm of his gloved hand.

He walked noiselessly to the shed door and pulled the small pack from his back. Within minutes he had gained access and disabled the very basic alarm system, surveyed the main room, and then turned his attention to the storage area. The door was heavy and impossible to open silently. There was nothing for it but to pull it open and close it quickly to shut out the bright light. He had chosen a night when the surf was pounding onto the beach, and hopefully that would mask any other sound.

He stood inside the room and waited. There were no sudden lights; no one came crashing into the shed to investigate. Finally, he checked each stack of black boxes in turn to find what he wanted. With precision and care he knelt down on the hard cool-room floor, opened the backpack and withdrew a large glass syringe, a glass vial and a pair of heavy gloves.

* * *

Mitchell was sitting on his deck reading a book about the history of chilli when a big, wet chocolate Labrador came charging up the sand and almost bowled him out of his chair.

'Merlot!'

The dog licked his face and shook seawater all over him.

'Do you want something to eat? Do you, boy?' He stood up and went inside. 'Come on, come and see what I've got in here.'

Merlot trotted obediently after him into the kitchen and stopped at the closed fridge.

'Oh, yes, you know where the meat is, don't you?' Mitchell put a plate of steak on the bench, cut a hunk off and dropped it on the floor beside the dog. As Merlot wolfed down the meat, his tail wagged furiously.

Mitchell watched him, then picked up the plate and walked towards a closed door. 'Come with me, boy, and I'll give you some more.'

* * *

'Hello, you two very fine people.'

Mitchell was strolling along the beach when he saw the Wilsons coming towards them. He waved to them.

Anna hurried over to him. 'Have you see Merlot, Mitchell? He's gone walkabouts and we can't find him. Our chocolate Lab.'

Mitchell frowned. 'No, I can't say that I have, but I'll keep a lookout. Could he have gone visiting?'

'We've checked with all the people he knows and no one's seen him,' Vinnie said.

'It's just not like him. He never strays from home,' Anna added, and Mitchell could see the worry on her face.

'Don't worry, my dear. I'm sure he'll be home when it comes time for dinner and a cuddle.'

* * *

Mitchell spent the minutes before he went to bed watching the dog stretched out in his spare bedroom. He had always wanted a cat, but he'd known his father couldn't be trusted around small defenceless animals, so it had stayed a secret desire. Then, when he grew up, he became a man who couldn't be trusted around small defenceless animals.

He considered his options. He could poison it and dump the body in the Wilsons' driveway or he could take it fifty miles down the road and let it find its own way home. But neither of those things was convenient. He knew that Vinnie was going away in the morning and Anna would be by herself, alone, grieving, vulnerable.

'You're just a little bonus, aren't you, Merlot?' he murmured as he smiled at the dog.

* * *

Vinnie hugged Anna and brushed the hair out of her eyes. 'If you want me to stay until he comes back, I will,' he said gently.

She shook her head. 'Don't be silly. He'll come racing in for his food anytime now. He never misses a meal, and he'll be starving.'

'If he doesn't, will you organise a search party?'

'If I have to.'

'And will you ask Mitchell to help?' he asked.

She pulled back. 'Do you mind?'

He hesitated. 'No, not really. But I do think he fancies you something rotten. I might have to teach him a lesson.'

She smiled at him. 'Should I hide the wine bottles?'

He laughed. Their humour was a barometer of the relationship. 'Pétrus is definitely too good for him!'

Anna poked him in the chest with her finger. 'Do you remember Louisa Logan, mister?'

He grinned sheepishly. 'Yes, and I get the point. She fancied me and we used to laugh about it.'

'Exactly. Mitchell can fancy me all he likes but the best approach is for us to laugh about it. He won't get anywhere.'

Vinnie kissed her on the cheek. 'Call me as soon as that scoundrel dog comes home.'

* * *

After breakfast, Mitchell put Merlot in his sports car and drove down the road to the Wilsons' home. Vinnie's car was gone and the back door was closed. Anna answered the bell and, when the door opened, Merlot shot past her and into the house.

'Merlot!'

Without looking at Mitchell, she turned and followed the dog inside. When Mitchell joined her in the lounge, she was on her knees hugging Merlot and having her face licked.

'Where did you get to? Naughty boy.'

'I went for a walk in the trees on the other side of the road. I called him and – wouldn't you just know it – he came to me. I was going to give him some steak but I wasn't sure what you fed him,' Mitchell said.

Anna got up and held out her hand. 'Thank you so much. I was afraid we had lost him.' She kissed him on the cheek and he returned the kiss.

'You're so welcome, glad I could be of service.'

Anna laughed. 'Oh, you're so delightfully American – a real southern gentleman.'

He gave a little bow.

'Would you like to have dinner with me this evening? To celebrate the dog's happy return?'

She gave a little frown. 'I'd love to but we have a problem with one of the batches, due to go out Friday, and it needs my attention.'

'Oh no. What kinda problem? If you don't mind me asking.'

She was obviously reluctant to share.

'If it's a chocolate issue, I'd be mighty interested to have a look. It could help with my research,' he added.

She seemed to make a decision to trust him. 'Oh, it's not a massive disaster or anything. When the girls were packing the white chocolates, they noticed that some of the boxes were stained. They opened them and the chocolates are leaking, possibly something to do with the coconut oil. But it's not every box in the batch, which is strange.'

He leaned towards her and put his hand on her arm. 'My goodness, Charlotte, how fascinating! What will you do with them?'

She couldn't help it, she wanted to show him how in control she was – it was written all over her face and that amused him.

'We can't sell them and we can't put them back into the next batch, it'll upset the balance. So we'll check every box and see how many are affected, then use those as give-aways, maybe donate them to a charity to use for fundraising.'

He grinned broadly. 'Well, I suppose as long as someone gets to enjoy them. It would be a right shame if they got thrown out.'

She gave a small laugh. 'That won't happen. There's too much investment in the ingredients, and there's nothing wrong with them.'

'Has anyone tried one?'

She shook her head. 'Not yet, but we will, before we give them away.'

'Surely you deserve a little break, just one night. They'll keep. I'll show you my chocolate research,' he added.

She smiled at him and sighed. 'How can I say no to that?'

'Splendid! Around seven-thirty and I'll barbecue you something special.'

* * *

Vinnie strode into the Chocolate Box in Parnell, his supplies in a carry-all box in his hand. 'Good morning, my lovely. How are you?'

The owner looked up from the shelf she was stacking and grinned at him. 'Michael Wilson, my favourite rep. And I need you – just about sold out.'

'That's what I like to hear.' He put the box on the counter and looked at the arrangements behind the glass. 'Wow, you are low!'

She climbed down the stepladder. 'And you have a fan. I had a lady come in asking for some chocolate she'd tasted and couldn't remember the name. We narrowed it down and it was you.'

'How did you narrow it down?' he asked.

'She said it was exotic, unusual.'

Vinnie was reading the backs of blocks of chocolate as he listened. 'Am I exotic?' he asked.

She nodded. 'By far the most exotic rep I know and, you have to admit, some of the flavour combinations are unusual, delicious, but unusual.'

'Ah well, you solved the riddle, that's the main thing.'

'I did. She wanted to buy direct but I told her she would have to buy through me. I suspect she was a tourist as she didn't seem to know the country.'

'What nationality?'

'English.'

* * *

Vinnie sat on the wall at Mission Bay beach and watched the ferry chugging across the harbour. It was on its way to Waiheke Island. He was trying to make up his mind. Something in the conversation he'd had that morning had rung a tiny bell in the back of his brain. He needed to check to see if a larger plot was swirling or whether he was suffering from old imaginary fears. He dialled a number on his phone. It rang three times before the call was picked up.

'Hello, Louisa Logan speaking.'

'Louisa, it's Dom Darcy. How are you?'

There was a small silence.

'Dom, how lovely to hear from you! Where are you?'

He smiled; she was as nosey as ever. 'Making an honest living, and missing you all. Lou, I have a question for you. Is that okay?'

'Of course, darling. Fire away.'

'Have you had anyone on a tour asking about us? About the winery?'

There was that pause again. 'One or two are interested in Rocky Bay, and they usually don't know it has changed hands. And yes, recently some have asked questions, wondered where you've gone, but I didn't tell them anything, naturally.'

He felt a slight lurch in the pit of his stomach. 'Thanks, Lou. Love to everyone.'

'But wait a moment, Dom, you –'

He hung up and pocketed his phone.

CHAPTER THIRTY-NINE

MISUNDERSTANDING

'That was a lovely meal,' Anna said as she sank into a comfy leather sofa.

Mitchell put two cups on the coffee table and sat down beside her. She looked surprised at his proximity, but recovered quickly, although not quickly enough.

He pointed to an armchair. 'Would you like me to sit over there?'

She shook her head. 'No, no, you're fine.'

He sighed contentedly. So far so good. 'I'm getting to like this barbecue habit.'

She picked up a cup. 'Didn't you grow up with barbecue in Texas? I thought all they ate was beef.'

'Not where I come from. We lived in the city and my daddy didn't know many cattle ranchers. We ate in restaurants.'

'Which city?'

'Austin.'

'What did he do?'

'Commercial banking. What did your daddy do?'

She paused. 'He was a doctor, a GP.'

'Noble profession.'

'Oh, he was anything but noble. He ran off with his nurse when I was four. I have three brothers and three half-sisters. Waste of space, all of them.'

He laughed. 'You're so direct.'

'You mean blunt – sorry. What was he like, your daddy?'

Mitchell gave a small grimace. 'To tell you the truth, he was a devoted churchgoer and a moral man, and he wouldn't approve of what I'm about to do.'

Before she could answer, he put his finger on her chin and turned her face towards him. Then he leaned across, took the cup and kissed her on the lips.

For a second he felt her responding, then she raised her arms and pushed him back. He wasn't expecting that, and he fell sideways into the sofa, spilling the coffee.

She stood up. 'I'm very flattered, Mitchell. But I can't allow this to go any further.' Her colour was high, and she looked flustered.

'I'm so sorry, Charlotte.'

She was looking around for her handbag.

He stood up and took her hands in his. 'I just thought, with Michael away … Actually, I wasn't think–' He tried to kiss her again but she pulled back and slapped him.

'Stop it! I'm not playing games. I'm sorry if I gave you the wrong impression. I could never hurt Michael.'

She had seen her handbag on the seat. He rubbed his face, stepped in her way and locked eyes with her. He saw the shock cross her face as his smile faded. Finally, he let the hatred and repulsion shine from his eyes. It was decision time. The bitch wasn't up for an affair, so what was he going to do? Stick to the plan or abandon it and revert to his true nature? She was at his mercy. Which would hurt Vinnie Whitney-Ross more?

'I … I need to go. Let me go.' Her anger had dissolved, and her voice sounded small and fearful.

He raised his arm to strike and she shrank back. Then, just as suddenly, he moved sideways and she darted to the chair and grabbed her handbag. In four strides she was at the ranch slider and had pulled it open.

He needed to keep up appearances, and it took him two strides. 'Charlotte.'

He grabbed her shoulders and spun her around. She was obviously shocked to find him so close and her fist flew up. He blocked the punch with his forearm and whacked her hard across the face.

She staggered back. 'Leave me alone!'

The cry followed her out the door and into the night. She didn't look back, and he could hear her footsteps down the deck. He smiled. This felt right. The stage was too big for a private tragedy. This revenge demanded a Shakespearian ending.

* * *

Anna stumbled as she ran down the beach, her shoes in one hand and handbag in the other. The moon was bright and she had no trouble finding her way. Her breath came in rough pants, almost sobs, and yet she didn't feel ready to cry. Her brain was churning. Who the hell was that man and what had just happened? What had she seen in his face? He had looked as though he wanted to kill her.

A noise to her right caught her attention, and she pulled up to a stop. 'Hello?'

There was no response.

'Who's there?' she called out.

Her gut instinct told her that eyes were watching her. For the first time in months, she felt a wave of real fear. The same kind of paralysing terror that had flooded her when Norman Lane had stepped out of the shadows and put a gun to her head.

Someone was up on the lawn, out of sight, observing her, following her. She broke into a run and ran as fast as she could all the way to her own deck, fumbled with the lock on the door and pulled it open, then slammed it shut and locked it after her.

Tipping the contents of her handbag out onto the floor, she grabbed her cell phone. Her hands were shaking so badly that she could hardly press the buttons.

The phone rang twice and then clicked over to voicemail. 'You've reached the phone of Michael Wilson from Aunt Muriel's Magnificent Chocolate Masterpieces. I can't take your call at present, but please leave your number and name and a brief message after the tone, and I'll call you back as soon as I can. Thanks for the call.'

She shook her head with impatience, and as soon as the tone sounded she yelled into the phone: 'Vinnie, call me! As soon as you can.'

* * *

Vinnie had decided he should be at home and had driven through the night. He needed the music playing loud to keep him awake, and so didn't hear his phone ring. He turned into his driveway at three in the morning, yawning.

It was a full moon, and he could still see the outlines of the house and the shed once he turned off the headlights. The surf crashed in the background, the ever-present soundtrack to their lives. Mary and Anna would be asleep, and he wouldn't tell them what he suspected until the morning. Anna would want to know if they were going to move again, and so he had rehearsed his answer. It might be nothing but, if anyone was coming, it was time to stand and fight.

Instead of going straight to the house, he walked down the side of it, between the house and the shed, and stood looking out at the moonlight glinting on the sea. Could it be Melissa Lane? What were the chances? Should he call Peter Harper and tell him? Would Peter think he was overreacting? A small part of him was glad that it had happened – this was the last one, and this time, when it was over, it would be over.

* * *

Inside the house, Anna lay asleep on the sofa, still fully dressed. There was a carving knife on the coffee table beside her. The sound of the car engine didn't penetrate her consciousness, but the door slamming did. Her eyes opened and she held her breath. Was it Vinnie? Had she slept through his call? Surely no one else would bring a car and risk being heard? Mary was in the house. Her fear was real, and she could feel it deep in her bowels. Eventually she forced herself to pick up the knife, get to her feet and cross the floor to the folding doors.

Vinnie grabbed the door handle at the same time she did and his face appeared out of the night. Relief engulfed her.

He unlocked the door and she threw herself into his arms.

'Hey!' he exclaimed as he caught her. 'What's this?'

He took the knife from her grasp.

'Vinnie, I was so scared! Did you get my message?'

He led her over to the sofa and they sat down.

'Nope, I must've had the music up too loud to hear the phone. For goodness sake, what's happened?' He raised her face and studied the bruise and the swelling around her eye socket. 'Anna? Who hit you?'

Suddenly the strange events of the evening, combined with her relief at having him back, became too much for her and she burst into tears.

CHAPTER FORTY

THE JEALOUSY TANGO

It took him an hour to quieten her, reassure her and take her to bed. He held her close until she fell asleep, and waited until her breathing was deep and regular. He hadn't told her about his fears. This closer threat was more immediate and had to be dealt with first. It was time to be a husband.

He slipped out of the bed and dressed warmly, took the carving knife and strode along the beach to Dawson's house. He let the anger boil with every step, and by the time he arrived at Mitchell's house, he was a seething cauldron of rage. Someone had threatened his wife for the last time.

The lights were on and the ranch slider was open. Mitchell was sitting in a lounge chair, wearing a bathrobe, reading and drinking wine, almost as though he was waiting. He didn't look up as Vinnie strode in.

Suddenly Vinnie had an unsettling feeling he couldn't quite put his finger on.

'I thought you were away,' Mitchell said finally.

'Apparently so.'

Slowly Mitchell raised his eyes and then he laughed. 'You brought a *knife*?'

Vinnie bristled. 'You assaulted my wife. You might be some kind of maniac.'

Mitchell laughed louder. 'And you thought a *knife* would help?'

'If I had a gun, I'd have it in my hand.'

Mitchell raised an eyebrow in surprise. 'Really? Now who's the maniac?'

Vinnie shook his head. He needed to stay in control and ignore the goading. 'What the hell did you think you were doing? She's mine. How dare you!'

Mitchell put the glass and the book down on the table beside his chair and pulled himself to his feet. His legs were uncovered, and for the first time Vinnie noticed that his thigh bones were long.

'I made a pass at your wife and she put me in my place. I'm sorry. I should never have hit her. It was most ungentlemanly of me.'

Vinnie locked eyes with him. The other man's eyes were ice cold. Something, he couldn't place it, but something ... 'Who the hell are you?' Vinnie asked softly.

The corners of Mitchell's mouth twitched.

It was a tic – Vinnie hadn't noticed it before, and it was strangely familiar.

'I'd like to say I'm competition, but Charlotte's far too noble for that. Or scared of you.'

Vinnie punched Mitchell in the gut. His fist bounced off the taut muscles as if they were concrete. Mitchell grasped Vinnie's shoulder and squeezed. The pain was excruciating. The nerves in Vinnie's arm went numb, his hand opened and the knife dropped to the floor.

Then Mitchell's other hand struck him across the face. 'I've wanted to do that for such a long time, you pompous ass.'

Vinnie regained his balance and launched himself at the taller man. They crashed to the floor, wrestling and landing half-hearted blows.

'Stay away from –'

'Oh grow up! Didn't that fancy public school teach you anything?'

Vinnie kicked himself clear and moved out of reach. Something about this man was all wrong.

'How do you know I went to a public school?' he asked.

Mitchell shrugged. 'Good guess.'

Vinnie's eyes narrowed. 'How do you even know what a public school is?'

Without waiting for an answer, he threw himself at Mitchell and caught him off-guard. He struck higher up, and felt rib bone crunch under the blow. Then he gripped two fingers in his hand and bent them back as far as he could. The joints and bones cracked loudly.

'Fuck! Let go!'

That voice, those bloody clipped public school vowels!

Vinnie spat the words into his face: 'Don't take no shit from nobody.'

The answer was automatic and involuntary: 'No shit.'

It hit him as sharply as it had all those years ago, so hard he felt winded. He let go of the fingers and scrambled away across the floor.

'*No!* No way! You're fucking dead!'

Vinnie's brain was swirling, and a roaring noise filled his ears. How was this even possible? And what the hell was he going to do now?

Marcus gave a short, humourless bark. 'I was tempted to call myself Lazarus, but I thought it might tip you off. Been fun watching you, and flirting with your precious Anna. She's a piece of work.'

Vinnie felt dazed and shocked, and very afraid of this ghost from his childhood. He knew Marcus could, and would, kill him without hesitation.

'Why did you come here?' he asked.

Marcus gave a triumphant smile. He seemed to be struggling with himself, with something he couldn't help but brag about.

Vinnie remembered what Peter Harper had said at the identity parade about Marcus's Achilles heel being his need to boast. 'How the hell did you find me?' But he knew the answer: the nosey woman in Auckland had been Melissa.

Still Marcus just smiled.

'What are you going to do to us now?'

Marcus didn't answer, but Vinnie could see he was desperate to share.

'I know who you are, so you might as well tell me what you plan to do, now that your cover's blown. You can't get away with –'

Suddenly Marcus laughed. It was a bitter sound, with more than a touch of hysteria.

'It's done! It's too late. My cover wasn't all bullshit: I *have* been researching chilli. Your precious white chocolates are injected with pure capsaicin, the oil in chilli. But this is from the ghost chilli, Bhut Jolokia. Less than four grams will kill in twenty minutes. Anaphylactic shock. An exquisitely painful death. It's so strong it burns through plastic. Those chocolates are now potent killing machines.'

Vinnie was almost lost for words.

'Why?' he spluttered.

'*Why*? Are you *completely* stupid? This makes you a mass murderer. You'll have no defence, and they'll lock you up forever. Trust me, there are things worse than death, and a life sentence is one of them.'

It was ingenious and cunning. But the person who would take the blame would be his mother. At that, a red mist of rage rose up in Vinnie and he let out a shriek as he flung himself forward and punched Marcus in the face. Marcus's head bounced on the floor with a sickening thud. They traded punches again, but harder this time, first Vinnie on top and then Marcus, who was hampered by his damaged left hand. Vinnie drove his knee up into the other man's testicles and Marcus screamed in pain.

Marcus pulled himself away and staggered to his feet, looking urgently around the room. Then he saw what he was searching for on the table, grabbed it and advanced towards Vinnie, his lips drawn back in a grimace of agony. 'Payback time, you murdering bastard,' he gasped.

Vinnie had been on his knees and sprang up. 'Takes one to know one. Did you know your father shot my dad? It wasn't suicide at all – it was murder. Norman told me just before he died in a vat of my wine.'

Marcus stopped. It was clear he'd had no idea. 'You're lying.'

For a moment they stared at each other and the years fell away. Two little boys on a bridge.

'No, I'm not. Your father shattered my world, broke my mother's heart and condemned us to a life of shame.'

Then Marcus started advancing again. 'He must have had good reason. Don't you think it's fitting that it comes down to us? After all these –'

'Vinnie! What the hell's going on?'

They both swung around. Anna was standing in the opening of the sliding door, her face ashen and another knife in her hand.

'Call the police, get the neighbours!' Vinnie yelled.

She fled, and, while Vinnie was still distracted, Marcus moved with lightning speed.

'It may be over but you're going to pay for killing my dad,' he screamed as he ripped open a case and drove the needle of a syringe into Vinnie's shoulder, depressing the plunger all the way.

The pain shot down Vinnie's arm and across his upper chest. He reeled back, the syringe still embedded. Marcus stood above him as he sank down the wall.

'Don't follow her,' Vinnie said quietly. 'Stay. Watch me die.'

Marcus smiled. 'Oh, I intend to.'

* * *

'How long did you say it takes?' Vinnie asked.

Marcus looked at his watch. 'It's been ten minutes. You should be in real pain by now,' he said.

Vinnie smiled. 'I hate to be a party-pooper but I feel fine, and Anna's gone to the neighbours. The police have to come some distance. They'll be a good half-hour, but the neighbours won't let you escape.'

Marcus shrugged. 'Where would I go?'

'Exactly. Only one road in and you'll meet the police coming.'

Marcus was sitting on the floor beside him. The adrenaline had subsided in both of them and, with it, the hatred and the fury of the confrontation. Vinnie wondered if Marcus felt as exhausted as he did.

'How's your hand?' Vinnie asked.

Marcus looked at it. The joints were swelling and red, and had to be hurting. 'I'll live. I had worse in prison.'

'Shame we can't have a chocolate,' Vinnie cracked.

'Do you remember Cookie's scones and jam?'

'Oh God, yes! And her lemon curd. And those sodas she made with coke and ice cream.'

'Do you remember duck racing?' Marcus asked.

Vinnie chuckled. 'You wanted them to drown, and they just sailed out the other side of the bridge. We couldn't tell them apart, and yet your duck always won. You were a competitive little shit.'

Marcus laughed. 'You wanted to be a pilot. What happened?'

'Life. Wine. Marriage. What did you want to be?'

There was a pause. 'I ... I wanted to stay at school. I'm sorry my dad shot your dad – I'm sure he didn't deserve it.'

Vinnie looked at him. It was hard to see Marcus – he looked completely different, but he was still under there. 'Nor did David Kelt.'

Marcus shrugged. 'Fair cop ... Feeling any pain yet?'

Vinnie shook his head and then ran his free hand through his curls. They were damp with sweat. 'I have a fucking great syringe in my shoulder, but apart from that I feel fine. Why didn't you just grab your second chance and go off and have a life somewhere? Mitchell Dawson could have gone anywhere – no one is looking for you.'

Marcus poked him. 'You've nearly destroyed me, Vinnie. You killed my dad.'

'Well, your dad killed *my* dad.'

'My grandfather worked for years to build his empire, and when you gave the police Kelt's notebook, it gutted our money-laundering business, the heart of everything.'

'Good! It was illegal.'

'You betrayed me and put me in fucking prison. For life.'

'You killed my employer! You nearly had me crippled once.'

'But I didn't, I saved you.'

'Let's be honest here: when you found out that it was me in Kelt's cellar, you would have had me killed, and Anna and –'

Marcus shook his head emphatically. 'No. If you'd come to *me* with what you had seen at Kelt's, I'd have given you the bloody money to start your vineyard, and none of this would have had to happen.'

'But your father –'

'Need never have known it was you. I'd have found some lowlife to take the rap. You've forced me to hurt you; I would never have chosen to.'

Vinnie winced. His shoulder was starting to hurt.

Suddenly Marcus glanced at his watch, and then slammed his fist onto the floor. 'Fuck! That conniving scumbag – you know what he's done?'

This is straight out of a French farce, Vinnie thought as he watched Marcus pull himself to his feet.

'No. Who? What? Has someone done the dirty on you? Heaven forbid.'

'Tom fucking McGregor. And he's taken most of the family money to do this.' Marcus started to pace the room. 'He came to me in that fucking Swiss clinic and gave me two vials of what he said was fucking pure capsaicin! Guaranteed to kill.'

His distress was driving him to walk faster. He lunged out and overturned a small coffee table as he passed it then picked up another and threw it at the wall. Wood flew in all directions.

While Marcus was venting his fury, Vinnie scanned the scene. His eyes came to rest on the wine bottle that had crashed to the floor and rolled across the room.

Marcus was being consumed by his frustration and rage. 'It was the perfect fucking plan: set you up as a murderer and then disappear before the crime is discovered. Enjoy myself as the new American boss of the Lane gang while you rot in jail. But now I'm going to have to slit that motherfucker McGregor's throat!'

Using his good arm, Vinnie grabbed the bottle and hurled himself back against the wall.

'Those chocolates should be lethal and you should be *fucking dead*!' As Marcus spat out the last words, he turned towards Vinnie, who shrank back in apparent fear.

'First, I'm going to have to kill you, Vinnie, and make my escape. No one else knows who I am, and no country pigs will catch me. New hair colour, glasses, beard, new passport and I'll be home before you know it.'

There was that heel again, Vinnie thought, the need to boast. He could use that.

Marcus picked up Vinnie's discarded knife and looked at it. 'Gutted by your own knife. How appropriate.'

Vinnie didn't answer. His good hand was behind him and he gripped the bottle by the neck.

'Aren't you going to tell me I'll never get away with it?' Marcus said in a mock whine.

Vinnie shook his head. 'You'll get away with it – you always do, you jammy bastard.'

Marcus beamed. 'True. You should have stuck with me, kid. I'd have made you a master criminal.'

He advanced swiftly, the knife raised to head height and pointing down. Vinnie waited for the perfect moment, then hit the bottle hard on the bronze statue beside him and felt it break. He rolled sideways and avoided the plunging knife, hitting Marcus on the shoulder with the bottle and then driving it into his lower stomach.

The knife fell away, and Marcus let out a loud roar. 'Fuck!' He flailed at the bottle neck with his right hand, but it was stuck fast.

Vinnie grabbed the knife and gestured towards the floor. 'Lie down. Stop thrashing about. You'll lose less blood that way,' he ordered.

'Get it out!' Marcus screamed. He clawed at the bottle and blood spurted through the neck.

Vinnie shook his head firmly. 'If I pull it out, you'll die from blood loss very quickly. It's in your stomach, not your heart. If you stay still, you might live.'

At least two high-pitched sirens broke the tension, still a little way off but getting closer every second. Marcus groaned in pain, but Vinnie kept the knife pointed at him.

Marcus stretched out an arm. 'Help me, Vinnie!'

'I am. I'm keeping you still. They're almost here.'

As the police burst through the door, both Marcus and Vinnie began to laugh, one in sheer relief and the other with bitterness.

* * *

Vinnie joined Anna talking to a detective on the veranda. The sun was coming up behind the house, and the dawn mist was lifting.

'I need to call Detective Inspector Peter Harper of the Met in London,' Vinnie said as he sat down. The detective looked up and nodded at him.

'I've already called him, sir. Do you think this Mitchell Dawson has anything to do with the Lanes?'

Anna sprang to her feet, panic on her face. '*What?*'

'He has more to do with the Lanes than you can ever imagine, Detective. Peter will want a DNA sample from him to compare with Norman's widow.'

Anna sat down. 'Why?' She sounded confused and shocked.

Vinnie reached out, took her hand and squeezed it. Here we go. 'Mitchell Dawson is Marcus.'

'*No!*' Once again the force of her emotion thrust her to her feet. 'You're lying! It's not true. *It's not possible.*'

'Anything's possible in this day and age,' Vinnie said gently.

Anna sank back into her chair and covered her face with her hands. 'I just couldn't have been that stupid,' she murmured, and then began to sob.

Vinnie picked her up and held her in his arms, stroking her hair and soothing her. 'No one could know. No one. He's got brains, determination and no conscience. You never met him. He was my boyhood friend and even I didn't suspect anything.'

The detective coughed.

'It was a brilliant plan, you've got to give him that. His revenge was to ruin my life. I'd be charged with murder on a mass scale and he'd be long gone.'

Anna pulled back and looked up at him. 'Oh, my God. I fell for his lies. I showed him around the shed, into the storage room. I'm so, so sorry. Can you ever forgive me?'

He smiled at her, brushed the tears off her face and kissed her. 'There's nothing to forgive: you called the police – you saved me.'

She shivered. 'I need a drink. Is it too early for a glass of wine, Vinnie?'

He kissed her again. 'It's never too early for wine, my darling.'

EPILOGUE

The young banker looked across the desk at the man in front of him, middle-aged but in good condition, stocky and fit. He handed over a piece of paper. 'The balance is correct, sir. Where would you like me to send the money?' His accent was Swiss.

He had dealt with enough clients to know that this man had undoubtedly been skimming his employer for years, regular amounts, too small to be detected, deposited into a Swiss account. Now it was time to disappear and live off the millions.

The man reached into his pocket, took out a card and gave it to him. 'This account, in Rabat, Morocco.'

English, London, East End, tough life. Unaccustomed to his very expensive suit, and using too much designer cologne.

'Certainly, sir. Account in the name of Tom Carter.'

* * *

'No doubt about it: Mitchell Dawson and Marcus Lane are one and the same person. When he's healed, he's heading back to jail for another very long stretch.'

Peter Harper looked across the room at Vinnie, Anna and Mary. They still appeared stunned by the news.

'How on earth did he do it?' Anna asked.

'There is brilliance to it all. Tom McGregor busted him out of the van, put in a body, blew up the van and flew him on a private jet to a clinic in Switzerland. The cover story was he was a billionaire who'd had an accident and been badly burned. The rest was medical magic: facial surgery, extreme body-building, contact lenses and a new identity, accent, back story.'

Anna shook her head in amazement. 'If Tom hadn't double-crossed him, he might have succeeded.'

Peter shrugged. 'I'm pretty certain Tom would have turned him into the law for attempting to murder Vinnie's clients. Tom wanted total control of the gang and all the power. He never had any intention of letting Marcus come back.'

'Will you talk to Melissa?' Vinnie asked.

'Got her. They arrested her yesterday. She's adamant she had no idea that Marcus was still alive. But she knew he was planning to escape. She spoke to him and he sang like a canary in a coalmine and stitched Tom up. We haven't found McGregor yet – he's disappeared. But we will.'

'So it really is over?' Anna asked.

Peter nodded. 'It is. What do you want to do? Come home?'

Vinnie and Anna looked at each other.

'We are home, Peter. We need to get back to work and replace all that stock.'

He grinned. 'Sounds good to me. What about you, Mary?'

Mary looked surprised. 'What do you mean: what about me? How can Aunt Muriel's keep going without a real Aunt Muriel?'

Vinnie reached out and squeezed her hand. 'It absolutely can't, and neither can we.'

Peter sighed and gave a small chuckle. 'You know, Vinnie, if you wrote this story down people would never believe what you've been through. But it is a really good yarn, you should try.'

Vinnie raised his eyebrows. 'I've always fancied writing a novel, and Michael Wilson is as good a pseudonym as any.'

'What would you call it?'

'*My Excursions Up a Lane*?' Anna suggested.

They all laughed, and Vinnie shook his head.

'There's certainly been enough blood, so I guess that should be in there.'

'And excellent wine – don't forget the wine,' Anna added.

'I never forget wine.'

'Can I add a vote for chocolate?' Mary asked. 'The happy-ever-after has to be the chocolate.'

ACKNOWLEDGEMENTS

The idea for this novel was born in London while drinking a bottle of very good New Zealand wine. The question posed was: 'What would you do if you went into witness protection, but the wine you made was so good that the world came knocking at your cellar door?' My answer was *Blood, Wine and Chocolate*. To me Marcus is Blood, Vinnie is Wine and Anna is Chocolate.

First, I would like to acknowledge Creative New Zealand and the financial assistance they gave me at the beginning of this project. It is, as always, most appreciated.

When I needed a vineyard, I emailed the Waiheke Island Winemakers and I met Mike Spratt. He invited me over to Destiny Bay and showed me around his incredible vineyard. The setting was perfect, and his wine is simply world class. Thank you for your patience and knowledge, Mike.

When I needed a chocolatier, I visited Bliss in Rotorua, and Mary Salter filled in the holes in my knowledge and gave me a bag of the most divine chocolates. I hasten to add that research gave me Marcus's story; I didn't make the acquaintance of any mob bosses.

During the writing of this book, my beloved mum, Thelma Thomas, was in a rest home down the road, and my day was split between writing and twice daily visits to her. She died peacefully on Christmas Day 2013. Her humour always lifted my spirits and she remains my inspiration.

I have to add a shout-out to the British musical theatre star Michael Ball. Not only did he provide the inspiration for the character of Vinnie Whitney-Ross, but his humour and his music bring sunshine into my life. God bless, my lovely.

I owe a great debt to my 'writing buddy', Reuben Aitchison, the best beta-reader ever and a constant source of crazy ideas and black humour, and to Lynne Johnston for encouraging and believing in me – you're a vital part of 'Team Thomas' and I love you both.

Once again, to my wonderful publisher, Finlay Macdonald at HarperCollins, who has supported me every step along the way, I so appreciate your commitment to my efforts. Cheers, let's raise a glass!